I0607497

Arcanium

ILLUSION

AURELIA T. EVANS

Illusion
ISBN # 978-1-83943-974-2
©Copyright Aurelia T. Evans 2021
Cover Art by Erin Dameron-Hill ©Copyright April 2021
Interior text design by Claire Siemaszkiewicz
Totally Bound Publishing

Published in 2021 by Totally Bound Publishing, United Kingdom.

ILLUSION

Chapter One

Bell closed his eyes in the golden lantern light backstage.

When Bell let go, spread himself wide over the web of Arcanium, he was its omnipresent god and omnipotent voyeur, from the thoughts of his cast backstage with him to the audience anticipating the performances, the guests putting in their last efforts in the midway and the Skeletons settling in for their evening meal. He could see what they'd done yesterday and what they would do tomorrow. Even when he didn't try, he had a finger on every pulse within the borders of Arcanium.

There had been nothing since Locke that had come close to taking Arcanium again. The fae hadn't even constituted a threat. They would have left with far more chagrin if they had known how distant they had been from taking Arcanium by force. And Locke was now a red diamond on Neve's finger, waiting for the day she was ready to kill him slowly.

Bell's opiate of choice had always been pleasure, but his taste for violence went in and out with the seasons. He hadn't the heart anymore for the punishment of man. He had enough of that to contend with in his cast's memories and nightmares—but he'd rediscovered the old joy in punishing the immortals who had exploited his Arcanium, even if he had to experience the act of punishment secondhand.

Man swallowed against the apple every second they breathed, and Bell burned with the same sadistic sickness as his fireborn brethren. He kept the Ringmaster in Arcanium as much to remind himself of the line he couldn't cross as to do the things he shouldn't.

No one had ever told him what he could and couldn't do. He was neither angel nor demon nor creation from dust. He had determined his own lines, chiseled his own moral code into his skin before Hammurabi had commissioned his scribes. He was free will incarnate, an agent of chaos to cast awry best-laid plans. He was his own, and so he made his world in his own image, populated it with free wills of all shapes and sizes to shape to his liking—which was often to theirs, because it pleased him to manipulate but not necessarily to control. Manipulation meant nothing without will. If he'd wanted slaves, he would have filled the circus with more convincing golems—like a flea circus of mechanical illusion but with zombies.

But where would be the fun in that?

Bell opened his eyes again, returning himself to the moment, although a blink could send him back out into the circus, forward or backward. All Arcanium and beyond was as accessible to him as the palace of his memories, but although grasping the world in his hands became easy when he made himself more of the god he was, he didn't see much fun in that either. He made things *easier* for his cast and for himself, imparting skills that they hadn't or couldn't have learned before, gifting talent, but even the demons preferred to work for their performances. Without effort, there could be no achievement, and without achievement, no satisfaction. Pleasure, as with pain, had to be earned.

Selena wrapped her arms around his shoulders from behind, her sharp smile against his cheek. She kissed him lightly. "Ready, darling?"

As a demon, Selena could twist her body into shapes that Valorie couldn't have hoped to create. In Valorie's case, Bell had wanted a contortionist human enough to be both awe-inspiring and credible. When Selena had offered her services as a demon, he no longer had to keep the contortions credible. He didn't need her to inspire awe. She preferred to inspire fear.

With her black eyes, dead blue skin and blood-stained hair, she was beautiful, but she was still a demon and plied most of her contortionist trade in the Haunted Funhouse rather than in the big top. For the big top performances, she'd taken over Maya's role as his magician's assistant and damsel in distress—at least, Arcanium's version of a damsel in distress, which rarely followed a traditional plot.

Selena retrieved one of the steel knives, gleaming silver as new for every performance, from the bandolier around his torso and brought it to his throat. He lifted his chin, threaded his fingers through her locked hair, breathed in her craving for impure blood. When she shifted her kiss to his mouth, he met that craving with his tongue, hissing as her sharp teeth caught him and she slid the blade over his chin. Then she kissed down to the trickle of blood and drank from the wound until he healed it under her mouth.

She fed from his corruption instead of feeding from his people or too many of his guests, and in return, she made him numb. She could render men into oblivion, but the best she could do for Bell was take both the pleasure and the pain away for a time.

Most of the human cast believed he was sleeping with Selena. Kitty knew better. Neve and Elizabeth had guessed otherwise. And, to his annoyance, Vivian suspected, although because she didn't know, she hadn't shared that information with Dom or Delilah. The demons and the faerie could tell just by looking at him, but they wouldn't share that information one way or the other. A jinni's business, like that of a demon's, was his own.

Selena kept his secret, liked keeping secrets in general, because secrets so easily corrupted, improving the flavor of that which she fed upon. It was only apt that she'd chosen an actual lover among his humans who was as ingenuous as they came. The fact that she regularly drained Victor of corruption that he had done nothing to earn satisfied Bell.

Selena licked the smear of blood from the edge of the blade before returning it to the bandolier. Then she jumped onto his back, wrapping her legs and arms around him. She was taller than him by half a head without heels, over a head with the ones she wore for the performance, but although taking a human form limited him in many ways, it didn't impede his strength. He caught her legs and tucked her against him as he carried her to the curtains. Chelsine would finish her fire dance any minute, which would cue the lights for Sera's aerial act. After Sera, Bell and Selena would enter. Though Selena should have been getting into place, Sasha and Mikhail had worked their magic, as they always did, and both Bell and Selena were reluctant to part.

Bell had never been so frustrated for so long.

Selena would find her own satisfaction after the performance, as most of his cast did. Some didn't even wait until they were out from backstage.

To be surrounded by the lust and love of his people, to feel it against his skin, against his teeth, to drink it like milk and honey, hum with the vibrations of their moans and screams, watch them dance around each other, caress, kiss, their pupils dilated and their cheeks flushed, the touch of their tongue to their lips... It was the torture of his own dungeon, to be surrounded by everything he wanted but not to partake himself, even when he was tempted.

Instead, he rested his head back against Selena's chest as her hair draped on either side of his face.

Selena slid from his back and kissed his shoulder. "Hard out there for a demon with a soul. You, of all people, should know better than to resist. God, Bell, there are so many willing victims. Why do you do this to yourself?"

He didn't have a word she would understand. Demons punished with ease, but they had little concept of self-punishment. The closest any of them came was limited self-denial.

"I'll see you in the ring." Bell would seem casual to anyone without an extra sense or two to detect the deception.

"Sure, handsome." Selena broke away, scurrying up the ladder to the heavens, where the trapeze swings, spotlights and aerial silks lived.

Neve was his crown jewel—the Spider, a black diamond he would keep in a vault if he could, but Kitty, who reclined on the chaise longue, was the life's blood, the very beating heart of his circus. Locke had understood that she was valuable but hadn't understood how much, or else he would never have allowed the Ringmaster to take her for himself.

Without an ounce of magic in her blood, Kitty sensed his attention, opened her eyes and met Bell's gaze across backstage. Though she couldn't see it, the Ringmaster's darkness seeped from under the curtains as he introduced Sera, but when it reached Kitty, it dissipated. She was a pink, floral oasis in a sea of smoke.

Bell sent her what love he could spare from a distance. She received it like a blanket warmed in sunlight, because she was his Kitty Cat and he could rest his head on her shoulder and hold her until the sun rose and set again. Even if she blamed him like the rest, she'd lost none of her love for him. If a human being could become family to jinn, they had bound themselves with something thicker than blood.

She was the only other one who truly loved the circus. The others, demon and human, dwelled within it, sheltered in its shade for a time, but they could all find shelter elsewhere. He had a number of voluntaries but none with so much to lose if they left. That she would lose it broke his heart for her. He cradled her heart as much as he could without making his hands a cage.

Sera's sweeping cinematic score faded. Bell closed his eyes again, gathering himself into the persona who people recognized and believed was him. Since Locke, never had he so wished to be the man people assumed he was. Not a good man, not harmless, but one who could be measured and fitted, warm and enticing as melting butter and honey, burnt cinnamon incense in a small world of cedar, silk and sawdust — the mysterious stranger who could manipulate emotions like clay on a wheel to make people feel flattered, comfortable, content, to lower their guard and put themselves in his hands.

"Here in Arcanium, we hope that you have survived your foray into the fantastic, into the dream and the nightmare, indistinguishable — deadly, dangerous, a glimpse into beautiful darkness for a short time. What has been real, what fantasy? We offer no answers." The Ringmaster's deep, resonant voice richened each word in his script, imparted emotional significance he was incapable of meaning. In some ways, the Ringmaster himself was the greatest illusion of Arcanium, but it was the only one that the audience never questioned.

"In this dream within a dream, let this be the finale of seem. During the day, he is a teller of fortunes, both good and bad, but with the setting of the sun, he weaves reality from the stuff of imagination. What is real and what is illusion? Let us blur the lines further."

The light on the other side of the red velvet curtains dimmed to near darkness. Bell let in the barest of lantern light as he entered, nothing but a shadow in the silence. As the curtains closed again, the darkness was absolute, but like the Ringmaster, Bell didn't need the light. He knew the big top like he knew his own mind, because it was his creation.

The lights flashed up in a splash of jewel colors, with the spotlight on him in the center of the ring, just as the music switched on, not the symphonic metal or sweeping cinematic pop of the other performances, but a bleacher-vibrating blast of Fall Out Boys' *My Songs Know What You Did in the Dark*. Because Bell, like most immortals, had an unhealthy appetite for irony. The only song that made an audience reel faster was when he used Britney Spears' *Circus* with unrepentant aplomb.

Selena descended from the heavens, untethered to rope or rigging. As with Sera, the audience strained to see whatever transparent cord held her hovering in the air. They could strain until their eyes popped out. Creating the illusion that there was illusion at all was one of his greatest joys that had nothing to do with lust, and he had precious little joy these days. Within the big top and fortune teller tent, the best he could hope for was glimmers, so he took what he could get.

Selena could do her portion of the illusionist danger act under her own power, but there was no need for her to exert herself when making magic look like tricks was effortless to him. What magicians did to make their illusions seem like magic took far more work than he needed to make magic look like illusion.

They also used his magic instead of hers to establish their dynamic from the beginning. Sometimes Selena even tried—and failed—to wrest control from him. It helped her maintain character and convinced the audience of his dominance over the scene, over magic and illusion, over his magician's assistant, over the audience itself.

There was benefit to submission for beings such as him. The demons in his care actually seemed to thrive, living under the consummate control of someone like him, someone who kept them leashed and collared and relieved them of the usual expectations. They liked having restrictions to push and pull against.

Selena could take or leave D/s games the rest of the time, but in a circus like Arcanium—a circus of leather, latex and enough innuendo to power a mid-size city— she was more than willing to play the part of the unwilling prisoner, with her left leg straight in the air by her ear, her arm wrapped around her thigh and bound to the collar around her neck to trap her leg there and keep her from being able to run.

Like Valorie, she was thin, her narrower curves setting off her flexible limbs and the purple latex she wore to unique advantage. She didn't reach the level of his Skellies — no one healthy and living could — but she made him seem strapping in comparison.

He conjured her down to the center of the ring with him. She struggled in vain against the leather bonds holding her, wriggling her beautiful body against his until she reached the ground. His chest to her back, he smoothed his hand up the length of her thigh to the delicate ankle then hooked his arm around her waist to bring her closer against him. He had much more license for lascivious intent during the big top performances, where children under thirteen were not permitted — at well-documented risk of life and limb, not that anyone believed the warnings.

He went through the motions of lust within their dance, Latin style mingled with his magic and demonstrations of Selena's flexibility and ferocity through her resistance, struggling against but never managing to shake either the leather bindings or the effect of his touch on her. The incubus and succubus had already planted seeds in the audience's heads. It didn't take much for Bell and Selena together to make them grow.

Until his magic flung Selena from the center of the ring to the wooden target that had appeared in front of the curtains. She slammed face-forward against the wood with real force that no sound effect could replicate.

"*Mmm, harder, darling.*" She writhed against the target, grasped the edge of the pallet with her free hand, but she couldn't budge from where Bell had put her.

He drew two knives from the bandolier that crossed his otherwise-bare chest. He paused only for the audience to blink against the shine on the silver before flinging both toward the decidedly squirmy demon twenty feet in front of him.

They hit right on either side of her waist. The audience winced for her. She only became more agitated.

Bell flourished his hand like a flower. Another leather shackle appeared in his palm, with no sleeve from which he could have retrieved it, not even the usual leather bag on his belt.

He pitched the shackle straight at her. The right leg and arm that had been free jerked to the side, so that her legs were arranged at twelve and three on the clock. The wrist that wasn't bound to the collar was now shackled to her leg just short of her knee. Selena could slip from each of these bindings if she chose—with work, given that leather and latex didn't lend themselves to slipping anywhere, especially on each other—but the audience wouldn't know quite how flexible or determined she could be.

And Selena wasn't actually trying to get free so much as challenge him by attempting to shake his magic off—like a goat trying to shake off a reticulated python. No mean feat, as his snake charmer could attest. Impossible, really.

This time without hesitation, Bell flung two more knives. They hit outside each of her elbows.

He flipped her around on the target to face him and the audience, proving that she wasn't bound to anything but herself. The chorus of *oohs* and *aahs* from the crowd barely made it through the music.

Rather than one of the knives in his bandolier, he went for the etched Bowie knife in the sheath on his belt and held it up for the audience to admire. Selena's eyes widened without guile—not the easiest thing for a demon to manage, but Selena had been passing for human for longer than her lover of choice had been alive, and before that, she'd possessed enough humans to learn how to pull it off.

The song determined the pace, and everyone loved a fast-paced danger show. He threw the Bowie knife directly at Selena's pretty face, square between her black eyes.

The tip of the blade dented the skin, but it drew no blood.

Bell called the five knives out of the wooden target, one by one, until they hovered in front of Selena's body. He quickly but casually removed the rest from their bandolier sheath and tossed them in front of him to hover in a staggered formation.

With a push to the air, the knives flew once again at Selena—face, neck, heart, gut, all potentially fatal blows alone, undeniably so together.

Selena fell back through the wooden target as though it weren't there, although it caught each of the blades with a series of *thunks*. She sank into the ground with a burst of sawdust and a high-pitched cry.

The music abruptly stopped.

In the midst of such a quick-beat act, Bell took his time turning around, his bare feet quieter than the brush of his cotton pants in the sawdust.

Hold the pause. The audience looked around wildly then back to him, because he was pleasant to look at and he held attention without having to hold on to souls to do it.

Then he pointed into the bleachers. Music burst through the big top once more as the spotlight found Selena in the middle of the audience, twisted into full demon-possessed, spider-like contortion, her mouth a dark, crooked cavern as black behind the snaggle teeth as her eyes.

Her deafening shriek blended with the music and the startled screams and laughter of the audience as she scurried down the bleachers, still in her contorted state—nimbler than anyone had any right to be with their limbs in all the wrong places and angles, going down headfirst and backward. She leaped from the bottom bleacher over the ring partition, unraveling herself and stretching out her limbs to strike him with her claws like a lion.

The magical web of his circus trembled.

Bell almost didn't catch Selena. If he hadn't, she would have landed on all fours like a cat, but she would have reamed him after the performance. But he saw her hitting the ground and blinked himself back to the present, back to the ring and snatched her from the air in a *Dirty Dancing* lift. She launched from his shoulders in a double flip to land on her heels—not quite stilettos but still not the best shoes for uneven earth. Little could make Selena fall when she didn't want to.

The web still shivered, the movement of someone with uncertain motives, certainly not the usual thought patterns of those who entered Arcanium—to enjoy a circus, to leer at the sun-glistening bodies of the more revealing of his cast, to terrify themselves in the unprepossessing funhouse. And from his cast, their efforts to entertain themselves and others, to serve the guests, to keep them politely distant or unprofessionally close. To make it through another day.

This wasn't that.

This was *nothing*.

And nothing was not good. It was a void, a gap in his sight as prominent as a dark cloud in his eye, like watching someone walk across the edge of a forest at night. The average person would never see anything, but demon and jinn made no distinction between a new-moon night and a high-noon day, and Bell was attuned to anomaly.

While he and Selena sparred in a dance fight that showed off the full extent of her gymnastic contortion and his speed, style and timing to the musical transition of Beyond the Black's *Hysteria*, Bell followed the invisible void moving through his circus.

The only reason he didn't stop or send one or more of his demons or monsters to meet the shadow was that it didn't seem malicious. It was at peace, calm, serene, its movement measured rather than furtive.

Locke had been more effective at concealing himself when he'd entered. Bell had only ever been able to feel the trail that his presence had left behind, never where he had been at any given moment. He'd cloaked himself in innocuous motives, predictable thoughts. Only the Spider's and Neve's memories had made his motivations better known, because he'd hidden himself less from them.

This was something that only cloaked itself from being recognized. Bell sensed curiosity, amusement, intrigue and trepidation like music from a staticky radio station. Multiple voices. A crowd where there should not have been one, because most of the guests still in Arcanium after eight came to the big top performances.

Bell conjured playing cards from his palms in a bird-flock rush. The ruby-backed cards fluttered around

Selena, herding her to the sawing table and transparent coffin, where the playing cards forced her in.

He called the decks back to his hands for a number of shuffling tricks that impressed audiences as much as any magic he offered, which was why he appreciated real skills within his circus more than the non-illusions that he peddled. He loved card tricks, juggling, tumbling and knife-throwing, and he had little patience for the usual mentalist game—not when the truth was more interesting to him than the trick.

The shadow came closer, toward the big top, an inverted storm eye.

A shrieking power saw descended from the heavens toward the coffin, set for a classic woman-sawn-in-half stunt. His version was far bloodier and pushed the limits of the illusion of error, but it was no less than what fans expected from Arcanium.

From there, he let the saw do its trick, which wasn't a trick at all, because Selena couldn't die from being cut in half. Buckets of blood splattered the sides of the transparent glass. Selena's guts quivered in place when the two parts of the coffin pulled apart.

Bell rolled the halves of the coffin around the ring with his magic. People would rave about how secretly high-tech Arcanium must be or praise the quality of their prosthetics team, when all a good demonic circus needed was a jinni with an occasionally gory sense of humor.

The saw would do as well as the knives and playing cards if what approached was worse than it seemed. For now, his curiosity met the shadow's own, although he was wary enough from the events of the last two years that, beneath his calm, controlled exterior, the core of his power was rigid and cold as steel.

Selena's body came together in the blood-strewn glass coffin on the other side of the ring, her blood replenished, the latex reconstituted. Selena, whole and unstained by the blood she'd lost, burst through the lid of the coffin to the cheers of the crowd, especially when she flipped from the coffin with a graceful scissoring of her legs and, popping joints the whole way, approached the cruel magician who had trapped her.

The shadow entered the big top.

Bell was capable of fear. He kept it within reach these days, like a bottle of bourbon in a nightstand. With fear came rare anticipation—not from within the shadow but within himself. Suspense only worked if one didn't know the outcome, and most outcomes weren't so necessary to him that they hid themselves from his sight. Of course, there were consequences to keeping himself ignorant, too—like Vivian trying to kill everybody. He hadn't hidden the future from himself since.

This outcome was genuinely hidden, which meant only that the outcome was significant, not that it was bad. And because the impression he received from the shadow wasn't angry or baleful, he strongly suspected that this was *not* another Locke or even a small faerie army come to take Arcanium away.

Hence, anticipation—anxiety and thrill all mixed into one heady emotion, headier because of how infrequently he contended with the effects.

"Your heart's not really in this tonight," Selena spoke in his head. *"What's up, doc? Do I need to show some skin, pull out a heart, bulge a few eyeballs to get some attention around here?"*

Bell didn't answer. He committed to the dance fighting that they'd resumed, this time with Selena performing more and more impossible acts until he'd tangled her in her own limbs and conjured steel chains from the heavens to hold her hostage.

He could never have done that with the older cast. Even some of the demons were cagey about being chained. Many of them could still stand the leather, because they had fonder memories of Sasha's artistry, but although demons could recover from torture, being chained was another issue altogether.

Bell held out his hand in front of Selena's chomping mouth and flexed his fingers outward.

The shackles pulled away in every direction, but there were no blood and guts, no need for repair or holding back pain. Selena tightened into herself like a knot on a string, deep into her torso, then kept tightening until she disappeared, all in a matter of seconds.

Selena would reappear backstage to take her leave from the big top tent, which left Bell alone in the ring.

He spun around with a master flourish and bowed to the usual thunderous applause. He liked an audience, but applause had never been his favored response — too predictable, too socially required, too strange an action for people to have agreed upon as a signal of appreciation. He took in the wonder lighting up their minds with color and sound instead, bowed until the applause subsided.

Except it didn't.

A single slow clap, loud and steady, pierced through the parting shadow.

Chapter Two

She emerged all in white, her broad, feathered skirt sweeping over the grass and sawdust but only redistributing it, not staining the hem. The Art Deco corset cradled a slender body significantly older than the last time he'd seen her. Her variant olive complexion was beautiful above the neckline. The kindness and smile in her eyes deepened her lines. Hair as rich and dark as when he'd known her, now shot through with slate and white, was bound high on her head to complement the platinum and diamond necklace that collared her.

The woman was tall, her step soft, her eyes white as the magic of her inner sight, so much so that some believed her blind. It had served her well when she'd been his apprentice and again when she'd broken away from Arcanium to continue the profession alone.

Bell hadn't resented her for leaving. Jinn, like demons, formed attachments as passionately as any human — often more so — but they didn't have the same drive, natural or social, to settle down. Mating for life could last millennia and even the most enduring of blooms faded. To a human, acceptance of temporary relationships seemed flighty or fickle, but that was only because a human's temporary seemed like forever. The jinn's forever was inconceivable. The length of time a companion had been with him did not measure his love for them.

That Fairuza had been with him in Arcanium for twenty-seven years didn't mean he'd loved her less than the demon Elspeth, with whom he had spent a hundred — or that he'd loved her more than Maya, with whom he'd had only five.

To everything its season.

Fairuza had been a few seasons ago, but she was as clear, vivid and vibrant to him now as she had been then.

She stepped over the partition as though there weren't yards of fabric and feathers to catch on the wood. Behind her sparkled the glitter and gleam of more people in the blanket of shadow. Then she tossed the shadow away, flooding his head with the thoughts and feelings of a sudden crowd, a cacophony of both knowledge and ignorance. They knew Arcanium, recognized it by reputation earned from members of Fairuza's cast who had once been his and now were his once more. Seth and Lars had left Arcanium together but separately after Locke — Lars back to some semblance of a normal life and in the bottom of a bottle on more nights than not, Seth straight into the arms of a less esoteric circus for a while — not that Fairuza's small world was without its own brand of magic. Caroline and her men had returned to Arcanium after a stint with Fairuza as well.

Fairuza continued to approach, unhurried, just as experienced at milking a dramatic pause as he, holding the silent note while the audience watched, entranced.

Bell waited just as patiently, testing the edges of Fairuza's mind and magic the way animals caught and studied scents. He searched for any resentment that some of her acts had transitioned to Arcanium. She wouldn't hold Seth, Caroline, Colm or Riley against him, but she would have taken the Albino Triplets and Chelsine, who'd been hers first, more personally.

There was supposed to be clear delineation between Arcanium and Illumina, complements rather than outright competition. Bell's was a classic carnival-circus hybrid that dwelled on the dark and impossible with his demons and oddities. Fairuza ran a circus of the newer breed, one based on the beauty of skill, with more elaborate and well-integrated productions, and although she hosted salons, something akin to the Funhouses was out of the question. She would never employ someone like the Spider, Delilah or Dom, the Sphynx or the Man-Doll, or even Kitty, although she might hire Neve or the clowns for seasonal work.

It wasn't better or worse than what Bell did. It was simply different.

There was no reason for Fairuza to be in Arcanium — and certainly not with her entire entourage of acrobats, aerialists, tumblers, dancers, street performers and assorted prettied-up freaks. Bell hadn't seen her in person or spoken to her since she'd left, before even Kitty had come to Arcanium.

Bell rarely saw his former charges again after they departed, unless they returned to serve. They didn't visit Arcanium to get their fortunes read or ride the carousel for old time's sake. His lovers returned even less often than the others. They chose to move on, to grow in a different direction, like vines he'd nourished from seedlings.

Fairuza honored him in her new profession, a woman with the strength to relinquish him, leaving the web of Arcanium to weave her own.

She puzzled him with her return.

Fairuza reached the center of the ring, her sparkling, luxurious formality stark against the rustic buccaneer that Bell created of himself.

She took his face in her hands and kissed him.

The kiss took him by surprise, but only for a moment. He grasped her wrists to draw her closer. Her touch was warm and eminently familiar, although he tasted greater depth in her, like whiskey that had seeped into the wood of its barrels.

There were cheers in the audience from those who still believed that this was part of the show — and from a few who just liked to watch — but they faded until the world was just him and just her, as though no time at all had passed. They found their old rhythms and neither would yield, which just brought Bell higher, because how often could he spar with an equal, even if she was an equal that he'd made?

He released her wrists to disturb her elaborate hair, tangling his fingers among the thick strands as he drew their bodies flush against each other, nudging her skirts back with his legs. God, it had been *so long*, and she was hot with the same fire and water that ran through his own veins. The things they had done... The things they could do again...

When they parted, Bell had no concept of the time that had elapsed. It was a consequence of slipping in and out of it, of registering time as less linear than human beings, although his human shell tempered the effect. If he'd been there for days, the audience had decided to remain. If it had been mere minutes, their patience would not have been too tested, not that he cared at the moment—indifference as rare as surprise.

"Hello, beautiful," she whispered against his lips. She looked up at him, meeting his gaze with the fearlessness that had led him to give her so much more than most humans could ever handle—power, magic, immortality, all wrapped into her wishes but not into Arcanium. They'd been gifts he'd given to her, not gifts to give to himself. "Now, disappear."

Fairuza snapped her fingers.

He didn't disappear. He still stood in the middle of the ring, but the audience could no longer see him, and they gasped as dramatically as they had when Bell had tied Selena into the disappearing knot.

Fairuza swept her grand skirt with her as she regarded the room. Bell got out of the way of the feathers to keep from disrupting the illusion. She hadn't offended him with the concealment. Had she genuinely tried to make him disappear, that would have been another story. He didn't change his routine often, but he was fully capable of improvisation when the need arose. Whatever made a good story.

Fairuza's smile dazzled under the lights more than the sparkle of her collar. "Arcanium is mine," she announced.

Lights out. Thunderous applause.

When the bleacher lights switched on, Fairuza had disappeared from their view as well, along with her cast. They crowded within the ring, which seemed empty to all but those who knew for certain it was not. They couldn't see him or Fairuza or each other, and either Fairuza had kept most of her skills from her cast or she'd never used this particular spell before, because they frantically spun around in dizzying circles, unable to see one another to move from where they'd been herded.

The audience started to leave, with their white-noise chatter and laughter, shouting over each other to be heard. Bell remained in the background of the audience and Illumina under cover of invisibility. Fairuza hadn't shared her plans with her cast, so there was nothing in their heads for him to mine, but he was willing to wait, and he contained his own cast backstage. Word had already spread that something different and potentially alarming had happened during Bell's act. Even those who never performed under the big top tent had flocked backstage to see, but the red velvet curtains wouldn't budge. Only the Ringmaster remained on this side of the curtains, a statue on his raised platform, suspicious but awaiting Bell's cue.

Bell knew that by trapping them in the big top, he risked worrying his cast more than necessary. More than a few of them would wonder whether Bell hadn't known this was coming, whether he'd failed again in keeping their circus protected.

And even Bell himself was uncertain. But Fairuza had no quarrel with Arcanium, nor did he sense antagonism or conquest from her. She was an intelligent woman. Any power he'd given her was his to take away again, which made her powerful to all except him. She'd know not to challenge him in such a way that he had to strip her of her immortality to protect his people.

Yet anything that made the future turn hazy as Iodolite kept the tension in his spine from releasing. All the more reason for revelations to come sooner rather than later. Bell expanded his awareness to the edge of the circus to compel all the guests to leave. Even those who'd considered lingering abruptly changed their minds.

Once all the guests had left the big top, Fairuza lifted the invisibility spells. Her cast reacted to reappearing less strongly than if they hadn't known about any of her magic. Bell didn't react at all. He sat on one of the partitions, taking in the sight of Illumina, drinking in the sight of her as she found him in the crowd.

Her cast backed away from her as she found a path through them to him. Oh yes, they knew she had power. She didn't have to give them any command. They anticipated her needs, climbing over the partitions into the bleachers to take their places like well-ordered students. A few grabbed discarded, half-finished food from the benches.

As the Illumina cast settled, Bell released his hold on the red curtains. The Ringmaster parted the velvet, hooking the curtains open.

The Arcanium cast stepped into the ring. Some of the tension in their necks and shoulders relaxed when they noticed Bell sitting at the edge of the ring.

Bell's heart ached that they trusted him — that they were still willing to — in spite of yet another potential threat from outsiders, because even other circus folk were outsiders to Arcanium.

The cast of Illumina all seemed to belong together, costumes and makeup complementary, their bodies strong, athletic and beautiful like airbrushed advertisements. In comparison, Arcanium was a mismatched patchwork, just the way Bell liked it, a collection of individuals rather than a proper group.

And they intimidated Illumina, which Bell also liked. They needed a little chaos where Fairuza had forged order. She'd become jinn, but Fairuza hadn't been born of fire, and she could never change that.

Standing before him, she extended her hand. When he took it, she drew him from the partition back to the center of the ring.

Seeing Bell so calm with her soothed his cast more, although Bell hadn't seen through Locke until it had been too late. The demons, however, recognized Fairuza, even after twenty-five years, during which she'd grown older, unlike them. She didn't need to any more than the demons did, which meant that she'd chosen to, and it thrilled him that she had chosen to — yet another way in which she had retained her humanity.

After reading the room, in which Fairuza made Bell and herself the spotlighted center, the Arcanium cast dispersed into the bleachers to join Illumina.

The Mountain — a giant almost as wide as he was tall but dense rather than fleshy, with a disproportionately small head — sat next to a cluster of comparably tiny aerialists. They looked up at him like dragonfly fae, afraid that he would crush them. He could have, but he was a placid demon — not unlike Ciarán — and if he'd intended to break bones, he would have used his boots instead.

Moss grinned a predator's jagged grin at the two Illumina dwarves, in case they dared to compare themselves. Ciarán wrapped an arm around Moss' waist to lift him to his shoulder and defuse the situation. Two halves of the same demon, they moderated themselves without too much struggle between them, given that they both functioned to help the other exist.

Seth, Caroline, Riley, Colm and the Albino Triplets settled among the Illumina cast like old friends, with enthusiastic greetings on everyone's parts but Caroline's, whose appearance visibly alarmed those who recognized her through the harlequin mime makeup and thick, overlapped surgical thread that wove her mouth shut. The alarm heightened all the more when they realized up close that the thread was real rather than part of some elaborate latex mask.

Fairuza squeezed Bell's hand. "I warned them what to expect, but hearing is not the same thing as knowing. Their experience with oddities and demons is quite different. Most of them have never been to Arcanium before."

"More's the pity," Bell said, "that they joined a circus without knowing what else they could have been a part of."

"More's the mercy that they didn't have to sign over their soul to do it."

"It's a rich, historied tradition."

"That doesn't mean we have to continue it."

She had always disagreed with him on how he brought people in and kept them like pets. Most of his companions did. He was a wish-granting jinni who needed wishes and who loved oddities and the wealth of things humans could do and become, with and without magical assistance. A circus seemed the logical end, keeping them close and collared, their wishes the logical means.

He understood her objections. She understood his. She was human in a jinni suit, and he was jinni in a human suit. They would never quite see eye-to-eye on the problem.

"And yet here you are." He spun her to swing her dress out behind her then slid his arm around the small of her back to bring her against him again. "I missed you."

"I missed you." Those three words held more layers within them than his own. She hadn't lived long enough to simply mean what she said.

She'd missed him, but at the same time, she'd moved on, viewed him very much as her past—a stage that she'd needed to go through and that had given more than it had taken, but which she had outgrown and left behind where it belonged. Which raised the question… Why she had come back at all?

They were too psychic to hide much. Psychics had a code not to peer too deeply without necessity, but although he revered mystery in the pursuit of performance, the circus was closed, and he and his people could do with a little less real mystery in their lives. He saw through her like the diamonds on her throat—refraction through facets, angles and distortions, but hard in their clarity.

He tightened his arm around her. "Fairuza."

"Don't hate me."

"What have you done?"

"I wanted you to see me coming. I wouldn't try to hide too much, even before…what happened. But I concealed her more, even though you wouldn't know to seek her in a sea of other shadows."

Bell drew his arm from Fairuza and turned, searching the bleachers, each face, each pair of eyes.

"I didn't know whether to tell you before I came or not—or which would be better."

Kitty stood with the Ringmaster in front of his platform, although the Ringmaster showed his possession in ways other than what most considered traditional and he and Kitty rarely displayed affection in public.

Bell met her eyes briefly as he searched, and she stiffened.

No one else would make him like this. Not Valorie. Not Fairuza. No one else made his skin molten and his insides shards of ice. Kitty stepped away from the platform and ran into the ring to peer into the bleachers as well.

She and Bell noticed her at almost the same time.

Bell couldn't understand how he hadn't seen her from the beginning, because just as Fairuza was the only one of her cast to wear white, Maya was the only Illumina cast member to wear red. They black-mirrored each other, their coloring similar with Maya's Mexican and Italian roots and Fairuza's Byzantine and Persian background. Fairuza played the wise white witch in swan feathers and diamonds. Maya played the more seductive, darker witch, with garnets dripping from her neck, blood-red still streaking her hair from her time in Arcanium—as though Fairuza had brought Arcanium into her circus on purpose, a touch of wickedness that skintight, low-cut costumes alone couldn't accomplish.

Maya was shorter than Fairuza but wore taller boots. She wouldn't have lost any of the preternatural balance that had served her on the high-wire and tightrope. He rarely took away an ability unless they requested it of him, and she'd cut off all contact—not that he'd tried the traditional ways, knowing how violently she'd reacted to just sensing him in her head outside of what had been Locke's Arcanium.

He hadn't blamed her for that. He'd withdrawn as soon as he could, because within her had been razors and garottes, needles, claws, teeth, gun muzzles and scalpels, each a thought, each a memory—and constant in her head. Being among his people after taking Arcanium back had been like rolling in a crater of broken glass and nails, but being in their heads was like being in a trash compactor of sharp objects. It had been excruciating, experiencing their pain—firsthand, secondhand, thirdhand—and knowing he was the cause.

He'd left her alone, although he'd feared what she would do without him to stop her, because any one of those piercing thoughts could have found an artery. Part of the reason Caroline had returned and asked for such extreme alteration, part of the reason why Neve had begged him to do even worse to her, was to keep from doing something unalterable to themselves. With Bell, in an off-label dungeon, he could give them all the pain they needed without destroying them entirely. He could bleed them and replenish the blood at the same time. But Maya had never asked that of him, hadn't so much as thought in his direction for relief that he more than owed her.

Yet she was there. She'd come back to Arcanium, a place she should never have wanted to see again, a place that should have resurrected memories that stabbed fountain pen nibs underneath his nails. He had set free all those who had asked it of him, and with her final wish, she'd already been free to leave at any time. There was no reason in the world why she would return, not with how deeply he had betrayed her— everyone—and the suffering she'd endured simply because he had favored her.

This wasn't right.

Not that it was morally wrong, although a case could be made. Maya would have been the one to make it, even if she hadn't always followed her own moral code, treading instead in the murky waters of moral ambiguity or swimming in deeper, darker pools in spite of the lighthouse she tried to follow.

This isn't right.

He slipped into her mind like a ghost. There wasn't so much as a piece of paper against which to give himself a paper cut. She carried no open wounds, no thick, keloidal scar tissue — neither continued pain nor healed surfaces.

No recognition. None of the fondness or hatred that recognition would conjure.

Superficial relief warred with the hellfire that would clearly be blazing behind his eyes as he met Fairuza's unblinking but unsteady gaze.

He couldn't find words for too long, manufacturing his own razorblades underneath his tongue. "She doesn't remember."

Chapter Three

"Bell..." Kitty pulled herself together enough to insert herself between Bell and the woman who had no idea who he was.

Fairuza remained an eye in his storm, unnaturally still and unwilling to move to his or anyone's indignation. He could strip her of power, but not without a fight. He had made her so that very little could frighten her anymore.

"No, she doesn't remember—not Locke, not Arcanium, not you. She knows that she was part of Arcanium, but only because I told her, because Seth came to Illumina and I knew it would come out on its own." Fairuza searched his face, but she did him the courtesy of allowing him privacy in his mind.

Grief was far from only a human emotion. Elephants, wolves, whales and pigeons grieved. Even demons grieved. That he could still experience grief after centuries of its particular needle digging into his heart wasn't a question. He felt thoroughly and well, and although his reactions and emotions were sometimes unspeakable to humans, they were as strong or stronger. Creator God, he hadn't yet finished mourning what had happened to her, what he had done, what he had lost.

Bell didn't speak. Tension mounted between the jinn like static-charged mist, spreading slowly from the center of the ring to the canvas, thickening the more they stared at each other, gradually not blinking. Like breathing, blinking was more habit than necessity.

Fairuza was the first to blink—literally and figuratively. Bell's magic swept around her like the tide around rocks.

"I come in peace, Bell. I didn't come here to fight. It would have been more suspicious to her if I'd kept her from Arcanium while I brought everyone else with me. As long as she stays with Illumina, this concerns her, too."

"If you had to bring her at all, you should have stayed away," Bell said.

Maya had never asked Bell to box away her bad memories like he'd done for Joanne and Christina, and even then, he'd told all those leaving Arcanium that he wouldn't take their memories of the circus itself. It was important that they remembered how they got into Arcanium so that they wouldn't make the same mistake twice. The warning had been especially menacing toward those who had been in Arcanium as punishment, although that punishment had been paid multiple times over by demonic torture that even Bell's Arcanium at its worst couldn't get close to meeting.

He hadn't sectioned out Maya's most terrible memories, and he never would have sectioned out the Arcanium memories for exactly this reason. Fairuza had hidden so many that Maya wouldn't know why she had fortune teller skills or the ability to keep her balance, no matter the surface on which she walked. She trusted the basics that Fairuza told her, and she'd agreed to come to Arcanium because she'd known she'd been there before, because of inevitable curiosity. This Maya didn't know better than to come back.

"This isn't about her," Fairuza said.

"The fuck it isn't," he hissed, and not in a stage whisper that everyone in the room would hear. "You brought her here when she doesn't know why she should stay away or even why she asked you to remove her memories. She just knows 'something bad' happened. A human mind with no concept of demons and what they are capable of will not begin to comprehend the horror of what she experienced. At least I left them with the sense to avoid Arcanium at all costs."

"I protect my own as well as you do."

"You knowingly brought her into the place she was adamant about leaving and never returning to. That should have been *her* informed choice, not yours."

Fairuza blinked again, with the first hint of genuine confusion. "Bell, Arcanium is safe now. Everyone knows it, even the demons considering taking their own stab at your security. I wouldn't have brought *any* of mine here if it weren't safe."

"Why *are* you here?" This time Bell didn't remain in *sotto voce*, nor did he conceal anger for the sake of appearances with his own people.

"Not all of us have wealth dating back to ancient Mesopotamia. I'm here because Illumina is not doing so well financially and because, in spite of a few new tricks and talent, Arcanium hasn't changed much since you first brought me in. That was almost half a century ago, Bell. There's something to be said for tradition, but

I think it's time to inject a little new life into Arcanium, don't you think?"

"And you believe you can do that with Illumina, a circus that's been so successful that it can't support itself without asking Arcanium for financial aid?" Bell crossed his arms. He didn't need to affect anger, but he did need to affect dismissal.

Because this was something he hadn't foreseen—not even a hint—nor was it something he'd ever considered, because no ordinary circus could be trusted with Arcanium's secrets. There were only a spare handful of supernatural ones, none of which would be foolhardy enough to invade Arcanium, even in a friendly way, and none of them were dungeon-based or willing to risk putting themselves in the position of getting trapped within one. Oh, there were a few circus-themed dungeons in the vein of Locke's Arcanium, but as inventive as demons were with their torture, they were less so with their themes, which was part of the reason why Locke had stolen Arcanium rather than make his own.

"Don't stand there and tell me that Arcanium *is* financially successful, even with your overpriced midway games, slightly more reasonably priced food and your encouraging tip jars. Having an independently wealthy patron who also runs the circus and who creates or steals most of the overhead doesn't make you successful."

"I think that definition is relative. Although you don't begin from a place of wealth, my dear, I gave you all the tools to create or steal that which you need yourself. Why run to me?" he asked.

"I can create lodgings but not anything that a body actually needs. I can steal food and the occasional minor windfall, but I can't take enough that it attracts attention or damages those I steal them from. And unlike you, Bell, I have to pay my people a salary, because they *can* have families and homes outside the circus."

"I don't see how this is my problem."

"This isn't your problem." Fairuza stepped to the side, restless and — dare he believe it — embarrassed. "It's mine. This is one of my solutions to my problem. And, my darling, this is a solution to one of yours."

"Ah, yes, my problem."

"I know you're of the 'if it ain't broke, don't fix it' school of thought, but I've been here multiple times in the last year, and something's broken, Bell."

"Do I not have enough glitter for you, love?"

"There's no need to be cruel."

The feathers from her skirt fluttered away, a few of the tips tickling under his chin before they came together to form a dozen white swans that flew out of the big top entrance. What they left behind was a thin, layered underskirt, but she certainly seemed more human, less of a caricature — although no amount of flannel and denim could make her less than she was, any more than cotton and leather could change him. No matter what form the jinn took, no matter how innocuous, people gravitated, responded, reacted, as though breathing in perfume and incense.

Fairuza let down her elaborate hairstyle. Beautiful thick hair spilled over her shoulders, messy and still stuck through with pins. She removed those next, to fall on the sawdust like petals. She spread her arms, as though offering this version of herself — stripped down, if not stripped away. Bell couldn't offer the same without stripping completely. Fairuza wouldn't be surprised by what he revealed, but Bell could think of a few people who would rather not have that sight indelibly branded into their brains. Fairuza was a far more appealing sight for all.

"I was glad that you brought everyone in, as I brought everyone with me. I care for my cast, Bell. I don't want to shut Illumina down, not when I'm so proud of what Illumina has become. It would not be my first choice to start from scratch, from nothing, to find something new that would work in our small, exclusive, changing, dying field. You and I both know there should always be a place for wonder, somewhere to escape from the mundane, even if people insist on returning to it, briefly sated, as though there is ever satisfaction for such things."

Bell allowed the swell of his magic to dissipate, return to its home, sharing the ring with Fairuza with less antagonism. He didn't forget Maya in the shadow, because now that Fairuza had let him find her, he couldn't unfeel her in his web, the shiver as unmistakable as each measured step he took over the vast silk. But her fear no longer trembled with her—nor did her hatred. She was not so loud or so sharp, and he could hate Fairuza less.

Such hatred could endure for decades, but he already knew this wouldn't last. It was a squall that would settle into a torrid rain then earthworms in puddles. He was angry because anger was a response to surprise. He could appreciate the rare experience of surprise and still suffer the emotions that arose from it. He would solve the problem of Maya in due course. Right now, his pain was his own and could be handled, as could Kitty's. Maya had no pain. Fairuza had made sure of that. He didn't need to deal with Maya immediately. Or possibly ever, if he arranged things well.

He didn't know how this evening would end, but he suspected, because he had a soft spot for his companions, even when they made bad decisions. That made him vulnerable, which made his people vulnerable. But although the line between demon and jinn was so thin as to occasionally seem nonexistent, his soft, vulnerable places were one of the things that distinguished him as jinn.

"I don't want Illumina to end, and to be honest, Bell, I don't think you want it to either. Or did I not sense you there when you considered using *my* circus to plant that wishing well?"

"I didn't." Bell saw no need to pretend he hadn't been desperate for wishes and the power they gave him so that he could take Arcanium back from Locke. In the end, he hadn't forced Fairuza to be party to his vices when they were part of the reason she'd left — the reason most of them left, even if they parted amicably, as he had with Fairuza. He'd chosen other venues for the well.

"No, you didn't, and I give you my thanks now, for not making me culpable in your particular brand of wish-granting." Fairuza could only grant one wish, and it had to be intentional, not idle. It was the power she had requested, certainly not an unusual one among the wishmasters of the jinn.

Those who worked in her circus weren't there against their will. They had contracts instead of soul-binding. She used the wishes judiciously and granted at her discretion, whereas Bell was obligated to grant any wish, intentional or not — a total of three — and his nature demanded that the wishes not always turn out as the wisher imagined. The fonder he was — the more protective of their heart — the more likely he would grant a wish in the spirit it was made, and unlike

Fairuza, he could continue granting a wish indefinitely, shifting it to his pleasure, as long as he justified the alterations in his mind. Fairuza's grantings were one-and-done, etched into stone, while his were unbaked clay.

"I came here to make you an offer, a mutually beneficial arrangement, because although Illumina languishes in a financial mire, Arcanium can do everything for my people and more. It can respect their contracts with me while you also provide your people's severance salary upon their release. Mere drops in the sea of your private wealth, Bell."

Bell sensed intrigue among both circus troupes. But although Illumina had employed a few demons, they were demons of the sort that were indistinguishable from humans, not just in appearance but in manner. No one could tell that one of the Albino Triplets was a demon unless told. Then most of them assumed the demon was Sin, although that was a bit on the nose. The assumption amused Marina more than anything.

The pretty little things that Fairuza liked to keep around her didn't know what they were getting into.

"And in return, Fairuza, what do you think you can offer me? We have fans all over the country — all over the world — by keeping things the way they are."

"But you know things need to change." Fairuza continued to circle him. Not the way a demon would circle. She'd always liked to move when she talked — and when she was nervous. "Everyone knows you're good with your oddities. Demons who don't have to pretend so hard, people you've cursed, people you've transformed... You're good at that. But you've known you had to change. That's why you started the Skeleton Band, which has pulled in so many more fans than even you must have suspected it would. Your diva's had agents come in to recruit her. Too bad she's stuck in Arcanium like the rest, no?"

Fairuza glanced back at the Skellies, at the sugarskulled leading lady in her usual studded leather jacket. Vivian narrowed her eyes, making no effort to curtail her suspicion, as keen from her natural inclinations as that of the cast who'd earned their suspicion of powerful strangers.

"You've kept playing the karaoke game, which is clever enough with its pleasant surprises among the rest of the ear-knives, then the coup that sets the tone for the rest of the afternoon and evening. But you don't even consider using the band in your big top performance, when you have such a collection of singers and styles that can keep that momentum going? You're a collector of individuals, Bell, but you only ever present them as a individuals and small teams rather than as a cohesive whole."

"It's an artistic direction," Bell said.

"It's a talent show of professionals who shouldn't be doing talent shows anymore. You've tried integrating acts, but you don't go much farther than two or three. Your instinct tells you that something needs to be done, but you don't have the eye."

Fairuza stopped behind him, her breath warm against the nape of his neck. "You're a collector. I'm a director. In my circus, *I'm* the Ringmaster. I respect yours, no mistake, but he's only a real Ringmaster after the circus closes. *You* are the Ringmaster, but you're not mastering the ring, because that's not who you are. You're a good collector, a good creator, a good MC. Your haunted funhouse is legendary, your Funhouse events even more so. You just don't know how to take the next step. You're a magnificent being, but there are some things you still need to learn, and you're usually not too proud to admit it. They say you've lost your nerve. You haven't. You eased your way back into things. Anyone who criticizes you for that doesn't understand what happened. But you need help, I need help, and I think we can help each other. Then our fans get to experience the other circus, which is just a bonus on both sides."

"What exactly do you propose?" There was no one better than jinn at maintaining a straight face. He blocked Fairuza from seeing into his thoughts without a less delicate touch, which would have been impolite, especially when she needed this alliance more than he did.

Except she had Maya, and he still wanted to throttle Fairuza for that, even as he didn't want to let Maya escape him again, not when she'd lost all the abrasive scars and sharp edges she'd had when she'd left. That was illusion, though, greater illusion than anything he did in Arcanium. He couldn't even look at her, much less hold on to her, now that she was here.

It would be better for everyone if he fronted Fairuza the money she needed to keep Illumina afloat for a while longer and spare Maya from returning to Arcanium on something other than her own terms. Yet he kept his peace.

"I suggest that Illumina and Arcanium join forces, travel together, perform together. You teach my people to find their inner freak, and I teach yours how to create a cohesive evening performance. It means less improvisation and fewer last-minute changes, because my people are not going to be able to make those adjustments without warning, but we can change the theme quarterly. My people remain contracted. They don't bind themselves to you, and they're paid every two weeks, with health benefits, et cetera."

"Honestly, love, it sounds like your people are getting the better part of this deal. My way, I keep Arcanium uprooted, sugar-daddy everyone and, in return, three performances a week change only slightly, even though they don't need to."

"I ask you to honor their contracts, but they'll also be at your mercy, Bell, like your own. And I'd care for your people the way that you care for them. Arcanium would benefit from having another jinni watching over them, adding her power to the spell threads."

Bell looked up, blinking slowly. "You haven't told them what Arcanium is. You haven't told them what being at my mercy means, because they've never had to be at yours."

"I didn't know whether you'd even consider accepting this exchange," she replied evenly, but she couldn't conceal her trepidation. "They can break their contract at any time, unlike yours. If enough of them refuse, we will look for another way to raise money or find another patron. But my people are dedicated and disciplined. That happens when they're part of something voluntarily, Bell, as I'm sure you've noticed."

"And I'm sure you've noticed the quality and dedication I gain, even from my involuntaries," Bell said. "Funny how that happens with the right disincentive for escape."

One of the male trapeze artists stood up from his group in the bleachers. "What kind of disincentive?"

"Death, for instance."

"Are you goddamn serious?"

"Deadly so. It's rarely the first option."

"But it's an option at all? Just for rebellion?"

"It's preceded by a great deal of pain." Bell stepped toward the edge of the ring, unwavering. He'd had enough people question the treatment of his involuntaries, and he'd made enough amendments to his original rules to assuage his own merciful proclivities. "But I assure you, it usually only takes a little for them to learn."

"Who the fuck do you think you are?" the man asked.

"Where the fuck do you think *you* are?" Bell jumped onto the partition. Although it was barely an inch thick, he didn't struggle for balance.

Another man stood among the same group, not a trapeze artist but a tall man with trimmed, striking facial hair and an iridescent teal suit. A magician.

How quaint. Yet a man after his own heart.

"You enslave them." The magician was indignant rather than belligerent, his chest puffed like a rooster to a wolf.

"Yes."

"And you brought us here?" the man asked Fairuza.

"You wouldn't be one of his involuntaries."

"But you're okay with bringing us into a place that enslaves *some*?"

"Without Arcanium, there would never have been Illumina," Bell said. "Your mistress was mine first, and she was involuntary as well."

"That doesn't make it okay. People have a right to —"

"You have *no* rights." Bell leaped from the partition to the bleachers then stepped up each bench without looking where he put his feet. He trusted Arcanium to keep him standing. "Human rights are rights you have as human beings among other human beings. As you would not expect a gorilla to respect your rights, there's no reason to expect such respect from me. You may try to fight me, Canton, but *I* am the one who makes the rules in my own little piece of the world. And just as there are things that make you human, there are things that make me jinn."

"Fairuza is jinn." To the man's credit, he remained standing, uncowed, steady, as Bell reached his row and stepped down onto the floor below the bench to stare up into Canton's eyes. He obviously fought not to squirm at Bell's closeness and how unflinchingly he stared, but as a man of the arts, he wouldn't be quite as uncomfortable with the deliberate homoerotic undertones in Bell's challenge.

"Fairuza was human. I *made* her jinn, a reward for her faithfulness. And after serving me for over twenty-five years, I released her freely. As part of Arcanium, you would still be tied to her, not me, although even if you were tied to me, boy, you'd still come in voluntarily, with all the perks therein."

Bell patted his cheek. Canton jerked his face away, but he didn't step back.

"It's not all puppies and roses. I protect my cast jealously, which may lead me to do things that you find distasteful, but you don't get to decide whether or not I do them. As an example... You have a child, a son, Alexander. He will not be welcome here at all hours. His life would be at risk if he were here when he was not supposed to be. This is why my cast can't get pregnant, and that would have to apply to the women of Illumina if they were to stay."

"You're insane." Canton clenched his teeth, the delicate bones of his cheeks and jaw more pronounced. Aside from the garish suit, he was pretty, dramatic in coloring with his paler skin and dark hair, long-limbed, long-fingered. Bell would consider bending him to a more flexible way of thinking under other circumstances, despite his strident cry for human rights.

Leave it to humans to torch the earth and enslave other animals for food, labor and companionship, destroy entire species then have the nerve to tell him not to do the same with them.

"What of it? A little madness is no terrible thing."

"But yours is a monstrous thing."

Bell smiled. Canton finally took a step back. Bell had none of the sharp teeth of his demons or the Sphynx, but he smiled as though he did.

"The clowns are monstrous things. They keep my circus from being exposed by children who believe what they see and grow up to become hunters."

"They're just children," Canton insisted.

"They don't stay that way. And considering what many of my cast get up to when the circus isn't in session—and sometimes when it is—I guarantee you don't want your son getting an eyeful of that."

Bell stepped up onto the bench and continued to walk its length, introducing himself to Illumina in every step and shuffle and the utter disregard he paid to the more apparent strength of the artists who'd had to earn every fiber built on their tight, lovely bodies. He could have a field day with them if they ever properly relaxed.

"My dear guests, you've entered *my* world. You are not the apex predator here. You have no strength, no power. You are here now, after hours, because I allow you to be. But if you do anything to threaten Arcanium, the clowns leave very little behind, and my incubus and succubus are always hungry, although they're quite well-fed these days. However, Arcanium isn't just sawdust soaking up blood. My means are little…unconventional, but it's done with Arcanium's safety in mind. Don't question it. Your questions will change nothing. All I ask is that you are careful with who you invite in and when. Children are welcome in Arcanium, of course—just before eight p.m. I normally don't take in parents, but accepting Illumina would require some adjustment to our usual procedures."

"Sorry to put you out." Canton's steady determination devolved into sarcasm, as though he had the wit to yield it.

"Do you know what happened to us? Do you know what people have tried to do? No, you don't, because you're a circus of gymnasts, dancers and bodybuilders, and your venues look much richer than mine. We appear leaner, more vulnerable, and my human oddities are subject to the basest insults of your kind— *their* kind. I once kept fifty prisoners, humans who had dared to attack my people en masse. They suffered every day and night in recompense for the suffering they caused just by breathing the same air as my people. Because I protect my own." Bell emphasized every word. "I use any means available to me, including corporal punishment, public humiliation and, yes…death. When I let my guard down for a second, it didn't go so well for my children."

"I thought you were supposed to be some kind of god." This time the speaker was one of the smaller tumblers, a woman with short blonde hair and eyebrow piercings to complement her facial glitter.

"You try keeping your finger on every thread in a tapestry at all times, past, present and future, give everyone a good show and see how far your influence extends. I was once worshipped as a god, and in comparison to, say…you, I am. But who wants to be a god of everything? I'm content being almost omnipresent and omnipotent here."

"Almost?" Canton asked.

Bell shrugged. "I am what I choose to be. I could be more. Would you rather I take *all* the reins, love?"

Canton scowled but didn't reply.

"As long as you follow a few fundamental rules, you will have all the freedom that those who are voluntary to Arcanium are permitted, although I still urge everyone to be careful and limit your time on the outside just for a while longer, or request that one of our demons—or yours, for that matter—accompany you. I can track them much more easily than I track you. There are far too many of your kind out there."

"Rules?" the blonde woman said. "Other than 'you're trapped and try to enjoy it, and you're safe but not'?"

"You're safer than houses in here. If nuclear war broke out, I'd keep you safe and fed until nuclear winter subsided. I don't have much recourse for the sun exploding, but perhaps you wouldn't want me to. However, the rules... Yes, the rules. More like laws, really, and not up for debate or challenge, because a circus as demonic as mine is designed to protect both the demons and the humans. The humans feel I give too much to the demons, and the demons feel I give too much to the humans, and that's how I know I've balanced their souls fairly."

Lennon raised his fist in the midst of the Skeletons without looking up. Bell met the fist bump without a pause as he continued around the bleachers.

Considering how deep-earth Lennon had been created, he would probably take umbrage to being called Bell's most well-behaved demon, but it amused him far more to play within the rules that Bell set than to struggle in every direction like his tentacles when he let himself get 'wriggly'—his words to describe the Cthulhuian nightmare he became when he showed his true self. Like Bell, he preferred his human skin to play in. The monster shape was a novelty, something to bring out when special guests had been invited to dinner. Jonas, the odd chef, also on Bell's well-behaved list, had never shown his true face in Arcanium, and the Ringmaster was spare with his own, saving it for Kitty alone. Demons, well-behaved or not, usually chose human skin. Destruction wreaked in human form made far more of an impact than anything done by a monster.

The Skeletons around Lennon — not including Vivian, but Vivian rarely included herself among their number, and they were just fine with that — shifted ever so slightly on the bench as Bell passed them. He'd spent less time with them than he had trying to keep Vivian from throwing a wrench into the machine that he'd just finished repairing, but he begrudgingly admitted that putting the group of struggling women together then refusing them satisfaction had not resulted in quite the effect he would have preferred. They were all doing much better now, from Vivian and Shane all the way to Alicia. That Lennon got to enjoy three of them at any given time in addition to his lovely mermaid was simply a testament to how a demon who played by the rules could get all the spoils.

Sometimes it just took a while. After all, it had taken fifty years before he'd found someone just for Mikhail and Sasha to enjoy. The incubus and succubus had almost forgiven him for what Locke had done to Neve, because they could be the ones to give her what she needed to heal.

"As you might have noticed," Bell continued, "Arcanium is a special circus with a particularly adult slant, although we keep that just within the realm of decency during the day. The incubus and succubus add an extra layer or five of sexual tension. That will make you newcomers uncomfortable for a while as you adjust to the desires that arise. But the incubus and succubus themselves, Lady Sasha and Lord Mikhail over there in the spare bits of leather, are off-limits to all except Neve, the woman with them, without their permission. To touch a person without being able to feed from them creates a mutual craving that ultimately cannot be met without murder, and they are charged *not* to murder the people they're meant to protect without *my* permission. Neve is the only one who can replenish herself after a feed, because I made her that way. None of the rest of you can be so lucky, not even me. I don't know if it would actually kill me, but I'd rather not test that theory, and as long as the three of us have to live with each other, I'd rather not make it harder than it already is."

Among those less accustomed to the regular string of innuendo in Arcanium, there were furtive, juvenile glances and snickers. His own cast was long over most of the double entendre to the point that they didn't even hear it anymore, especially when he was in the middle of grandstanding. Kitty was reaching the end of her own patience for him taking over her job. She was more abundantly clear in her instruction, while he liked the sound of his own voice far more.

He usually used Kitty to introduce individuals to Arcanium, but this was different. This was another forty or fifty guests who needed to adjust to the idea of Bell holding their fates.

"To summarize," he said, in deference to Kitty's anxiety, "don't touch the sex demons. Just enjoy or endure their effect on the circus. Which brings us to the next but not less important law. It's the law most often broken, but as with trying to escape, it usually only happens once. Because of my sex demons, you will experience a substantial boost to your libido. If you have a partner or five, this can work in your favor. But even in the midst of a Funhouse event—which is ultimately a celebration of sex—all my people are permitted to say no. It doesn't matter how much our guests contribute to the event or how many vacation homes they own or if they gift an oddity with a shiny jewel. Consent is *required*. If someone says no, my dears, that is when you *stop*."

Bell stopped behind the Spider, who sat with the Creature. Elizabeth knew better than anyone how thin the line was, and how important the distinction.

"If you don't stop, I will know. In Arcanium, it's best to behave as though I will know *everything* you do and think. Most of time, those things aren't that interesting to me, but if you do what I've expressly and with no ambiguity told you *not* to do, I will know. This law is designed to protect my humans from the demons and my cast from outsiders, but it has been invoked to protect demons from humans as well. Violence between anyone is forbidden—and ignoring the withdrawal of consent is violence here."

Bell stepped down from the bleachers then jumped back into the ring. "Guests who commit grievous harm against my cast are offered a choice—to give themselves to the clowns or give themselves to me by wishing into the circus, to become whatever strikes my fancy. Once a wish brings you into Arcanium, it is my decision when you leave. Even wishing yourself out won't necessarily guarantee I will allow you out. All of you would enter Arcanium under Fairuza's contract, and I would honor that, unless you fuck up, at which point you would become mine. But whether you are mine or not, the punishment for hurting one of my people or trying to force yourself on them — no matter whether you think you need it or they deserve it or want it — is ten lashes from the Ringmaster, who's a demon with a bullwhip, and that isn't a metaphor."

The Ringmaster descended from his platform. Lennon could hide what he was from anyone, had hidden it from Bell for a good five years because it had been such a long time since he'd taken his original form that his more human-like demonic visage had presented even to Bell as true. The Ringmaster, on the other hand, though a tall, dark, handsome stranger, could be nothing but what he was, in spite of his human skin. If any of Illumina thought that Bell was full of shit and Arcanium so much smoke and mirrors as a front for a sex shop, the Ringmaster quieted their dismissal when he shook out his bullwhip and cracked it so loudly that everyone who wasn't Bell or Kitty winced.

"My Ringmaster has been at sixes and sevens without prisoners to punish multiple times a week. He'll make the most of the ten. At his worst, he cuts to the bone."

One of the young tumblers, a nineteen-year-old boy, raised his hand tentatively, as though afraid the Ringmaster would snap it right off if he noticed. Bell played teacher and pointed to the adorable cinnamon roll, who reminded him of Seth in his early days, although slighter.

"If you need us to work for you, how is beating us to the bone, shredding muscle, supposed to let us do that? We can't perform if we're disabled. Even if we heal, there's no guarantee we'll be in any shape to perform again. Most of us have had serious injuries before. It can be months of rehab…or years. Sometimes no amount of physical therapy gets us in the place to do what we were doing."

Bell crooked his finger to the Ringmaster and turned his back just enough to present a clean canvas.

The Ringmaster didn't hesitate. He raised his arm, sending the lash into an elegant, serpentine curve before bringing it down on Bell's back.

Not just the Illumina cast gasped, although the Arcanium cast recovered more quickly, and none stood in shock like the strangers.

Struck to his knees, Bell glanced up as blood trickled down to stain the waist of his pants. Pain sang through his back with every shift.

Maya was on her feet, too, just as concerned as the rest of Illumina — an innocent civilian once more. Oh, she'd never been completely innocent, but her vices had been comparatively small and normal to those of some people he'd brought into Arcanium. A sweet, slightly lapsed Catholic girl entering Arcanium, however, had triggered the old guilt quickly and completely. One night, she would agree to let him tie her to a post for the entire circus to sample, and the next she'd wrap her arms around the plain wooden bench he used for punishments and take twenty lashes of the Ringmaster's whip, in the absence of a priest to confess to. Bell hadn't needed her to confess to him, but his knowledge of all she would confess was why she could kneel before him.

That had been before, a Maya who had been wished in by an unfaithful, unappreciative boyfriend, a Maya trapped in a tempting hellscape that offered slices of heaven she never would have dreamed of before stepping foot into the circus. This was pre-Arcanium Maya, a Maya who only knew Illumina.

He still had her, the Maya of Arcanium. He had her as though she were in his arms right now, before Locke had taken her away. He had her in his bed after a session with the Ringmaster, smoothing his palms over her back as the potion cooled the sting and stitched together the tissue. Even a hellborn demon knew the difference between perdition and absolution, and because the Ringmaster loved Kitty and Kitty loved Maya, he hadn't struck her as hard as he could have. But absolution without damage was empty, so the demon had done his damage. Then Bell had erased the damage, with his hands or with the potion, held Maya while she cried, surrounded her with heat, warmth, love and home, punished and soothed her as he'd sunk into her and she'd cried, moaned, came. He was with her now, even as he saw her in the bleachers, watching him bleed.

Time, like water rocking in a storm, brought him back and forth, between the Maya he'd known and the one before him, as he staggered back to his feet. Let the Illumina cast believe what they wanted about why he'd permitted a lash. Their opinion of him didn't matter. Fairuza's did—and she watched him carefully, guarded, contemplative, but she didn't interfere.

"If you have earned my mercy—and precious little does once you've caused harm to anyone under my care—I will heal you myself."

Bell called the wound together, repairing the damage with his magic. Immortality didn't make him hurt less or depreciate the pain. It just made the recovery time faster.

"If not, you'll receive this." With a flourish, he revealed the electric blue potion that he kept for just such an occasion as this. "It'll heal any injury and prevent infection. It's not a universal panacea, however. Arcanium heals and cures disease, but if you have a little something you want fixed, you'll either need a wish or a serious amount of good will, and that, like mercy, is earned."

"So if we punch someone, we get whipped by... whatever he is," Canton said. "Doesn't that seem —?"

"Excessive? Sometimes the only way to make sure something doesn't happen again is to let it happen once and allow the person to learn better. I may not be able to stop everything, but I can damn well put myself between my people and danger, even if that danger is you. Clowns or a wish, Canton — which would you pick?"

Canton sighed, lifting his hands in something between a shrug and nonchalance, but Bell could read between a magician's actions and the glint of fear in his eyes.

"Being circus folk isn't easy. Even your circus, one built around skill rather than strangeness, understands that. We're subject to ridicule, scorn and, yes, violence from outsiders and newcomers. Our oddities have it even harder. Those brought in against their will never chose that kind of vulnerability. It's my responsibility to make sure they only ever have to fear two things — the Ringmaster and me. That may not be much comfort to you, but to ease your mind, a single punch isn't likely to get you anything but a scolding. A barroom brawl isn't advisable, and I suggest that if you're a mean drunk, you abstain from alcohol while in my world. A slap, a shove...? If they're mild enough, nothing will happen. I know that, in the heat of the moment, sometimes emotions spill out. But after the initial moment, I expect you to control yourself. Do you understand?"

Bell eliminated the bloodstain on his pants and the drying drips of blood from his back, leaving no trace of what the Ringmaster had done. The Ringmaster's fingers around the handle twitched, but he wound the whip once again. Bell wasn't nearly as fun to him as humans. Though immortals allowed him more lashes, there wasn't much of a thrill when no amount of blows could kill them. That Bell wouldn't permit humans to die under the Ringmaster's whip didn't matter — only that they could.

Fairuza rested a hand on Bell's shoulder, her fingers cool. Most jinn ran hot, but she'd always had colder fingers. He'd kept the small details, which — as every artist knew — were the most important.

"Arcanium is a demonic circus run by a jinni. I'm jinn, but I was human, and that informs everything I do," she said, both to Bell and to the rest of the room. "Illumina was never about magic, although I help where appropriate. All you wonderful people rarely require my help, but then we were never trying to achieve beyond what was possible. Arcanium is horror-themed, less disciplined, less rigid and more dependent on magic for more fantastic results. It has its benefits. You'll never fall, and any injuries can be healed in a matter of moments. Performances and practice will feel easier. Most of the people performing in Arcanium don't know how hard you've worked to achieve what you do, but most of them who have these abilities without working for them were brought in against their will and can't leave. There's *always* a trade-off. Don't allow resentment to interfere with collaboration. Teach them what you can do without magic, and they will teach you what you can do with it."

She stepped away from him again, the tips of her fingernails brushing over his skin.

He prickled with the same desire she'd evoked with her kiss. He wanted to follow her, press a kiss to the base of her neck, wind his arms around her waist, show her people what she'd once been to him. To her people, she was a leader—powerful, intimidating, arch, inaccessible, the woman behind the curtain in many ways, no more a part of them than any boss among employees. She'd stepped over the line of professional more than once, he could already tell, but that didn't make her one of them.

But she was still his, no matter what she had become, no matter how powerful he had made her. Just as he still had Maya as she'd been and always would be to him, he had Fairuza, experienced their last night as though it were now, with less pain than he had with Maya.

"I won't make this decision unilaterally. I've had a few of mine abandon Illumina in favor of Arcanium, and I don't take that personally—much." Fairuza smiled softly at the members of Arcanium she recognized. "Especially those who started here. If you want to stay, even if the rest of us go, I won't hold that against you, as long as you go through all the paperwork with me. However, for those of you with perfectly reasonable reservations about whether we should all stay, might I suggest a trial period?" Fairuza glanced back at Bell. "Would you object to a few exclusive circus days during the week? I remember how quiet it was when we weren't traveling, but I don't know whether you have a Funhouse event or something else planned."

"We have nothing planned this week, although we have a Funhouse event scheduled next week," Bell said. "Illumina is welcome to it, as guests or entertainment, although as guests, we'll have to get you something...nicer to wear."

"I'll have you know that I spare no expense on my costumes. You're only disdainful because you have

Sasha working the leather and Kitty doing everything else." A note of playfulness crept into Fairuza's voice. Both of Bell's costumers had gained fame as well as notoriety in the circus world.

"I just think that if my usual clientele sees one hint of iridescent polyester, they might choke on their champagne," Bell said.

"Well, one look at Sasha in leather and I'm pretty sure my clientele would choke, too. Sticks and stones, love." Fairuza shook her head, but she was smiling. "I propose that we experience each other's circuses over the next two weeks between open days. Illumina visits Arcanium this week to become used to you and your circus' idiosyncrasies. Arcanium visits Illumina next week, and Illumina experiences a Funhouse. Then we decide if we want to become a part of it."

Fairuza turned back to her Illumina audience, but she passed her gaze over those from Arcanium as well, acknowledging the unanticipated invasion of Arcanium's dubious privacy. "Majority rules, as usual. If enough of mine decide they want nothing to do with Arcanium, which I anticipate a few might, then we will move on, leaving only footprints, taking only memories. You'll never have to see us again."

"If they're going to stay, Tragedy, Comedy, please don't jump our poor, unsuspecting Illumina guests," Bell said mildly. "Do forgive the clowns if they need to smell you. I'd rather a moment of discomfort to a moment of maiming. If you're unsure, bring them to me or Fairuza and we can confirm whether you're allowed to eat them."

Canton stood again. "You're actually going to let the clowns eat people if they're not one of us?"

Bell respected someone willing to take the responsibility of mouthpiece, but he could already tell that Canton was going to be a problem. Every single alpha male among Fairuza's cast had learned how to bow before a woman, but that would make them all-the-less prone to bow before anyone else, and every word that spilled from Canton's mouth was shot through with shrill self-righteousness that would quickly become tiresome. Bell didn't like bringing in alpha males who thought he'd never heard these objections before or who believed anything they did would change how he chose to do things.

Strong women were never this annoying to him, perhaps because they never believed that their power and dominance was a given.

Bell sighed. He liked conflict—really, who didn't, if they were honest?—but he hated this kind. What did a magician really think he was going to do against a jinni?

"Clown-mauling was literally the first thing I warned you about," Bell said. "If they were Rottweilers, they'd take a bite out of the ass of anyone climbing the fence. Since they're demon clowns, they take a bigger bite. Are we going to have a problem?"

"You don't even pretend that you're not demons. You just come out and say you're evil. And you still brought us here, Fai?"

"You slept with this mouth-breather? Did you really think his ego needed the boost?" Bell muttered just loud enough for Fairuza to hear.

"Look who's talking," she muttered back with good nature.

"My ego is not overinflated. It's an appropriately earned size."

"You know you can always depend on me to keep it from growing too large, which is part of the reason why I'm here. Remember?"

It was good to see her smile, though.

"Besides, don't pretend you don't want a bite yourself as soon as his ego deflates and something else needs attention." Her breath brushed the shell of his ear, just short of a caress as she stepped around him.

"Do you recommend?"

"Why do you think I slept with him more than once?" Fairuza patted his shoulder and raised her head back to Canton in the bleachers. "I'm jinn, too, my darling. Did you forget that when you signed my contract?"

"You didn't start out that way." Canton crossed his arms in a way that seemed both assertive and defensive at the same time, but the way that Fairuza looked at him, he'd lower his arms to surreptitiously cover his groin any minute.

"You didn't know that when I gave you your choice. It may have just been pen to paper, but it was still your word, and contracts are as binding with jinn as they are with demons. No amount of lawyers you ever bring into a courtroom will change our agreement. Bell and I are both made of the same thing, and unlike angels, demons and jinn have free will, the same as you. Do most demons make it a point to put a railroad spike through your soul? Yes. Do all of them? No. Most of the demons in Arcanium now have been with Bell for over fifty years, and never have I met dirtier polite gentlemen in my life."

Lennon wolf-whistled among his Skeleton harem. Moss howled to join him, compelling Ciarán to low his own deep, resonant sound, somewhere between groaning and an enthusiastic blast of a tuba. Selena spread her legs on her place on the lowest bleacher near the curtains, laughing with Mayumi, whose long, wet hair threatened to swallow them both up.

"I understand that Lord Mikhail's had a few lapses," Fairuza continued, "but he and Lady Sasha are probably the most controlled people I've ever met, considering the feast they're surrounded by, pretty things they can't even touch, in spite of all the pretty things that want to touch them. Can you say the same, Canton?"

The magician opened his mouth like he was going to respond. Bell practically heard him go through every version of a response that tried to justify each slip of his control as something beyond his willpower, in comparison to a sex demon subverting their own, far-more-driven drive. Canton may not have known much about sex demons, but he wisely decided to close his mouth again and sit down.

"Good boy," Fairuza purred. "Now, does anyone else have any objections beyond the usual jitters one might have about considering Arcanium as a home? The laws apply across the board, among cast and guests. There's only one that Bell hasn't shared yet, because he's an asshole. Strike the word 'wish' from your vocabulary, unless you're prepared to accept the consequences of a capricious jinni granting it according to his own assholish whims. Something as innocuous as 'I wish I had some pizza' can get you in trouble if he's in a mood or you're not in his good graces. He is what he is. Most of us have just learned to work around that."

"You're not like that," the younger, blonde tumbler said.

"I'm a different kind of wishmaster, but even if I were, I hope I'd do things differently. Now, I can use the word 'wish' as often as I want, because I've already used all three of mine. Unless he has good reason to force a wish out of you, such as if you've egregiously broken one or all of his laws, please don't make it easy for him to play. And don't think that just because he's not there, he can't hear you. If you're in Arcanium, assume he'll hear. Understood?"

"If he's such an asshole—" Canton began.

"He's not always. He's not most of the time. But wishes are where the devil in him finds its way into the details. If you know that going in, you'll be more prepared to choose your wishes strategically. He can twist them no matter how specific they are, but it helps if you know why you want something and you've proven yourself beneficial to his circus. If you go into the fortune teller tent just out of curiosity, for God's sake, don't make a wish. It's all good fun until someone loses an eye…if they didn't want to lose it."

Neve raised her hand in acknowledgment of the conditional amendment, her eyepatch sparkling. Sera, sitting among Carlo, Lazarus, Magda, Salem and the Horned God, chose not to comment. She hadn't lost her eye because of a wish, and she was holding on to one of her wishes to get it back one day, which would not be any day soon.

"Did I about cover it?" Fairuza asked Bell sweetly.

Bell maintained a blandly pleasant expression, but he really didn't mind that Kitty and Fairuza warned people against wishing. People ended up wishing anyway. "All I would want to add, for both casts, is please be kind and patient. Don't hesitate to bring any reasonable grievances to Fairuza or myself. Reasonable, not complaints about the lack of five-star hotel rooms. We're a traveling circus. There are portable toilets and whatever you have in an RV or trailer. Magic means we don't have to attach to plumbing, but we make do with what we have."

He neglected to mention that the Skellies had a decent community bathroom and shower as part of their group tent or that the two odd food booths had bathroom facilities as well. It was up to their occupants to share that hidden gem, if they wanted to. Bell doubted that Vivian or Jonas would bond with the newcomers, but the rest of the Skellies could potentially bring a boy or four home, so the secret might get out eventually, at their discretion.

He *could* have brought a five-star hotel with him wherever they went, nothing but the best for his children. The golems were almost as good as waitstaff, and he could hide a hotel in just a series of tents, bigger on the inside the way it was for the Horned God, Kitty, the Skeletons and the food booths. But Bell didn't like perfect. Everything he provided, magical or otherwise, was everything anybody needed. Even he lived in an RV, and it wasn't the nicest in the caravan. They had all the circus to roam if they need space. That was more than most people enjoyed and had enjoyed in the past.

"There are tents waiting for you by the caravan. If you came in cars, you can sleep in them if you want, but the tents will be perfectly comfortable until I determine how to split you into vehicles. I'll take most of your cars and keep them in a safe place so that they don't have to drive along with the caravan or take spots from our paying guests. I'd do it now, but I haven't the interest in expending the energy tonight."

Bell turned away, dismissing them, annoyed that he needed to think of logistics when he hadn't planned for a sudden influx of guests. Already, he was figuring how many people would be able to tolerate each other at any given time, who were already sleeping together, who were family, who needed space, who just needed somewhere to sleep, et cetera and so forth. For now, he provided single camping tents, cots with decent mattress rolls and sleeping bags, which would be waiting for them when they arrived at the caravan.

"I'll help with that in the morning. I've been working on it for a while," Fairuza said quietly. Where Illumina called its home base, they had homes and families, but Illumina did a national tour every year, traveling by bus and sleeping in motels. They'd crammed into motel rooms and apartments before, but it wasn't the same as cramming into recreational vehicles. "The tents will do. It's my fault for springing this on you without enough forethought on my part. Don't worry about the cars, though. We came on the buses."

"Shouldn't you know that?" Canton asked. "Aren't you supposed to be the fortune teller? Isn't that how Fai learned her version of the craft?"

Bell shared a glance with Fairuza, begging her to let him throw knives at the man. Fairuza tried not to smile, but she shook her head.

"I can know everything you're thinking about that you don't want to be thinking about but you can't help thinking about now that I've made you think about it." Anyone who knew Bell would recognize that he was losing his patience, and he hoped he wasn't being too subtle for strangers to tell. "The question is, do you *want* me to know everything? Because I don't, but I can. And I can share. Except the circus is closed, I'm tired, and my people would like to leave the tent for some well-earned privacy. And while we're on the subject, if you see anything sordid, mind your own damn business."

Chapter Four

Bell dimmed the spotlights to the ring and walked through the red velvet curtains, effectively ending the conversation and forestalling any further protest. The bleachers shifted, little trembles in the earth, and the cluster of souls they'd carried dispersed through his circus. With the release of so many strong and loud personalities, even though most had been silent, Bell closed his eyes, rubbed them then dropped onto the pink chaise longue.

"I can't believe you still have that old thing."

Fairuza untied her skirt and draped it over her arm, leaving her in just the bodice, underwear and heels. Anywhere else, that would have been considered a come-on, but circuses, like theater, were well-accustomed to skimpy costumes and nudity. Fairuza could walk a tightrope in what she wore now, and the only reason anyone would blink was that she chose real diamonds to do it in.

People would be surprised how often the jewels were real. He had a whole cache of them, not even counting the demon prisons. Why not use them? The silk was real, the leather was good and Neve would have been stunned to learn that the eyepatch she thought was rhinestoned was actually gemstoned, to go with her demon diamond.

Fairuza's impeccable posture released just enough for Bell to know how tightly she'd been holding herself for both Illumina and Arcanium to admire. Jinn bodies didn't tire, but their minds did, and the mind made the body feel tired. She sat on the end of the chaise, her legs kicked out in front of her.

Bell leaned forward to unbuckle her right shoe, which was the only one he could reach. She sighed with a smile and worked open the other buckle so that she could release both feet at once.

"I'll never get rid of this old thing," he said. "It's lasted longer than anyone. Nothing has been as reliable as this chaise longue. You only wish you could say the same about anything else you own."

"You're not wrong. Remind me why we got into this business?"

"Because it wasn't the *business* we wanted to get into."

"Too true." She tossed her hair over her shoulder and leaned back, bracing her hands on the cushion. "You're not mad, are you? I don't mean about Maya. I know you're mad about that. I mean about Illumina."

"No, I'm not mad." Bell reclined into the corner of the chaise, tucking his legs up with flexibility and ease no man his presumed age should have had. "Perplexed. Tentatively curious. Concerned. Whenever I take this many in at once, things slip through the cracks, and it's usually the people who don't deserve it who get screwed over."

"Don't knock yourself out trying to control my people. I may do things the 'hard way', but I've gotten quite good at that thing you do of keeping an eye on everyone to protect them. I have my own spells. I just don't tie them to a place."

"I don't just tie them to a place anymore," he muttered, resting his chin between his knees.

She touched his foot lightly. "You can watch over them all, but I'm watching, too, and they're still more scared of me than they are of you right now. You can tell them to fear you till kingdom come. They won't believe it until you show them, and you've always been stingy with your real magic."

"Oh, I imagine I'll have a few converts when they visit the fortune teller tent in a few days. How long have you been thinking about joining forces?" He didn't have to explain how he could know things but didn't know everything to Fairuza the way he had to do with humans. She understood that sometimes it was better not to know, even if one could.

"Since doing it the hard way meant doing it the broke way. I've cut a few corners, magically. It's difficult to stand on principle when rent is due. But I'm not like you, Bell. I can't steal from Peter to pay Paul then make sure someone pays Peter a little extra later so the books balance. Or rather, I won't," she amended, obviously anticipating his response. "It offends my ethics. You understand that."

"So you'd rather I do it for you, and that doesn't offend those same ethics?"

"I trust the balance that you give to the vendors you steal from, because you have the reserve to guarantee it. I'm living hand-to-mouth right now, and I didn't want to fire any of my people, not when we've reached something amazing. But just because something's amazing and people know it doesn't mean *enough* of them know or that they're willing to pay more for it. There's plenty of amazing out there that goes unseen because of basic economics. I've been thinking about blending Arcanium and Illumina ever since you got it back."

That didn't speak to economics, though, because there was nothing about Bell taking Arcanium back that would make any circus interested in becoming a part of it, lest the massive target on the circus' back lead to collateral damage. But Bell didn't comment on that, and Fairuza didn't expand on the discrepancy.

The secrets she kept made him warier...but not afraid.

"When did Maya find you?" Bell asked quietly.

"Three months after leaving Arcanium. That was around the time Seth, Caroline and her men came to me as well. I guess that was how long it took for them to realize that they weren't going to be able to return to normal after what happened. All of them had looked into other circuses, putting their feelers out for supernatural elements, and found me around the same time. I gave them the confirmation they needed that we were someplace they could talk about what had happened to them without someone prescribing antipsychotics—although mood stabilizers or antidepressants probably wouldn't have been amiss for the PTSD." Fairuza closed her eyes, a line forming between her eyebrows. "God, the minute they came to my table... I get a lot of trauma at that table, Bell, but that... You live with that every day. How do you bear it?"

"I bear it because it's easier for me to bear it through them than for them to have gone through it, and because I'm the reason they had to bear it at all."

Not even accounting for the trauma that some of his cast had experienced before they'd stepped foot in Arcanium... Elizabeth was still his beautiful disaster, her abusers the only prisoners still left in Arcanium, although Dez had a few more freedoms than before Locke's Arcanium. Still, freedom as an armless, legless, mouthless, earless Human Torso was relative. At least he got a feeding tube now and didn't need a colostomy bag. The Man-Doll, however, still had his cloaca, because Henry was a notoriously slow learner.

One of the only reasons he still kept Vivian around — other than being a prodigy with the voice of an angel and a demon, depending on her mood — was everything she'd gone through that had helped turn her into the human monster she'd become. A little empathy had gone a long way toward making her psychopathic tendencies less prominent, as well as the support system of a reformed hellborn demon and two tremendously decent gender anarchists — one quieted the worst in her and the other two fed the best. No self-sabotage since the almost-mass-poisoning incident.

And none of that spoke to what he'd visited upon all of them with his wish-granting, but he likened what he did to pushing them into freezing water — the way a body seized, contracted, reacted, before adjustments were made. There was a reason why Caroline, Riley, Colm and Seth had returned to him, in spite of what they'd gone through. The minor trauma required to bring cast members into Arcanium was necessary for Arcanium to work, but he tried to provide hot chocolate and heated blankets after his people managed to climb out of the freezing water. Until then, he was more accommodating of their emotional turmoil.

They didn't know that, but God, the second, third and fourth chances he handed out like candy... He bent the rules so far that they almost broke to keep from hurting them or allowing them to hurt themselves. But that was the part they never saw.

Locke was different. If his people hadn't known that before, they knew it now, but that didn't always make Bell more palatable just because he wasn't sadistic in comparison. That was why, of all the people he had released, only four had come back.

Some had managed to put a semblance of a life together, even if they couldn't tell their therapist everything that had happened. Some had taken his offer to lose their memories of Locke's Arcanium, so while there were still residual effects, like aftershocks, much of the worst had been alleviated. And some had gone down a path of self-destruction well away from Arcanium, away from Bell's influence.

Bell poked and prodded at fate around them, but he couldn't fix them without complete transfiguration, which would be less painful but would shift their soul into something unrecognizable. It wasn't dangerous, but it was unconscionable. Locke might have been rendered a cringing thing trapped in a red diamond, but even now there were ways that he'd stripped power from Bell beyond the seven months of holding Bell's power in his hands—when Bell's shoulders had felt lighter but he'd barely been able to reach for a cup of coffee without exhaustion.

"I didn't mean to bring up all the feelings and memories at once, darling."

"It can't be helped."

Fairuza slid closer on the chaise, interlocking her fingers with his. "You've been punishing yourself. Does anyone know how much — or do they each only have a piece of it?"

"How I pay restitution for breaking my vows is my business."

"You paid enough in losing your heart in the first place. Getting it back and relieving the debt of others rendered your debt paid in full." She brushed the curls over his forehead. They were too dense and short for her to move much.

He resisted leaning into the touch, but he'd had precious little tenderness for two years.

Fairuza searched his eyes. "You never used to be like this. You don't believe in karma. There is no balance, and there is no real restitution, no absolution, no matter how many times the Ringmaster bloodies your flesh. You watched Maya try so hard to wash sins she didn't have away, and now you do the same?"

"You cannot look into my eyes as you do now and tell me that I have no sins."

"We're jinn. Even if sins as the books tell us exist, they're for humans, for mortals."

"We die, too."

"If you're so afraid of heaven, Bell, for heaven's sake, why do you still run Arcanium like this? Only someone with no fear of God does the things that you do. You've never feared God before. You certainly don't fear Maya's God, or else you'd find yourself a priest."

Bell snorted in spite of himself. He could always have himself a prophet if Lizzie's father ever rallied that promised spiritual army behind him to storm Arcanium. Elizabeth had spoken to her father since

Arcanium had been restored, and Bell could only assume that Lizzie had convinced him not to come after her. Bell hadn't asked, hadn't searched for Thomas Petros in his future — if it was, in fact, possible for him to see what a prophet had seen or what a prophet could do. Real holy men, of both good and evil ilk, staticked through his abilities like a bad ham radio.

Bell had never seen anything more impressive than demon or angel, although he knew he was created. He'd seen the creative fires from which jinn and demons were born, and there was nothing biological about it. Bell didn't have any special insight into the end of the world and what came after it, if anything, or what happened after death. The only things that walked the earth were those who couldn't know.

Some souls went to hell, but most demons trod earthside, even the hellborn, which suggested the population of hell wasn't nearly as high as the stories told. And Bell had never met anyone from heaven. Angels forgot once they fell, and when they weren't fallen, they were neither seen nor heard. Bell didn't think angels had souls for him to read, which opened up one of a series of incredibly interesting religious debates he'd never had with Maya, because she would have never truly believed him if he'd tried to convince her out of her beliefs.

Yet it was Maya's beliefs he had turned to in his grief — this incessant need for some kind of assuagement, exculpatory penance that would somehow erase the consequences of what he had done. But there wasn't a way to erase it. The penance would never end. It was irrational and ordered, far from the wanton chaos he had embraced within his very nature. If there was something to demons, to hell, to angels and heaven, and if there were indeed prophets, perhaps there was something to penance. And if he persisted long enough, perhaps he would reach the point when he'd paid enough.

Or, on the day Thomas Petros finally came for him, perhaps then it would be time for Arcanium to end. Fate was as capricious as he, but he saw her waters and the riverbeds where she'd been. There was a downhill path from the prophet to the fortune teller, and Bell suspected that one day the rains would come and wash the circus away.

"If that's where your thoughts are headed, Bell, then I've come right on time." Fairuza gently pushed his legs down, crawling closer to him at the head of the chaise.

"You're not going to change my mind."

But as she drew her cool fingers up his chest, his breath hitched.

"You're right. I'm not. Maybe I'll just give you a new way to atone." She leaned across him to press her mouth against his neck.

Cool hands. Hot mouth.

He threaded his fingers through the hair that threatened to cover him like a blanket and pulled her head back.

She didn't resist. She'd lived in Arcanium long enough to know where the lines were. She wasn't going to force him to do anything, but he hadn't told her to stop either. They were in the gray area where Bell had lived most of his life, where he'd taught Fairuza to lie comfortably with him.

She brushed her thumb over the corner of his mouth. "You haven't had sex since Locke took Arcanium, and you spent the bulk of the time since being driven mad by the incubus and succubus you keep to drive everyone else mad. I've gone that long, but not with sex demons infusing my very spell web with their magic."

Fairuza took his hand and brought it to her thigh, watching him every moment, careful of any resistance, which he didn't give. "Just because you don't experience arousal like they do, just because you can hide it, doesn't mean you don't feel it. I know what you feel. I know you're torturing yourself with all the women and men that you want, none of whom you're willing to take because of what you've done to them. But you didn't do anything to *me*. I walked into *your* circus with all my cloak and dagger, stole your spotlight in front of your entire crowd, and you would have kissed me until midnight if I hadn't stopped you. You may have been resisting your cast out of some newfound sense of decency, but you don't have to resist *everything*."

She drew his hand up her thigh until she didn't have to guide him anymore. He pushed between her thighs, stroking over the folds through her white panties then pressing the heel of his hand against her clit as though not a second had gone by since the last time he'd been with her. Twenty-five years bred such familiarity in the bedroom, and the twenty-five years apart had bred enough of a distance that returning to that familiarity was as far from a chore as possible—not that Bell ever really tired of a companion.

Fairuza brought her mouth to his, not quite kissing but breathing him in, inviting. "God, it's such a relief not to have to instruct."

That surprised a smile out of him, and he angled his head to kiss her again.

The spark between them hadn't died from the ring to backstage. He just hadn't been allowed to let his erection rise in the middle of the ring. A bulge in leather was to be expected, but most of his men kept their bindings tight for a reason. Bell had chosen loose cotton that evening, which threatened to show everything if he released his control. He could do nothing for his arousal, which sang deep inside him, but he could control his cock. Arousal was part of what he was. His cock was just an appendage of the body he'd chosen, as subject to his will as his arm.

He had control, but to release that control made both of them groan as she reached down to feel him and he swelled quickly to fill her hand. She crawled away from his hand between her legs and climbed up to straddle him, shifting the angle of the kiss. Rather than meet him, their battle evenly matched, she retreated in her aggression, yielded as he took more and more from her. He caged her tight against his hips by bending and spreading his legs on the chaise, wrapping his arms around her back.

To have a woman touch him, to have her want him to touch her, went straight to his head like good wine. The diamonds of her collar marked his chest, but her bodice undid itself to pull away and fall to the floor with her shoes.

His kisses became hungrier, bringing forth her moans and the rock of her hips against his, until they both dampened his cotton trousers. Her lust was as heady as his own, and such a taste after self-denial for so long while the sex demons ravaged the circus left him swept in the middle of a tornado of repressed desire. All the times he'd wanted the ones he loved and lusted for came to a head.

Bell deftly twisted them around, pressing Fairuza down into the tufted cushion of the chaise.

He sensed her pleasure at being able to submit with him, because such power dynamics changed nothing of his regard for her. Whatever battles they fought, the victories were shared. She'd had no such luck with most of the men she'd chosen for her bed — poor souls who'd needed to be taught because they'd never allowed themselves to be taught before, who needed to be ridden because they needed to remember who owned them, who couldn't be given a moment's power over her. Bell could afford to stay small, innocuous, but Fairuza couldn't falter for a moment, lest a strong personality believe himself stronger. Lady Sasha, too, was at greater risk for falling prey to men who thought they deserved her than Lord Mikhail fell prey to women, and he could wear the blades that dissuaded contact, while Sasha was expected to make herself accessible, even for a mere fantasy of possession.

But Bell could play both sides of power at his whim, just as he could be a woman if that was what he chose to become, although even his natural form was undeniably male and he felt more comfortable as a man. In Arcanium, he was the last word, and Fairuza was a guest. She could submit to him without repercussion from anyone who caught her — as people tended to be caught in Arcanium — and relish how that submission did nothing to change what anyone thought or felt about her.

She slipped her hands under his pants to grasp his ass when he thrust against her, forcing her legs to spread farther. Another thrust compelled her to close her eyes, arch beneath him, giving in a little more every time.

Feeling her let go and allow the pleasure she was made for wash over her was like stepping naked into secret hot springs. All at once, the loose pants he wore were too much. The bracelet that shackled his upper arm didn't bother him, but he sent his desire to Fairuza through his touch and she pushed his pants down his legs, reaching between them to unhook the fabric from his erection. Together, they kicked away his trousers. Then she worked her underwear off, and all that was left was the diamond necklace and the golden bracelet and the costume of their skin.

But as his cock slid heavy over her abdomen and she twined her legs around his to draw him even closer, he twitched violently and jerked back onto his elbows, looking down at her.

For a moment, he had been everywhere at once, with every person who had warmed his bed. He felt every betrayal, every resistance, every sigh, every moment that they succumbed, every moment that they relented, every time they left and why, all at once—the hottest mouth lined with cold teeth wrapped all the way around his cock like a lamprey. He stayed hard—he'd had all manner of things around his cock before, and the threat of teeth wasn't enough to wilt—but the arousal pooling at the base of his spine turned cold.

Fairuza framed his face with her palms. Her frustration wasn't the most important thing to her, and for that he felt sorrow that she hadn't yet found something to satisfy her in all these years, that frustration was too normal a state for her to be in. It was an indictment against all the men she'd brought into Illumina—although, to be fair, she didn't bring in people by how interesting they'd be in bed. More was the pity, but she wasn't running a sex show on the side like he was.

"Locke tortured you as much as he tortured them."

Bell withdrew, fighting the disgust that pushed against the top of his stomach, revulsion as reactive as fear. These things didn't come to him often, but that didn't mean he wasn't subject to them.

Fairuza sat up, not allowing him to put distance between them, but it obviously wasn't intimacy that she sought to reconnect. She didn't pull him back to her, not when everything about him clearly told her how much he wanted her—but also how much he didn't want her to touch him.

"He could have taken you with him, could have pulled you along with Arcanium into his world, stripped you of your power until you were little more than the meanest demon. Then everyone could have taken a piece of you while you also had to watch, helpless, as your cast suffered the same fate. In leaving you behind, Locke cut you deeper than anyone's dorsal spines. He left you a ghost town and no way to find where he had taken them, no way to know what he was doing to them. In keeping you away, he separated you from their suffering, so that they had to suffer alone—and you knew they suffered alone. Then when you found Arcanium and took it back, you had to take the weight and pain of everything you feared true. They don't understand that secondhand is firsthand to you. They *can't* understand that. But you made me like you, Bell. I understand *exactly* what you feel. Locke did everything in his power to hurt you worse than if he'd put his hands on you. In your entire physical battle against him, nothing he did, even crushing your skull, hurt you more than when Maya blamed you, did it?"

Bell sat back on his heels. "She wasn't wrong."

"No, she wasn't." Fairuza did him the courtesy of not telling him otherwise. A god's hubris was far more tragic than a man's, because he could fail so much more spectacularly. "But that doesn't change what you went through. Different things affect different beings. Pain, pleasure, you have a place for both. But your people's pain, the pain of those you love, past and present all at once, with that pain always there and stretching into the future... Even when they've finally developed some scar tissue in their soul or they've died, you will still carry it. He didn't take you because this was how he could torture you."

"So because Locke wanted to torture me, I shouldn't torture myself? This isn't about Locke. He's a hellborn demon. He did what hellborn demons do. *I* failed. *I* betrayed. That is what I must somehow repay."

Fairuza's white eyes flickered with candlelight that wasn't there. "There is no way to repay. There is no balance here, Bell. It's in the past, present and future now. You'll need to live with that pain, just like them but longer. Letting yourself blow off steam with someone who doesn't cringe when you touch them isn't going to change that. Hey." She clasped his shoulder before he could stand from the chaise and guided him back down. "Starting tonight, you have twice the cast to hold in Arcanium, and we both know Illumina's going to test boundaries like a bunch of hormonal teenagers. We also know that when they enter your fortune teller tent and drop a few w-bombs, you're going to be in a terrible mood. One night of release isn't going to tip the cosmic scales any more significantly than they've already been tipped. This isn't about me, Bell. Even I know it's about you, because I feel how much you need it. You never fought against your own nature before. You've been a deterministic son of a bitch from the beginning. I'm not saying that people can't change, but I've always admired your certainty. Please, my darling. Let me help you."

He didn't try to leave again. This time, he let himself lean into the hand on his cheek. She guided him by touch back over her, although he didn't lower himself onto her body.

"There are going to be a hundred horny cast members in your circus starting tonight, with Sasha and Mikhail feeding off all of them. And Maya's going to be there, walking through your circus, feeling all these things without any sense of context. Are you going to be prepared to keep her safe if you're just as lost as the rest...mmph."

Bell descended, possessing her mouth, untying the last thin knots of restraint. He'd gone longer than this without sex, but in his long life, he couldn't think of many times — and never with an incubus and succubus working at his will. Ever since he'd acquired cast for Arcanium, he'd never been without.

The arousal in his abdomen churned cold, but he kissed Fairuza until heat returned, closed off his mind to the rest of the circus. His spells would tell him if something went wrong. Right now, he wanted to shut everything off — his thoughts, his feelings, his past and present, the sometimes terribly beautiful chaos of the future. He wanted to lose himself in a willing body, in the pleasure he prized.

There was nothing special, spicy, acrobatic or artful about what they did. They locked their arms and legs around each other. When he tried to kiss down her body to the fragrance that called to him, she pulled him back up and caught his lip between her teeth, sucking sweetly until he groaned and tightened his fist in her hair.

"I have people for that. They can't fuck me like you do. I want you, Bell. You need to be inside of me." She reached between them to stroke the length of his cock, pre-cum and her own arousal slickening her way. But she didn't linger, didn't tease, didn't do anything to prepare herself before bringing the head to her cunt and gripping his ass to pull him in. Her fever, wet and dripping, wrapped around his own. Her moans grew higher and more desperate the deeper he went, almost a cry when he snapped his hips to sheathe himself completely.

Like demons, he was big, and like demons, he could make anything accommodate his greater length and girth—or else Ciarán would never be able to fuck anything—but what jinn and demons made people feel when they were taken had nothing to do with length or girth or how effective those things were. The fireborn reached deeper than the physical, their natural magic designed to tempt and bind those they chose to favor. Humans who partook of demon or jinn lived the rest of their lives vaguely disappointed that sex never fulfilled them the same way again.

It was a point of personal pride to please a woman or man, because pleasure went both ways for demon and jinn alike. The more pleasure he felt, the more he could share. The better it felt for him—with her hot walls surrounding him, tight and squeezing with every trembling contraction—the better he made her feel to have him inside her. And to be inside her was exquisite, because her pleasure, the need pulsing through her with each strong heartbeat, made him feel more as well.

The sex demons' magic, too, was filling the circus with greater intensity, which meant they were taking their own pleasure with Neve—the closest thing he'd ever had to being able to experience sex with an incubus and succubus himself. Bell knew he wouldn't last long, although that didn't mean anything for their kind, because he could stay hard after orgasm, could stay hard indefinitely if that was what his partner needed.

But this wasn't about making love all night, playing a companion's heart and lust-strings like a six-hour symphony for the sheer delight of watching them fall again and again. He'd had twenty-five years to make Fairuza's knees and spine melt under his ministrations, twenty-five years to make pleasure leave her trembling and weak in its wake, twenty-five years making her beg him to give her more or give her relief. He'd taught her everything he knew about pleasure then released her into a world that mostly found her pleasure confounding or secondary, unless she prioritized it for them. All the more reason to guarantee it now, to show her what she should demand — not just capitulation but devotion.

There were so many different ways to taste pleasure, and one of them was what they did now, yielding completely to sensation alone, because if he let himself think, he wouldn't be able to go through with taking her like he was, thrusting hard enough to make the chaise longue creak and crack. It had suffered greater strain to its structure, including a few repairs over the years. It would survive this as well.

He didn't quicken the rhythm of his thrusts, but he did fuck her harder the tighter and tighter his lust concentrated around his cock and scrotum, becoming more and more physical as it worked toward release.

Fairuza raked her nails down his back, drawing blood through thin scratches. He grasped the back of the chaise with a deep groan against the ache under the skin she'd scratched, like that which preceded the shifting of his form. He kept himself contained, but his need to come pushed out every which way, too large for the container.

Bell dipped down to take her mouth again, to run his tongue over hers in the same rhythm that he possessed her, reaching to the edge of her, until they squirmed with an identical itch. They muffled their moans in each other as they strived to reach a shared relief for everything that had built up over years of inadequate or absent sex.

The kiss broke as they came together, their orgasms joining forces to rock them back and forth as one body, locked in an embrace as close as his Human Knot had once been. His mind was in hers, her mind in his. The explosion that hit was shared, shuddering through them as she clenched around him and he filled her, the power of the climax shocking to both, for their separate reasons.

Gasping, they wrung pleasure until there was nothing left to twist out, until sweat and seed cooled on their hot skin.

Fairuza opened her eyes and brushed his forehead, tenderness achingly sweet in their still-shared minds. He sensed her sadness that a simple gesture could cause such a powerful reaction, that a man like him who thrived on contact and intimacy had denied himself that luxury in a circus where he fully encouraged it in everyone else.

Sex with another psychic was a special kind of disorienting, even for someone with as varied a sex life as Bell—like standing in the middle of his Hall of Mirrors and looking into a mirror that showed him looking into a mirror into infinity. Extricating himself from her mind was a delicate, painstaking process. The population of sapient beings on the planet was a giant archipelago, but where one or more were psychic, the tidewater could recede into a land bridge. Bell didn't know on his own what it was like to live lonely, without constant connection — because he had land bridges, rope bridges, planes, all manner of means to reach other islands — but tidewaters always had to rise again. To leave too soon reminded them too starkly of the islands they were.

Bell wiped the tears from Fairuza's temples and kissed her deeply, easing his cock from inside her before he even considered completely removing his mind. Her nails dented his shoulder to pull him back down so that he could blanket her through the removal of the last of his thoughts. Although he was still open to her and her mind open to him, the absence left him with the same grief with which he had started. But the frustration was gone. From experience, that satisfaction wouldn't last, but it would also take a good while to reach the same level of angry, caged tension.

Fairuza stretched her legs and arched her spine as she set adrift the last of her own pent-up lust.

Bell hadn't been able to enjoy the details of her body during the rush of momentum that had raced them through what he normally savored. Now he smoothed his palm up her abdomen to her breast, playing with the nipple until it tightened and peaked again. Sparks from the flint of his contact threatened to raise another flame, but he was content with sparks for now.

"Are you okay? I didn't mean to pull you down so fast with me."

"Yes, you did. That's what I signed up for." The scratches she'd made had already closed. She stroked his unblemished back, humming as he continued to tease her. "Are *you* okay? More importantly, Bell, are you ready?"

Chapter Five

When morning came without irreparable friction between the two factions, Bell considered that a win, even though he woke up alone.

He didn't necessarily need sleep, and he shared other people's dreams rather than have his own—Neve's and Lizzie's dreams had a particularly powerful pull—but after he and Fairuza had parted ways at the caravan, she to a tent and he to his RV, all he'd wanted to do was sleep. After a weekend of an open circus, everyone needed to reset their batteries. He wasn't the only one to sleep in.

The golems, of course, had been programmed to arise early enough to satisfy the odd early birds' gastronomical demands, and before going to sleep, Bell had set them to bring their usual breakfast feast to the caravan rather than to the big top tent. Catering trays had been set out on gingham-clad picnic tables for Arcanium's new guests to whiff awake at the scent of bacon. He'd accommodated the Spider's veganism for several years now, so he had plenty of non-animal alternatives for the few vegetarians and vegans within Illumina's cast as well. Satisfied stomachs improved any view.

The circus itself stayed closed, the mood at the brunch more like a day-long picnic than a considered alliance. None of his people wore costumes, although Neve wore her eyepatch and Sasha brought along her venomous cobra, Amil, to discourage anyone from trying to get close to her. Bell's warning and Mikhail's baleful glower at anyone who even looked at him or his women supplemented the serpentine threat.

In addition to Bell, a few people remained conspicuously absent. A crowd of humans without a single suppurating sore was too much for the Ringmaster's black heart to take. The clowns preferred their own kind, although a hive of two had become lonely for them, and even Caroline's return hadn't been enough to lift their ennui. Vivian and Jonas stayed in his food booth, taking care of their respective unique needs, and Delilah and Dom, although social creatures, avoided the crowd. Outside of the context of a freak show, they weren't sure how they'd be received.

Circuses attracted people with a similar sense of separation from the rest of the world, but Illumina's focus on skill meant that they had little understanding of how it truly felt to be an outcast, no matter where they went. Del and Dom were lovely people who'd unfortunately learned caution. Kitty had learned the same caution, but she'd also developed authority in her bearing that made most people hesitate to mock her to her face. Bell overheard some mockery well out of her earshot, but they would eventually know better on their own. They wouldn't be the first to have trouble seeing beyond the beautiful fur on her face and body at first interaction.

He watched Maya from a distance. He watched her smile, laugh with Illumina and even some from Arcanium who knew her, although Kitty also stayed away, every glimpse of Maya like a knitting needle to her chest.

However, the Arcanium cast, even the demons, had quickly realized that the Maya who'd entered the gates with Illumina was not the Maya they'd known. All the qualities they recognized were still there, but they lacked the context from which they'd naturally emerged and flourished.

Maya knew that she had voluntarily asked Fairuza to remove her memories. She'd been told that she'd been part of a dark freakshow circus and what kind of skills she had—although Fairuza had conveniently left out any of the psychic abilities Bell had gradually given her to do her own fortune-telling one day. She'd hidden those skills deep within Maya's memories so that not even other people's minds could trip a wire that would blow down the walls built for her protection.

She knew her boyfriend had cheated on her and that he'd suffered a terrible accident, but Maya had lost how her wish had been the reason why. She carried none of the blame that had once tied her more closely to the jinn and demons of Arcanium, who had fed her masochistic need for cosmic balance. She'd lost the memories of the cultivation of her passions that had led to intimate knowledge of far more Arcanium cast members than she would believe. Lennon, Ciarán and Moss spoke with her, and Moss leered and played the lascivious jester that he'd always been, but he didn't insist on an encore, nor did he reference anything he and Ciarán had done with her on a regular basis. He was the voice of his and Ciarán's rampant desires, but even without warning, he was observant enough to realize that this Maya would immediately take offense to any suggestion.

In her entire time with Bell, Maya had never been so relaxed or free. He'd expanded her mind, her boundaries, her appetites, but even when her last wish had set her free, she'd chosen to remain in his ornate, iron cage. He'd taught her to embrace her chains, cry under their covers while he made her skin sing, but she'd never known freedom in Arcanium, and if she hadn't lost the memories, she never would have found it again.

He still kept birds in his cage, some of whom had stayed, even when he'd opened the door. Freedom wasn't everything. There was value, sometimes, in captivity, especially for the broken. But nothing kept her from flying now. She wasn't caged, because she wasn't his. She was an outsider looking into the quirky aviary, a skilled performer unaware that she'd once been in bed with the very oddities who fascinated her now.

He wanted her like this. And to keep her like this meant keeping his distance.

He would have to confront her sooner or later, but the more time he could put between his initial shock and that moment, the more likely he wouldn't step on any landmines when she spoke to him. The walls around her removed memories were sturdy, but the right equipment — a landmine, for instance — could tear down even the best of walls.

* * * *

In their street clothes, Illumina became a small, disproportionately pretty collection of almost-average people, if it weren't for the dense, lean muscles exposed as they walked through Arcanium in shorts, tees and sundresses. Well into summer, it was a time when the skin Bell's circus showed wasn't as out of place as when winter came along and his people still strutted around in briefs or corsets. Now it was more impressive that his people wore leather under the sun. Sasha stitched magic into every piece to ensure the leather was buttery smooth and durable but, most importantly, flexible and didn't overheat the person wearing it — warm in winter and cool in summer, as breathable as the cotton he wore.

Bell assessed when his people were in place then stepped out among Illumina in his own costume that really wasn't a costume anymore. He so rarely left the circus that he only had a few things in his wardrobe, and all of them he could wear while the circus was open. Most of the demons had at least a pair of jeans, but he didn't like the material himself. He'd donned his bohemian summer ensemble — the gold bracelet around his upper arm, ivory cotton pants, loose cloth belt on which he looped the leather bag that would hold his earnings for the day and gave him something convenient to put his hand in to pull an object from nothing.

Today, there would be no earnings, no tips, no charge, no payment at the food booths or the midway — although if any of Illumina had a burning desire to win a stuffed skull-and-crossbones or steampunk teddy bear, they could absolutely take the prize with them back to their tents. Bell supported anything that sparked a little joy, which was why he had fuzzy prizes in the first place.

He stepped among the Illumina cast — which parted before him, whether they were aware of it or not — and headed for Fairuza. She wore a white tank top, skinny jeans and sandals and looked like nothing less than a rich, beautiful woman on a sunny vacation.

Maya stood with her in a DIY off-the-shoulder tee and patterned leggings. Gold hoops peeked through her loosely bound hair, twisted up and held together with a decorative chopstick. She shifted back and forth, expectant and excited to visit Arcanium for the first time, although she knew she'd been there before. He sensed more than the usual amount of curiosity, but he backed away from her mind before he could see too far in, because just seeing her happy was enough for him — to feel her happy would be too much of a good thing, acupuncture sent straight to a lung.

Bell focused his attention on Fairuza, stepping to her other side so that he didn't have to stand next to Maya, to whom he smiled as he would to anyone in his circus — warm, inviting, intimate without being suggestive, polite without being distant. Fairuza let him keep up the illusion, as she always did, and she slipped her arm through his as a gesture of support.

He hadn't anticipated how hard it would be, being this close to Maya and barely acknowledging her. But he'd made a career out of being a conman of conmen, an illusionist with no illusion in the midst of profound illusion and he could fool almost anyone into believing anything. He could convince Maya she meant nothing to him.

"Remember to be kind. Look but don't touch, unless you're invited. Feel free to act like guests. You don't need to impress us with anything except your humanity. So help me, Canton, if you comment on my lack of it, I will put you in swim trunks and a snorkel, and you can spend the rest of the day like that." He gave a dazzling smile to the rest of the Illumina cast. "Take pictures, tag Arcanium, have fun and try not to point. It's rude. Food, games and rides are on the house, and the bar is open. Drink responsibly and have a good time. Big top performances begin at eight."

Bell walked with Fairuza to the circus proper, leading the rest of Illumina with them. They dispersed at the big top, some going left to Oddity Row and the courtyard, others heading toward the rides and midway to the right. Behind the big top, Caroline once again reigned over the carousel, although she no longer lived in the nook he'd created underneath it. She couldn't stand confined spaces anymore. He'd given her a hybrid trailer that let her open the fabric flaps in the bedroom to feel the air when she slept, Colm on one side and Riley on the other—easy egress if the nightmares were too terrible.

These were the kinds of things that Illumina had never needed to think about and that his guests were never supposed to know. His regulars believed they'd suffered a contagious illness that had left them out of commission for a year to recover, but not all of the cast had recovered enough to remain. The lie wasn't so far from the truth.

Of the few carnival rides, the carousel was the most Arcanium, but they also had a decent steampunk Ferris wheel and now a tilt-a-whirl, bumper cars and a pendulum. In addition to rides, he had the metal jungle gym—with warning signs about potential injuries, given that the jungle gym was actually for adult

performers to share space with their younger guests —
and as soon as he gained a few more animal acts, he'd
offer animal rides again. No matter how well-trained
his Bearskin, there wasn't a safety regulation in the
world that would allow him to offer children rides on a
grizzly bear.

Bell had tucked the expanded haunted funhouse
behind the midway. There were fewer cast exhibits
within it now. The funhouse had been where he'd kept
most of the prisoners, playing off their misery and
torture as tableau theater, but since he'd let most of his
prisoners go, there were simply fewer people willing or
able to spend their time in a place that mirrored the
torture already done to them. The cast that remained or
had returned to Arcanium accepted their place in a
horror-themed circus, but they preferred it in the light,
in the open. Bell kept the last few of his prisoners in the
funhouse, in a less tortured capacity, along with a
handful of demons and monsters. The rest of the
building offered a series of experiences typical of other
funhouses — perspective disorientation, disembodied
limbs, the famed Hall of Mirrors, as well as illusions
masquerading as advanced-technology animatronics.

Oddity Row showed off Arcanium's oddities in their
red velvet display tents. Closer to the big top,
translucent red canvas draped over poles for makeshift
shade — precious real estate in the summer, and misters
made it even more so. Here, oddities spent their time
on performing platforms if they wanted to interact
more directly with guests. A series of elaborate selfie
platforms had been set up against the big top for people
to snap social-media-ready pictures by themselves or
with the cast.

Under the canopy, the Spider hung in her web to oversee the care and appreciation of her insect and arachnid menagerie as well as Sasha's snake collection. Sasha took breaks from Oddity Row to teach groups of children about snakes and pose in pictures with them. Prepubescent children were immune to succubus charms and Sasha was good with them, as long as she took care who she came into contact with, given that teenage boys also loved the snake collection. Golems were programmed to help Sasha maintain distance, and the Spider often dropped down to interfere as well. Her many limbs creeped children out, but teenagers tended toward fascination that briefly distracted them from Sasha.

Also under the coveted shade, golems sold merchandise associated with the oddities — resin accessories, photos, paintings, prints, Sasha's leather work, Kitty's knitting that didn't go to charity, the kinds of things they also sold on the Arcanium website.

Along the midway and under the courtyard canopy, his performers walked through the circus and gave mini performances. There was usually a makeshift ring near the jungle gym for just that purpose, especially for performers who preferred not to interact directly with the guests, such as the clowns. Their monster face paint dissuaded most children from approaching them and fueled many intransigent cases of coulrophobia, but that didn't mean it dissuaded everyone, and the clowns weren't allowed to eat during open hours.

Between the carousel and the haunted funhouse was an empty stretch where they set up the main series of food booths — two manned by golems that provided traditional fair food then Jonas and Vivian's respective booths that offered the culinary versions of Oddity

Row. In the field behind them, the Skellies set up to play in the afternoon, with live karaoke for guests and cast members alike before Vivian took over with her expanded set of rock and metal covers.

There were still things Bell wanted to do with Arcanium, things he'd lost that he still needed to replace and things he simply didn't have the ability to take on yet. He would never have a rollercoaster, because anything he offered would be weak in comparison to theme parks, and anything he did to make it more impressive wouldn't suspend disbelief. If he thought he could get away with it, he'd create a proper Tunnel of Love, but he exorcised that impulse with the Funhouse events. He still wanted to set up a more varied play area, with complicated slides, swings and web ropes, but he planned to wait until Halloween, when Arcanium's business went through the roof.

He'd always wanted an Oddity Row parade of some sort for his less-lauded oddities to show themselves off — like Edna and Donald, his octogenarian husband-and-wife team who had come to his casting call while Arcanium had been in Locke's possession. They were so old-school oddity that they were cool again. Edna was a virtuoso on spoons and popping her joints, and she made many of her own one-woman-band instruments. Donald had rubber-like skin and hypermobility that had wreaked havoc with him in old age. Arcanium had given him new vitality. The Parrot was another voluntary from the casting call — a champion impressionist as well as an expert mimic of animal and mechanical sounds. A parade would also give Kitty a chance to go full Mardi Gras on her costume-making. With Illumina to round out the pretty, that dream could actually be within his reach.

He also wanted to employ a few face-paint artists to provide elaborate, theme-consistent designs. Kitty had plenty of face-painting skills she'd developed while helping with everyone's makeup, but the woman was thoroughly busy during circus days. Troy offered professional tattoos both during circus hours and off-hours, depending on the scope of the project, and he occasionally did henna or paint versions of his tattoos for something more temporary, but he also had enough to do. So Bell continued to search for other types of creatives who could add new features and exhibits to the carnival part of his circus — spray-paint artists, caricaturists, perhaps a few writers in residence — eventually a convention-type setup for everything circuspunk, steampunk and horror. It was all entertainment to him.

To the right of the big top, in the midst of all of the flashy, colorful exhibits, was his cozy little fortune teller tent, unassuming on the outside and an incense-fueled hallucination on the inside, with crystals, candles, scarves and beads, parlor tables and chairs for his readings, several decks of tarot, a steampunked version of the Magic 8-Ball and a small collection of crystal balls. He didn't need any of them, any more than he needed phrenology or palmistry, but he liked using props now and then.

Fifty people spread out much thinner than their usual crowd, but Bell anticipated that they'd be much more polite and more inclined to join in with impromptu performances, which his tumblers and acrobats would enjoy, especially if it became friendly competition. Of course, his people automatically had the edge of magic, although a number of his human performers had been as disciplined as the Illumina cast before they'd been brought into Arcanium, including Carlo, Larazus, Magda, Okeyo, Chelsine and two of the Albino Triplets, who'd arrived in Arcanium already circus veterans. But it would be beneficial for both sides to experience routines outside their norms, given that Illumina tended toward more serious art and Arcanium leaned toward vaudeville and burlesque.

Bell extricated his arm from Fairuza's and kissed her cheek before ducking into his fortune teller tent alone to wait for the first brave soul to meet with him. Unlike every other guest who came into Arcanium, they would know that he, like Fairuza, was the real thing, which automatically changed the fortune-telling dynamic. In addition, a fortune teller's tent tended to compel wishes — not as effectively as a wishing well, but desire underlaid hopes for the future and desire bred wishes.

In the corner, a high-backed, winged armchair remained, although there was no longer an apprentice to occupy it. Bell sat at the parlor tables, leaning back with his legs stretched out in front of him. He didn't look forward to see whether anyone would come or not. Half the fun was not knowing, and since his entire guest list knew what he was, that took away the other half.

As he waited, he spread his magic to the edges, followed the movements of Illumina among Arcanium, sensed their mutual wariness and mutual joy, felt where the sex demons accelerated existing sparks, found the early stirrings of respect for the oddities who had inspired reflexive disgust — both atavistic and societal. Physical appearance alone was never Bell's first impression. He couldn't hold the average person's unchosen limitations against them as much as he wanted to. All he could do was foster the kind of environment that gave his freaks time to prove people wrong.

He returned to himself at the approach of footsteps.

Platinum blonde hair in a pixie cut, delicate face, trained in cheerleading, dance and tumbling, part of the floor routines because her size allowed her to be thrown into the air for all the impressive falls.

"Good morning, Cecilia." Bell straightened and retrieved his tarot cards to shuffle. "What can I do for you today?"

* * * *

Bell had twelve productive sessions — albeit none with a wish — before Kitty stepped into the tent and closed the flap.

"Do we need words for this?" Bell asked. "Or should I just get the tequila from the sideboard?"

"You need to send her away."

"Because it hurts to have her here? If that were the case, I'd send you all away."

Kitty took a breath then settled into the seat across from him at the parlor table. "This isn't about how her being here makes me feel. And it's not about how it makes you feel. I know how much it hurts — the things we were powerless to stop, the things that didn't happen to us and that we'll always be on the outside of. I'm not talking about us. I'm talking about her. Fairuza shouldn't have brought her here, and you can't let her stay."

"She doesn't remember anything."

"I know how it works, Bell, because you told me. You don't extract the memories, because that causes serious neurological problems when the brain tries to refill them with shit that didn't happen. The memories are still there, which means she can have them again."

"That's not going to happen. She's happy, Kitty. She's happy with Illumina, which she went to of her own free will, and she's happy with Illumina in Arcanium. I won't make her a special project. She'll be no more and no less than the rest of Illumina — under my protection but not my oversight. She's Fairuza's responsibility now."

"Something's going to go wrong. It's going to go wrong because this is the kind of place where things go wrong. People don't stay happy here."

"Kitty."

"Adversity is the spice of life. I get it. I embrace it. But she got out. That was her free will speaking. Joining Illumina was her free will. Getting her memories cordoned off was her free will. But Fairuza bringing her here was not, because Maya didn't have the damn memories that would have warned her to *stay away*." Kitty reached across the table to take his hand, as though she were the one about to read his palm instead of the other way around. "Fairuza doesn't understand. If she did, as soon as she took Maya's memories, she would have fired Maya and pointed her in the direction of a normal life. She wouldn't have brought Maya back to the scene of the crime."

"You're right. Maya doesn't have the context to know to stay away from Arcanium. But that's exactly why she'll be safer here than before. Because we have the context to insulate her."

"No, that's exactly why it's dangerous. People aren't just the sum of what they learn from their valleys. All the terrible things that happened to her weren't what drew her to you or you to her. All those things are still there. She's going to repeat patterns she followed when she was in Arcanium, because now she doesn't have the memories telling her why that's a fucking bad idea. It won't go the exact same way—after all, she has no wishes left—but it'll still end badly."

Bell covered Kitty's hand with his, sending her peace from both sides, until the shuddering tightness in her abdomen settled. "It won't if we stay away from her. I've already sent notice to those with whom she shared intimacy to avoid her or remain distant, to not forge the same ties. Maya has closer relationships with Illumina now. She will not venture out from them as long as her prior relationships remain severed."

"It's not enough." Kitty swiped tears that had fallen down her cheeks. "Do you know the reason Fairuza brought her, the reason she didn't do the right thing?"

"I don't peek too far into the minds of other jinn. It takes far too much effort and usually backfires, because they reach just as far into mine. Her intentions are good."

"I don't know her like you do. She'd already left by the time I arrived. And maybe her intentions *are* good. But they're selfish, too. She and Maya are lovers. Not as you loved her, closer to what she had with me. That's what I mean by patterns, Bell. You need to get her out of here. You need to insist that Fairuza cut her loose."

"She already knows she was part of Arcanium and that something happened to cause her to remove those memories. If Fairuza cuts her off now, that will only arouse more curiosity."

"Don't let that curiosity reach a point that she can more efficiently pursue it. Outside of Arcanium, she has no recourse to investigate."

Bell released Kitty's hand and stood, turning away. "Outside of Illumina or Arcanium, she doesn't have the same protection. I'm *relieved* that she found Illumina, where Fairuza could keep an eye on her. While Maya still had her memories, she could watch out for anyone following her, use the power I gave her to protect herself. Once she lost her memories, she was in good hands with Fairuza, better hands than mine. That she and Maya are lovers doesn't surprise me. Fairuza is a good woman."

"She's jinn," Kitty said.

"She wasn't always."

"Is that what you wanted to do to Maya? The little transformations, training her in magic and fortune-telling?" Kitty approached him from behind, placing gentle hands on his shoulders. In the name of their shared grief, she remained patient with him. "I noticed, Bell. We were close enough for me to notice. I don't know how much Fairuza changed from when she was human, but it makes a mark, transfiguring humanity — as though the fire burns it out. It doesn't have to be bad, but it *is* different. It's not just the blocked memories that changed Maya. She's different, and she doesn't know why she's different, but she can sense it. I understand why Fairuza wanted to take all the pain away, and like I said, maybe her intentions are good, but they're not human anymore, and that's going to get Maya hurt."

"There's nothing we can do to keep Maya from getting hurt, love. We can save her from the worst if we force a change in the patterns." He drew her hands from his shoulders to his chest, pulling her arms around him. She rested her cheek on his back. The soft fur of her face and arms soothed his skin. The beard had been braided, but her hair was loose and surrounded him. It had been quite a long time since she'd been this close.

"You had sex with her last night, didn't you?" Kitty muttered against his skin.

"I just established that I intend to keep my distance."

"Not Maya. Fairuza. She seems like the kind of woman who would make her will known, and she wouldn't be intimidated by you."

"You're not intimidated by me."

"I'm intimidated. That just doesn't change what I say or do, and my lover is more intimidating than you." She smiled against his back, but Bell didn't think it would reach her eyes. "You have blind spots where the people you favor are concerned. Don't let Fairuza be one of them."

"Do you not trust her?" Bell valued Kitty's assessments of character. She'd needed good instincts ever since she'd become the butt of everyone's jokes and had to anticipate how people would react to her. Accepting the courtship of a hellfire demon with very little expression had only honed her skill.

"I don't think she's being completely truthful, although I admit I have blind spots with the people I favor, too. I'm inclined to be suspicious of a woman who brings Maya here on purpose."

"Does the Ringmaster sense anything?"

"He's not concerned. But if she doesn't want to lie down in front of him and ask him to whip her, he loses interest."

"He's not as simple as you make him out to be," Bell said, entwining his fingers with hers. If the Ringmaster's motivations were so small, Kitty would never have caught his interest, because the Ringmaster never got to torture her.

She hummed in acknowledgment. "I'm being unkind. He's noticed Maya, noticed that she's changed. He wants to cut at her flesh, but he holds himself back from even mentioning that he wants to, which means he knows it's no longer an avenue available to him. If he's concerned about Maya in more ways than how it affects him, he hasn't shared that, although he's softened his treatment of me in response. He also doesn't seem to be worried about Fairuza—maybe because he knows her. But if he's not worried about Fairuza, it's because he doesn't believe she's powerful enough to challenge him, much less you."

"I sense no malice in her," Bell mused. "That's enough for me to trust her here. Her cast is pleased with her as a leader, far more than Arcanium is pleased with me. I don't think whatever secrets she keeps, if any, are dangerous to us. She was human longer than she's been jinn, my dear. She didn't want to become me, and she hasn't."

"You'll watch her, though."

"Always." Bell turned back around in Kitty's arms, pressed his forehead to hers. "And I'll play Maya's guardian angel, watching her from afar as well."

"No." Kitty backed away, color draining from her face and lips. "Don't try to play angel. You can't pretend to be anything other than what you are. The harder you try, the more you'll be the devil whispering in her ear. Enlist anyone else—but you stay away from her."

Chapter Six

The first day of introducing Illumina to Arcanium was such a rousing success that almost the entirety of the Illumina cast—including Canton—eagerly anticipated returning to it the next day.

Rather than offering a repeat of the previous day, Bell didn't have to work hard to convince his cast to adopt a more Halloween approach. Arcanium was most popular at Halloween. Popularity meant greater crowds, and more people usually meant more problems—more people trying to impress friends by insulting the freaks, grabbing at things they shouldn't, attempting to steal a Madagascar hissing cockroach or set a rattlesnake free and so on. His people were far more amenable to Halloween in May with guests old enough to behave better.

Face paint became more elaborate, and the costumes and performances trended more horror than steampunk or Renaissance faire. Bell switched from ivory cotton pants to black leather, with eyeliner and eyeshadow added to an admittedly limited repertoire, but he rarely felt the need to make himself more terrifying. People entering a fortune teller's tent already made themselves vulnerable, even if they didn't believe he was real.

In addition to discussing highly personal aspects of their lives, he was also a half-naked man often alone with his client—usually a woman—in an enclosed tent. They put themselves at risk, even if he were just an ordinary mentalist. Because he knew how dangerous he was, he ensured that his clients were safe with him in all other respects—safe to flirt with, safe to desire, safe to open up to. In the danger that they expected of him, he tried to put them at ease. The danger that he actually posed was, by nature, unexpected. He could guarantee them nothing if they spoke a wish aloud, and God help them if they'd already pissed him off. He tended to have more problems with men in and out of Arcanium, but problems were by no means exclusive to them.

He, as well as the other men in Arcanium, received significantly more appreciative glances by the women and some of the men of Illumina when his cast donned tight leather. If they hadn't noticed before, they wouldn't be able to avoid the suggestiveness of what such fabric cradled, front and back, given the generous attributes of Arcanium's demons. Whenever someone looked at Ciarán, their response was so strong that Bell practically wanted to cross his own legs. That didn't mean Arcanium's giant—in more ways than one—didn't still get a few extra glances his way.

Fear and fascination. Some things never changed.

After dreams of dying under the sexual appetites of his sex demons, Illumina hadn't been able to tell if they were fantasies or nightmares. The dreams had been wet either way, and Bell had tasted every one of them as they'd awakened, cleaned themselves off then left their tents and RVs for a new day of confronting the source. A few of his and Illumina's cast had already found a moment to hook up, but contrary to their usual behavior with Arcanium recruits, the demons had remained aloof of Illumina. They kept to the people they'd already found, possessive even when inclined to share, protective in the face of strangers staying so close.

Fairuza hadn't come to him in the evening. Even if Illumina stayed with Arcanium, their moment had passed twenty-five years ago. They would likely enjoy other sessions, but they'd grown apart, changed, their experiences no longer shared. Memories were good enough for now. And Bell was still resistant, although Fairuza's warmth for him remained and thawed some of her cast's reservations.

His Arcanium had done the rest. It wasn't the Arcanium of old. Flesh-eating viruses, oozing boils, eviscerations and lash marks among too many human bodies would have incited Canton to lead a human rights riot. Of course, in the old Arcanium, Bell wouldn't have even entertained keeping Illumina within Arcanium, and Fairuza wouldn't have dreamed of bringing Illumina to Arcanium in the first place.

He wasn't sure that was a good thing, nor did he think it was a necessarily a bad one. Who he was today was not the same person he had been a hundred years ago—and further and further. He was what he was, but that was far more flexible than some people believed— perhaps because they measured that change by human development rather than his. But like humans, he could change slowly or he could change all at once. Locke had forced a slow change to become a fast one, because Bell could no longer take joy in retribution as long as his people had suffered for nothing other than his company.

Bell opened Arcanium to Illumina in Kitty's company this time.

She was resplendent in her Halloween best, coppery orange with black lace accents, her skirts full with a crinoline underneath. She'd pinned monarch butterflies in her ornately arranged hair, and her braided beard had been woven through with matching ribbon. If Illumina hadn't introduced themselves to the prize of Kitty yet, Bell hoped that showing her as the treasure she was would lend additional appreciation.

He kissed her lips in greeting rather than her cheek like he had with Fairuza the day before. Kitty was startled into responding. Their affection mostly ran tactile, as innocent as Bell was capable of, but they were sometimes reminded that their chemistry ran hotter on the rare occasion they initiated it. It wasn't something they needed from each other, but Bell still hesitated in pulling away, chaste though the kiss was.

Kitty smiled, an impish gleam in her eyes, then curled her fingers around the base of his skull and pulled him back in. Her heels required him to raise his chin and lift himself up on his toes to kiss her on a more even level. Lace rasped against his bare skin and the skirts rustled around him, but he grasped her hips and jerked her closer, parted his lips to taste her.

She couldn't keep a straight face as the Illumina crowd cheered, whooped and wolf-whistled, and neither could he, in spite of her racing pulse under his fingertips. They stopped kissing to laugh, and Bell embraced her again. She rarely engaged in public displays of sexuality, although she had more than enough in private to last lifetimes, even without the Ringmaster. Maya had been her first real introduction to exhibitionism. Kitty had always been so self-conscious about people performing disgust around her rather than admitting they'd fuck her in a heartbeat if she asked. Whenever Maya had kissed her, it had given a crowd of outsiders the woman they were allowed to holler for, which permitted them to holler for Kitty at the same time.

Bell hoped he also gave Illumina permission to show her the love and lust she'd always deserved. He kissed her again, through their smiles. "You are magnificent," he whispered in her ear before pulling back.

He guided Kitty around to walk with her toward the circus proper, which had been bedecked with more skulls than Vlad the Impaler could shake a stake at. "Follow the Halloween Queen and stay creepy, my friends. Remember, though, that you're far more afraid of them than they are of you."

"Have I mentioned this week that you're not as clever as you think you are?" Kitty muttered as they passed the big top and approached the fortune teller's tent.

"What would I do without you keeping me humble, Kitty Cat?"

Kitty slipped from his arms, her smile faltering. "Just another normal day."

"Just another normal day. Albeit on a day we normally wouldn't have it, and by most people's standards, it is far from normal on so many levels."

Both of them determinedly avoided looking in the direction that practically screamed at them.

Bell's tent didn't change much through the seasons. It was atmospheric enough for any time of year. Usually, the only difference at Halloween was a jack-o-lantern, but he'd be the only scary thing in thing tent today.

Although he hadn't looked into the future for her, he wasn't surprised when Maya came into his tent later that afternoon.

The sun couldn't damage his cast's skin, which mean getting a tan was a hopeless endeavor, but Maya looked sun-kissed without effort, her cheeks flushed from the heat. She'd spent some time under the mister. The top half of her shirt was damp, and water still glowed in her low-maintenance ponytail. In comparison to the circus outfit she'd entered Arcanium in, she seemed so delightfully normal. With contentment added to the normality, he glimpsed what might have been if she'd never come to Arcanium in the first place.

There were other universes in which Maya would have found a way to Arcanium, alone or with her boyfriend or a handful of friends. Of the infinite scenarios, Bell brought her in far more often than not, sometimes by her own wish and sometimes when he used someone else's wish to bring her in. In every universe, she intrigued him, this normal girl with nothing ostensibly special about her except what she could become — strength she couldn't know, power she couldn't comprehend, darkness and desire she'd never fathomed until she'd needed it and he had given it to her.

The Maya who entered his tent was a curious blend of the Maya before Arcanium and the Maya after, because she *had* sought out Illumina when she hadn't been able to return to normal. Memories had been tearing her to pieces with no recourse, even though her mother had tried to get her to find a psychologist or even just someone to give her something so that she wouldn't wake up screaming every night.

Those memories were no longer part of her history map, but they had shaped her direction anyway, because she'd remained with Illumina, and she had a blueprint of what had happened to her as well as sketched knowledge of most of the skills he'd given her, skills she'd applied to a different circus. And she'd developed an arrangement with Fairuza that echoed the ones she'd had with Bell and Kitty, as Kitty had already assessed.

Knowing what had happened to her, even secondhand, had taken some of the normal from her, as had living as Fairuza's houseguest.

Maya wasn't the only member of the circus who roomed in Fairuza's house. Fairuza had set up dormitories in the guest wing for single cast who didn't want an apartment when they'd be touring for several months every year anyway. Fairuza treated Maya as special, but not in a way that was discernable to an outside observer. She protected Maya, kept her close in case the walls around the blocked memories shuddered, sculpted her into a new magical shape with the skills she could allow Maya to access.

The whole trail mix of information Bell gathered just from her stepping up to the open tent flap swept through his mind in a matter of seconds. He concluded with some relief that Fairuza's intentions with Maya had been purely proprietary.

Whether bringing Maya with her to Arcanium had been just as proprietary was still uncertain, but even their close relationship had developed so that Maya wouldn't always have to sleep in the women's dormitory, because Maya's dreams still ran toward nightmares. Her mind could no longer pull from the memories that had created them, so it made its own monsters. Fairuza ensured that she didn't remember them on mornings she awoke in Fairuza's bed, tested them to make sure that memories hadn't seeped out to poison the groundwater.

Within Maya's mind, Bell found Fairuza's fingerprints everywhere, each one a sign of care rather than subtle malignant influence. Whether Fairuza's actions were wise was a question for another age. In Maya's experience, she'd treated her well.

Bell slowly approached her, but although he reached out, it wasn't for her hand. Instead, he gestured her in. When he twitched his finger, the tent flap fell closed and knotted.

Being in a room alone with Maya was not the best of circumstances. Kitty chided him in the back of his mind—just her voice, not Kitty herself. Kitty didn't know Maya was there with him, and he could control himself.

"Welcome, Maya. Please, have a seat."

She chewed on the inside of her lip, a tingle of anxiety on the surface of her thoughts, but she followed him to the parlor table, where he pulled out the chair for her. Then he stepped around the table and sat across from her.

"What can I do for you today?"

Maya fidgeted with the tablecloth. "Fairuza's our fortune teller and resident illusionist," she finally said. "Canton does card tricks and some danger magic, but it's hard for him to compete against the real thing."

"I imagine Canton has trouble handling that."

"You might have noticed that he could use getting his ass kicked now and then. The man does like to hear himself talk."

Bell winced. "Are you suggesting we have something in common? Why would you say that to me?"

Maya laughed, genuine but strained. "Truth to tell, I think he likes that a woman shows him up in front of everybody. He doesn't whimper when she shoots him down. Well, maybe a little. But when she does it during a particularly strident rant, that's when he ends up in her bedroom, and I don't think he's on top."

Bell smiled. "It would be irresponsible for me to confirm or deny."

"You don't have to. We've already established that he's loud."

"Amusing though it is, you're not here to discuss Canton's predilection for humiliation."

Maya tucked one leg up on the chair, holding on to her shin. "You're Bell Madoc. You taught Fairuza everything she knows. You made her everything she became."

"I'd say your cold reading's impressive, but most of that is public knowledge—at least between our two circuses."

"What did you do to me?"

Bell raised his head. Her tone was even, but accusation threaded through each word.

"I know the bare bones. That's what Fairuza gave me after she took the memories—enough bones to know why I asked to lose them in the first place. When people from Arcanium came to Illumina, I thought they might know, but they were... I couldn't ask them about

Arcanium. Caroline and Riley couldn't even speak. Seth was twitchy, always with his back to the wall. He's better here, but Caroline... Caroline's not...okay, is she?"

"Each of my children has had to find a way to cope with what happened to them. You aren't the only one who chose to lose the memories. It was the only way Joanne was going to be able to survive in this world."

"Which one was Joanne?"

"She was the Siamese twins."

"She was the..." Maya's expression showed she was trying to work out the pronouns to the nouns, but no matter which way she turned the block, there must not have been a hole to put it in. "How is one person twins?"

"Like George but less unsettling." George was the Two-Faced Man of Arcanium. Bell wouldn't go as far as to call him a prisoner, but he hadn't been accepted into Arcanium under the most welcoming circumstances. He'd assumed that the developing Skeletons had been asking for a certain kind of attention with the clothes that had threatened to fall off their shrinking bodies. During the day, when the circus was open, the demon face on the back of his head mostly mugged for the audience, with a few words here and there. It got chattier when the sun went down and there was no one but George to hear it.

"How is 'like George' less unsettling?"

"Joanne started out as one indecisive girl. I made her two so that she would learn to better work with herself." It had worked, too, until Locke had decided to sew shiny buttons over her eyes and sew her mouths shut, without the courtesy of keeping the thread soft and gentle and the wounds clean. She'd come out of

Locke's Arcanium catatonic. Bell had had no choice but to take her memories if she was going to do anything in her life other than walk over the edge of a cliff. "She was a favorite oddity of Arcanium, and I miss her every day. As for your continued alarm about Caroline, rest assured that she's taken care of. She has all the time in the world here to recover."

"Recover? She has cadaver thread in her *mouth*. Neve has Frankenstein scars all over her body and she's missing an eye. Sera looks like she was hit by a car. Vivian still has the whip marks."

"Sera's state is separate from your own. She's a recent arrival. And Vivian earned every blow. Why is between her, Jonas and me, but every day she breathes is a blessing I bestow. She'll have the marks for the rest of her days in Arcanium. As for the more self-destructive inclinations of my children, this is the safest place for them to indulge such impulses."

She played with the end of her ponytail, staring at her hair so she wouldn't have to look at him. "I don't have any scars."

"I heal most scars."

"Did I have scars?"

"Not many. He healed scars, too." The fun of breaking toys as a demon was that the toys could break over and over and over, and they'd always come back together again.

"How bad was it?"

"Do I need to answer that, Maya?"

"The others, you removed their memories of Locke's Arcanium. Fairuza removed the memories of your Arcanium, too." She dropped her hair and forced herself to meet his eyes. "So what did *you* do to me?"

"You clearly didn't want to remember, love. Fairuza filled in enough of the gaps for what you need to know."

"Then she brought me back here, to you?"

"She brought you to Arcanium, not to me."

"Bell, I can tell when people are being evasive. Fairuza plays that trick on dozens of suckers. This whole circus is evasive. They're not mean, but if there's even the slightest recognition, they avoid me. Seth and Caroline avoided me in Illumina, too. Everyone treats me like I'm fine china, and I've never been fine china in my life. Or have I?"

"They're respecting your wishes to forget, love. Curiosity about what you forgot is part of the risk." Bell sat back in his chair, crossing his legs, which was a special feat in the leather rather than the cotton. "Do you not trust that you made the best decision for yourself?"

"Is that real gold?"

Just as Maya recognized the enigmatic evasiveness of fortune tellers, Bell recognized the misdirection of illusionists, but he would wait to see where the sleight took him.

Bell worked the bracelet from his arm into his palm then lifted it into the air and floated it over to her. She stretched out her arm, enchanted in spite of herself. She'd grown accustomed to magic from Fairuza, but none of the other Illumina cast had psychokinetic skill.

The gold bracelet slid up her arm. He didn't react, but he fought not to swallow, blink, shift or show any number of the physical reactions of his human form. The bracelet was too big for her. He adjusted the fit, molding the gold like clay.

Once, he'd wrapped her wrists in leather, bound her neck in a collar, and when he'd freed her, she'd picked them up from the ground and buckled them back on, carried his magic with her. Even when she'd worn nothing else, she would wear the cuffs or the collar for him.

The gold wasn't meant to contrast his skin tone or hers but to complement it with a gaudy display of luxury that no one could believe was real. Its weight assured that it could be nothing else. With all the outdoor exposure, anything plated would flake off under the elements.

She traced the curl of the gold, tested how it felt when she lowered her arm. Like most things in Arcanium, it would be more comfortable than she'd expect. He wanted to step around the table to wrap his hand over the bracelet and remove it from her, its shadow caressing her skin, her warmth joining with his in the metal.

"What if I were to wish for the memories back?" Maya asked, still stroking the gold as though confirming its worth with each smooth run of her fingertips.

"You've made your wishes."

"What were they? Fairuza never told me. Or can you not tell me that either?"

Bell gathered the tarot cards to shuffle, both for something to do with his hands and to distract her at least as much as she distracted him with her fingers on his gold.

"The wish that brought you into Arcanium was not your own. Your boyfriend made a wish in a moment of ire, vague enough for me to use as I pleased. Your first wish was to punish your boyfriend for his indiscretions

119

after having locked you into Arcanium without regret. Your second wish was to protect yourself from my previous companion, who had not responded to your entry into Arcanium with grace. Your third was for me to set you free."

"And that was when I left Arcanium?"

"No. You stayed. You simply had the freedom to leave whenever you chose. Which you eventually did, and I made no effort to stop you."

"You didn't want me to come back," Maya said.

"What makes you think that?"

"You're good. You don't reveal a lot, even when you're surprised. If I didn't know what I was looking for, I wouldn't be able to tell when you're surprised at all. But Fairuza doesn't get surprised often either. It's like she's surprised that she's surprised. Since the demons here are expressive as hell, I think it's an illusionist-slash-fortune-teller thing, not letting the audience of one or a thousand see where you're going before you go. But when you first saw me, you looked like you'd seen a ghost, and there's nothing vague about seeing Mommy and Daddy whisper under their breath."

She was good, too. She'd learned while under Bell, but after losing the memories, Fairuza had retaught her everything she'd needed to know about schooling her expression, and she hadn't allowed Maya's perceptiveness to wither.

"No, I didn't want you to come back like this, because *you* didn't want to. Otherwise you would have returned to me instead of fleeing to Illumina."

"I don't think I would have fled to *any* circus, do you?" Maya let her leg fall then took the tarot cards from him.

He let them go, observing without a word as Maya took over the shuffling tricks. She'd learned on both smaller and larger decks, so she fumbled a bit before finding her rhythm.

Bell had never taught her card tricks. Canton had been responsible for that new skill. On her own, it would take about three to five years of continued practice to fully develop her skills, but she was adequate, already developing flourishes. Bell resisted the impulse to give her every skill she needed, to smooth her gestures and trigger her imagination. Maya was no longer his. Even if Illumina were to become part of Arcanium, he would not be responsible for anything but her safety.

"Being in a circus makes you an outsider. What happened to you makes you more of one. To flee to something that makes you feel less so seems reasonable to me. It's why, even after leaving, several of my children came back to Arcanium, the very place they thought they wanted to escape more than anything else in the world."

"But that's because Arcanium isn't really a circus, is it? Neither is Illumina, but it has more people in it from a circus or carny background. What the fuck kind of tarot deck is this?"

Maya had flipped over the middle card in her latest shuffle, revealing the Calliope.

"My own, a collaboration between Troy and myself. It certainly shakes things up when people come in thinking they can read the cards for me." Bell tapped the Calliope. "This one seems especially pertinent to your point, love. Please elaborate."

"I guess when you create your own tarot, it's a lot easier to make shit up to fit whatever narrative you're looking to spin." Maya resumed shuffling, but she left the Calliope card on the velvet tablecloth. "I knew Arcanium wasn't a typical circus when I was looking for one. I don't remember why I was looking anymore, but I tried other circuses and carnivals before Illumina. Imagine my surprise when I couldn't understand half of what they were saying or doing, even though I said I'd been with Arcanium for five years and that seemed to mean something to them. Then I arrive at Illumina, and everything's so much more what I was used to, because Fairuza's not real circus folk either. She learned from you and she built off that. But when real performers came to Illumina, they actually had to unlearn the language they'd absorbed, because Fairuza quietly kept using the one she learned from you."

"I started entertaining alone or among Romany troupes," Bell said. "Not because they believed me to be one of them, but because they were too afraid to tell someone like me no. It's not often that the spirits you ward against actually show up on your stoop, thoroughly unwarded. I've learned many ways of referring to this life. I chose my own."

"I've been walking around Arcanium the last two days, doing the inevitable compare and contrast. It looks like a circus. It sounds like a circus. It tastes like one. But it doesn't feel like one. Because your people don't act like it. You've brought in some carnies, but they've adjusted to your world, and most of your people weren't born into it and didn't choose it. This isn't a circus. It's a music box that plays *Put on a Happy Face*."

Maya turned over another card. The Prison. She glanced up at Bell, suspicion furrowing her brow. "Tell me this isn't an enchanted deck."

"This isn't an enchanted deck." He raised an eyebrow, daring her to challenge him, but she just resumed her shuffling.

"It's a dungeon, right? That's the... What's the word? That's the *template* you used. But a prison retrofitted as apartments is still a prison, while we're following a theme." She pointed at the Prison card with the corner of her deck. "It's not a coincidence that you use iron bars."

"It's a complete coincidence. Iron abhors magic, but it doesn't abhor me, so it's good at keeping my magic in and other people's magic out. My fence is also very pretty."

The furrow smoothed when a smile curved her lips before she could stop it. "You like to pretend you created a dungeon-themed circus, with all your demonic influences and horror elements, but really, you just created a circus-themed dungeon—and it shows."

Bell sighed. "Here's one of the moments that remembering Locke's Arcanium would be quite handy. I have a dungeon-themed circus. *He* had a circus-themed dungeon."

"I'm not arguing that yours isn't better. I'm saying you're not as good as you think you are."

"Who said anything in the world about good?"

"How about kind? Not cruel?"

"I have my moments with both. I know exactly what I am, Maya. I've never hidden that. Just because I expect more kindness and less cruelty from outsiders doesn't mean I don't allow my own when appropriate. I have strict rules, though. I follow them and expect everyone else on the inside to follow them, too, these rules designed to protect my people. Locke's laws didn't give a shit about the safety of his cast, as long as they didn't die and came back together in the morning."

Maya stopped shuffling. Bell raised his chin to hide the biting of his tongue. It was easier for her to consume the information he gave her with no emotional context, but consuming the wrong thing could have such catastrophic results that it was his burden to keep what he served palatable.

He closed his eyes and took a breath. "What was your aim in coming to me, Maya? I'm just a fortune teller during the day. Would you like a fortune told?"

It was actually useless trying to tell her a substantive fortune, but he couldn't explain that to her, because for all that she'd gathered from Arcanium so far — which was impressive, given everything that had been deliberately withheld — she hadn't gleaned what she'd been to him. She knew that she'd been his, but in no different way from the rest.

"I can tell my own fortune these days, thanks." She put the third card on the table next to the others, face down. "I came here because you know something about me, and I can't think of anyone else here who could have fucked me up enough that Fairuza would take all my memories just because I asked her to. I need you to tell me."

"You *want* me to tell you. But you *needed* to lose the memories. And I won't take your own choice away from you, not when you're free."

"If Fairuza gets her way, I won't be free forever, will I?"

"It will be a collaboration. You'll still be hers. You'll always be free."

Bell turned over the last card. The Caged Bird. An ambiguous card — the door didn't have a lock.

"I think I've made my point with the enchanted deck, don't you?" Maya said.

"What makes you think the cards were for you?" Bell swept the cards together and beckoned for the rest of the deck.

She reluctantly handed it to him. Her finger brushed his.

Air forced itself out between his lips, as though someone had taken the Mountain's fist and jammed it into his gut. He recovered quickly, but he couldn't take back what she'd seen. She'd caused him pain. She wouldn't know exactly why, but she would understand that she was significant enough that a simple brush of her skin had been a fight-club blow. He paused, still holding the deck over the table.

She slowly withdrew to sit down again, the furrow back between her eyebrows. She didn't realize she was doing it — or why her cold reading was often so apt — but she was probing him for the reason for his reaction, too untrained and ignorant of her own abilities to get very far.

Bell did a simple shuffle of the deck. "These are for you." He placed the first card down. "The Lock. This can be taken extremely literally, if you like, but it's not meant to be. It means you were or are bound to something, and you feel trapped within it. You seek to escape, but you don't have the means to do so. Not without…" He placed the second card down. "The Key. You escaped, my dear. But in doing so, you had to lock a part of you up again, so that you could be more whole than with the whole of your memories. You'll have to live with your key, because Fairuza isn't going to remove the lock."

He placed the third card onto the table.

The Bell.

Curse me and my own damned vanity to put myself into the tarot deck.

Of course, like the Lock — which he'd created before Locke had stolen Arcanium and hadn't removed for the exact opposite of his vanity — it wasn't meant to be literal. Still, it was Maya's turn to raise an eyebrow in challenge, and he wasn't entirely sure she was wrong. Because the deck *was* enchanted to save his energy during a reading. Even if he couldn't read her future, the cards didn't have the same attachments.

If only he could read the cards without his own magic getting in the way.

"I'm going to remain the thing in your way, Maya." He set the cards next to his Magic 8-Ball. "That is my task. I have a responsibility to protect you, along with everyone else within the prison-bar boundaries of this circus."

"But you failed." She stood, and he stood with her, walked with her to the tent flap.

"All the more reason not to fail again."

She reached for the tie. Then Maya swerved to the right to plant her palm against his chest. She wore rings, but like the gold, they'd warmed from her body and the sun. Her hands were small in comparison to his, tiny in comparison to Ciarán's, and her palm was softer than that of other performers, with more delicate tricks up her sleeve.

He was hotter than her, but her touch burned him like a brand, and he was once again flooded with memories he would strip from his own mind if it were possible. He could never scrub through all of the various dimensions of worlds in which he'd had her. His chest constricted, hitched under her hand, and there was nothing he could do to hide that — nor was he sure that he wanted to.

Bell didn't turn away from her, nor did he yell or demand that she leave, although perhaps he should have.

She was being the Maya he remembered, testing boundaries wherever she could find them, even when she'd believed herself trapped and in the hands of a demon rather than jinn, sometimes in the hands of the devil himself — although Locke, as impure a demon as one could be, had made no effort to ingratiate himself. Locke was designed to destroy, and for most of Arcanium, steady, unrelenting destruction had been his aim. He'd brought more subtlety to his relationships with Neve — and, to a lesser extent, Elizabeth.

But oh, how he'd loved having Maya as his centerpiece. It hadn't been just about money and favors, not with Maya, not with a woman whom demons knew had belonged to Bell and whom he could no longer protect. Locke had been unable to play with Kitty, and Valorie hadn't been as fun for him, because although she'd been Bell's companion for longer, anyone with the slightest prescience could tell that his favor for Maya had been greater. Special.

And Bell had once made no effort to conceal that. He wasn't one to pretend that there was no favoritism in his circus. Most of his cast preferred to stay out of his highest favor, happiest when he didn't pay attention to them, just let them go about the struggle of their lives, and Bell was content to give them that as well.

The only problem with unfettered favor was when that favor no longer imparted additional protection to compensate for the increased risk.

Bell didn't look away from Maya, gave her no more satisfaction in the reaction she caused than what he hadn't been able to control. He recognized the moment she realized it might not have been the best idea to touch him when she'd already known how strongly he would react. Her eyes widened, dark eyes darker in the dimmer tent, and she tried to back away.

He covered her hand with his. He didn't trap her against him, but she stopped retreating, stopped breathing. Beneath her palm, his heart beat like that of a human under skin as hot as if he'd been standing under the summer sun for hours instead of sheltered in a fanned, ventilated tent.

She couldn't breathe, but her lips parted and she shifted her hand, smoothed it along the plane of his chest, the heel of her palm brushing the small nipple. He didn't look away, but now she didn't meet his eyes because she stared instead at the half-bare body in front of her, the rest covered by something that hid very little — skin over skin, designed to stimulate sight as her touch stimulated him. Without anything to warn her away, she responded as she had when she'd first entered Arcanium, immediate attraction that had been mutual, when he'd known her better than she'd known him. In Arcanium, contact could mean so much more, enhanced by the incubus and succubus, and he and Maya were affected by both, which could be a special kind of heaven along with a special kind of hell, depending on how much sex one was willing to have. Locke had complicated that for everyone.

Including Maya, even if she wasn't the one shying away from it anymore.

With her hand on his chest and her arousal simmering under her skin, within her skull, rising and warming between her legs at the very suggestion that her touch had made and that their privacy and the fantastic atmosphere encouraged, Bell wanted nothing more than to bring her against him—pull her up against his chest and take that sharp-tongued mouth, taste her heat to meet his fever until she melted under him. He could have her, happy and safe as though nothing had happened, and she wouldn't resist him, because she wouldn't know why she should.

That was a future he could see, a future that was possible, because he wanted it so hard that the chest under her hand ached, his heartstrings pulled all the way through his body, and in spite of his intentions, his cock swelled. He silently quelled himself, but it took more effort not to get hard for her than it had any right to demand. He had to think of a former prisoner, the Rotting Man, to bring himself back down.

"I think you need to leave, *golam.*" He drew her hand from his chest, touched her cheek lightly before undoing the tie to the tent flap himself.

"The tent or the circus?" Maya allowed her hand to be manipulated away, but she didn't move, even when the tent flap swung open and let in blinding light.

"You *should* leave the circus, but that's for you and Fairuza to discuss, not an issue for me to force. You *need* to leave the tent."

"What did I mean to you?" Her question had changed—although in a way, it hadn't.

"You were one of my own. I never forget my own. And I cannot be forgiven for what was done to you. You are not safe here."

"Safety isn't what I'm looking for." She started out of the tent but hesitated, one foot in the light and the other in shadow. "Don't you want your bracelet back?"

Bell closed his hand over the gold that wrapped around Maya's arm. Her shoulders and neck tightened, and though her thin T-shirt was loose and she was wearing a bra with the straps showing on her shoulders, he could practically see through the clothing to what lay beneath, which had changed little since she'd left Arcanium. Of course, while in Arcanium, she hadn't physically changed at all, except to strengthen and tone and grow more flexible for performance purposes. Psychological turmoil after she'd left had withered her appetite, and Illumina, a circus that required actual skills, had thinned her more through its physical demands, which made him want to sit her in front of the odd chef to feed — even though it wouldn't make a difference in Arcanium. *Self-created irony.*

The sensation of his gold embracing her, denting the flesh so that it wouldn't fall, compelled him to encircle her arm with his hand. He stepped closer.

She tilted her head up. Apprehension did nothing to dampen the desire that flowed between them, that begged on its knees that they satisfy each other because it would be so *good* when they did. That feeling wasn't a lie, which made it all the more difficult to resist.

"Keep it."

"Are you in the habit of giving away hundreds of dollars' worth of gold to just anyone who walks into your tent?" She shifted closer to him, drawn as high tide to shore.

All he could do was guide her into the sun then slip back into the shadow, parting them and imparting some space. But he could still so easily reach for her and pull her in after him, close the tent flap, have her in the middle of the room without even a bed or a table. Just hold her and kiss her and love every inch of her that he had worshipped so many times. And the sounds she would make...

"It's not unheard of. I can always make another," he managed to say without revealing what played out in his head a million different ways. "Please enjoy your stay here in Arcanium, but I think you should not return to me. You should break the contract with Fairuza and leave far from this place."

"Then I guess it's a good thing I don't always do what I should." She stepped back, but she made no move toward the Arcanium gates. "You and I aren't finished here."

The buzz of a vibrating cell phone in his head alerted him to Fairuza peeking in on the conversation and indicating disapproval. But she was the one who'd risked Maya finding her way to Bell again in the first place, so Bell wasn't inclined to consider Fairuza's feelings on the myriad thoughts in which she found herself swimming. He did the psychic version of the middle-finger salute and shut her out. Immature but effective.

"I'm afraid we have to be." He closed the tent flap then knotted it to ensure that he wouldn't be disturbed—at least for another fifteen or twenty minutes, the usual time for a client.

'This isn't a real circus. It's a circus-themed dungeon. A music box.'

Bell lowered himself not into his chair but to the sturdy Persian rug that made up the floor of the tent. Lying back to stare up into the prisms and scarves that colored the ceiling of his tent, he tried to peel each fantasy, memory and possibility like sunburnt skin from his mind.

Chapter Seven

After the two days open to Illumina alone, Arcanium had to reopen for outside guests, and the strain started to show.

They were so used to boredom during the week, but now they understood why he didn't push them to stay on for strangers every night of the week. Three days of physical demands, mixed with the kind of enthusiasm that burned out hundreds of thousands in customer service like old Christmas lights every year, was enough for anyone. To not have the week to recover left the more introverted among his cast strained to the limits of their tolerance by too many people trying to touch, by taking pictures, talking, flirting and so much goddamn smiling.

After such a quick turnaround between circus days, Bell didn't think his people had ever slept so hard.

Bell stopped sleeping after Saturday. Neve and Lizzie were usually the ones pulling him into their dreams, sometimes Caroline, but after visiting him, no one else could compete with Maya.

Although she hadn't returned to the fortune teller tent, she hadn't completely avoided him, and the sex demon magic continued to work within her. It didn't help that Mikhail had touched her before, which made her all the more susceptible to him.

She tried to work off some of the resultant sexual tension with Fairuza in the evenings, when the sexual magic in the circus was at its peak, but Maya wasn't the only lover returning to her, nor had she been Fairuza's primary partner prior to coming to Arcanium. Maya couldn't control with whom Fairuza spent her nights when she had a wealth of partners from whom to choose who also didn't know how to handle the hormonal wave that the sex demons triggered.

Unlike her first tenure in Arcanium, Maya didn't have multiple outlets for her sexual frustration. She wouldn't even *consider* multiple outlets, unthinkable to a Catholic woman for whom sex with a woman was apparently tolerable. Bell had long since given up trying to understand how people justified their actions, because he understood more than most how uncontrollable many actions were and how important justifications were to allow for them.

In the absence of any other outlet, her dreams gave her Bell, and they dragged him under, drowned him in her desire until he couldn't breathe. He woke up so hot that he thought he would set the RV on fire, his cock full and hard and angry that he wouldn't let it have what he so clearly wanted while Maya's dream continued to play in his head—violent and delicious, reminiscent of their earliest days when she'd still been ambivalent about him but not the sex that he gave her.

By the time Monday arrived, he was ready to insist that Fairuza give her a generous severance package to learn a new vocabulary and join a more conventional circus if she was so insistent on staying within the circus fold.

But at that point, Fairuza was working all day and some of the night with her cast and the golems to prepare the circus to shift from Arcanium to Illumina. They wouldn't need most of the carnival accoutrements—Illumina wasn't that kind of circus—but the performers didn't trust Bell's assurance that they couldn't fall, even if they tried, and that they didn't need to use a net. They rehearsed all Monday and Tuesday in preparation.

Prior to the Tuesday evening performance, Fairuza met him at the picnic tables set up among the caravan. He still hadn't given the Illumina cast more than tents and cots. A number of them had found themselves in trailers and RVs a few times since arriving, and the tents and cots were far more comfortable than they'd anticipated, so no one had openly complained yet. Bell didn't want to expend effort to create what they needed until he knew that they needed them at all.

Given his present mood, the Illumina-Arcanium merger was far from a foregone conclusion. Little got in Maya's way when a notion entered her head, and she had him in her head now, which brought him into hers. And so the dilemma continued in its ouroboros cycle.

Fairuza crossed her arms as she looked down at him. "You've been a bad man."

"Thank you."

"I'm being serious."

"Then don't start the conversation with 'You've been a bad man.'" Bell stood from the bench and met her gaze as though she wasn't considering stabbing her stiletto into his eye. A woman could stand to be more violent when there would be no real lasting damage.

"I told you to stay away from Maya."

"You *brought* her here — where it's impossible for me to truly stay away from her, where she can come to me, where if I go to sleep, she's the one whose dreams pull me in. You can expect me to control what I do with her, but you can't expect me to control *her* or the very wanting itself." Bell crossed his arms as well, mirroring her, although with less skin showing. He wore his Henley over the leather pants to distinguish himself as a guest of Illumina, long sleeves in spite of the heat. He was hot enough that summer felt cool, and winter couldn't begin to touch what burned at his core. "If you want *her* to stay away from *me*, then *you're* the one who needs to put a leash on that woman."

"You gave her a pure gold bracelet that marks her as yours. They recognize it, Bell, both of our casts. If yours starts to whisper a little louder, they'll start to talk — and Maya always hears."

"And whose fault is that?" Bell didn't mind sounding like a teenager, because he'd done right by Maya in letting her go. If Fairuza struck a match over gasoline, she shouldn't blame the gasoline for the fire. "Will you let her go now?"

"She's free to leave at any time. You know that as well as I do, and it matters whether she chooses it. I've never fired anyone, and I'm not firing her because you're attached."

"Then fire her because *she* is."

"She doesn't *remember* you."

Bell clasped Fairuza's shoulders. "Which means she doesn't know *not* to get attached. Patterns, Fai. Kitty saw it coming before you did."

Fairuza blinked, her anger shifting into troubled concern. Despite the fact that Kitty hadn't a psychic cell in her body, her intuition more than made up for it. "What can I do that doesn't involve pushing Maya away? Because she'd just come through the gate when the circus opens and pay for the privilege of torturing us both. You know that."

"I can bar her."

Fairuza sighed, stroking his cheek. "You barely even bar demons. No, I think the trick here is to nip the curiosity in the bud. Throwing her out is just going to make it worse. What do you need me to do?"

"Have more sex with her so she's not so frustrated when she goes to bed?"

Fairuza smiled. "I can try, but I have more than her to take care of, you know."

Bell released Fairuza's shoulders to walk with her to the fortune teller table she'd set up outside the big top entrance. "She's the linchpin, Fai. If you can't satisfy her, find someone else to do it."

"You know perfectly well that her having sex with me is stressful enough. Poor girl has had to contend with the moral struggle versus her physical needs all over again, and she doesn't have a demon anymore to whip her in lieu of priestly absolution. She doesn't actually seek me out as much as you think she does, and coming to me so often here has already worn on her. She's going to want confession on Wednesday."

"She's going to want confession *after* Wednesday."

"Perhaps she'll leave on her own," she replied mildly. "This isn't like when she came here before, when she couldn't leave the grounds to visit the nearest cathedral. Maybe Wednesday will be the deciding factor and her moral code will overwhelm the curiosity that keeps her here."

"Here's to good Catholic girls and their hang-ups." Bell saluted Fairuza's hand with a wry bow.

"And their ex-Muslim and pre-Islamic deity lovers." Fairuza curtsied, spreading her white-feathered skirts once more. She had more than one costume, but she'd chosen something familiar for tonight. "May the more tortured soul win."

"How far should I take it?" Bell asked.

"As long as you're not the one taking it... Go nuts."

* * * *

Fairuza enjoyed sweeping orchestrations, the kind that wouldn't be out of place in a high fantasy movie, and the Illumina performance told an equally sweeping story—or rather, a series of stories—of creation. Which one was right was immaterial. Only the stories mattered.

A collection of tumbling dancers and trapeze artists recreated Eden, with two dancers in skin-toned body suits dancing around a Tree of Life—which should have been the Tree of the Knowledge of Good and Evil, but Fairuza never let details get in the way of a good visual. Silk aerialists rolled down from the branches in bright red costumes, apples that glinted tantalizingly in the lights as several contortionists joined together to form the serpent tempting Eve.

The primary contortionist lured Eve into a dance that reminded Bell all too much of his courtship of both Fairuza and Maya. Both women had viewed him as the devil in their lives, even if Fairuza thought she'd made peace with it. He seduced his women into embracing pleasure and sensation in all its forms, but so many religions condemned such decadence as somehow contrary to the natural order and, at the same time, too natural to be pious.

Despite the inventiveness and artistic inspiration of religion, it left a bad taste in his mouth. He'd needed to put so much effort into convincing every human companion he'd been with to give in to the powerful, varied desires that they'd been taught to resist. Picasso had said that it was much harder to learn how to paint like a child. Bell found the same when it came to reverting to one's animal lusts—for food, drink, company, sex, oblivion, sometimes for something as simple as a flower garden...or an apple.

After the exile from Eden, the big top tent darkened. From that darkness, bright LED colored lights shone over the costumes of dozens of dancers to form the dragon Tiamat—dark, primordial chaos in the Babylonian creation myth. Then they broke away into a light dance show, followed by fire spinners with uncanny timing and a propensity for throwing their poi in a complicated juggling act between each other.

The lights came back up dim and blue in dizzying, constantly moving colors. Illumina aerialists, trapeze artists and a series of solo and duo cyr wheel acts spread through the ring to become the swirling chaos of the birthed cosmos.

When the palette changed to one he was more familiar with, crimson and cream, strength and Russian bar acts played out the somewhat gruesome beginning of Greek mythology. The strength acts in particular reminded Bell so much of Lars and Seth together that his chest ached. Lazarus and Magda couldn't hope to replicate the yearning between the two men — always secret, always shameful, as though the fact that Seth liked men as well as women and Lars liked Seth was something that made them lesser men instead of more. Illumina's strength actors were a beautiful mix of embraced desires, but insecurity had always brought truer beauty to Arcanium's less sophisticated act.

Following the Greek myth, Canton, Fairuza and Maya brought their brands of magic to a more symbolic representation of Nordic cosmogony. Maya was fire in red, Fairuza ice in white and Canton was the silence and darkness between them in a suit black from head to toe, shimmering like the night sky. Here was the mix of illusion and real magic that Bell was more accustomed to, and for him, the first real spectacle of the night, because it was the first glimpse of the impossible. Maya's and Fairuza's real magic blended with Canton's illusion into something that transcended childlike wonder. Awe from the impossible could also be quite adult, wonderfully complex in the emotions that it wrought.

When Illumina completed their performances, Bell joined the rest of Arcanium in a standing ovation, swept up in the fresher enthusiasm of his cast.

Even so, Bell wasn't swayed.

Illumina deserved more than barely meeting their expenses, but while the acts were cohesive and even impressive by human standards, nothing truly surprised him.

He supposed he wasn't the best audience when he knew how the proverbial sausage was made. Mild magic mixed with acrobatics entertained his cast, but when Bell could predict the choreography, when he practically heard the eight-counts, when he knew how illusion was made to look like magic, it didn't impart in him quite the same level of admiration. Traveling circuses and freak shows were dying—for some good reasons and some bad. Even so, acts like this were all too common on the Cirque circuit and television talent shows, and in a way, that was just making them die more quickly, because people kept wanting more and better without any sense of the work required to push the human body this far.

Such physical feats moved him, but there was a reason why Arcanium, of all places, had a regular cadre of fans, some so devout that they traveled with Arcanium to visit almost every weekend. Arcanium didn't only offer what looked impossible. It offered the legitimately impossible—just enough to whet an appetite for awe dulled by computer-generated effects and hoax videos. When people recorded Arcanium performances, comments decried them as fake, but they inspired enough interest that skeptics came to the circus to confirm the gaff themselves. Bell's Arcanium had long baffled even professional skeptics who made a career of debunking magic, including other magicians.

He deliberately provided more conventional acts like Lazarus and Magda and the Albino Triplets—although, as a demon, Marina added another element to the Triplets that made them seem more otherworldly, even alien, if not necessarily impossible. The conventional made novelty acts like Carlo and Okeyo more surprising, and it made Sera's flight in the middle of her aerial silk routine all-the-more jarringly beautiful. As his lady of the high-wire, Maya had once stunned people by spinning around the wire on nothing but her toes, only her magical inability to fall keeping her from striking the ground. But no one had known that. They'd been more impressed by an impossibility that only *looked* like skill.

Bell had an aesthetic. Illumina merely confirmed it.

But his people were impressed by the narrative of the performance rather than the variety show that he usually presented. Maybe his vision was more limited than he would have liked to believe after years of absorbing human imagination through their wishes. Fairuza was jinn now, but she still had a human breadth for fantasy.

His pride was just a little too big for him to swallow. Instead, he rolled it around in his mouth in consideration.

Bell made his way down the bleachers from the top row—a big top performance needed to be as thrilling from the back as the front—while some of the Arcanium cast entered the ring to speak with the performers they knew best. Many didn't, though, in spite of their generous applause. Enough of his people were still naturally suspicious, even after a week of acclimation. But that wasn't the only reason.

Neve tucked herself closer to her incubus and succubus. Caroline surrounded herself, shielded herself, with her demon and her boy. The Creature had his arms and wings wrapped around the Spider. And Kitty sat alone.

His Kitty was as solitary as she was social, but sometimes her two selves collided into loneliness when she was trapped on the outside of something she wanted more than anything—the easy conversation between lovely people that she could never be, even though she was lovelier to the people who loved her.

She'd shed all of her wishes to lose the opportunity to change her appearance, because that was capitulation, knuckling under oppression that seemed so tempting and limitless from the outside. She'd built so much of herself around what she looked like, because everyone who saw her did the same, forcing her to fortify the foundations of what she couldn't change.

She'd been sitting on a solution for years now, but it wasn't something Kitty would ask anyone else to give to her when she'd already ceded her last wish for a vanilla and chocolate twist ice cream cone in July.

She had to know that if she asked that of him, he would give it to her without hesitation. The wish that had brought her into Arcanium was enough for him to give her whatever her heart desired. But she still hadn't asked, because she couldn't admit to wanting it after having fought so hard to love what she was.

Where was a place for her in the world that Illumina would create within Arcanium?

Bell sat next to Kitty and kissed her neck. It was dark in the bleachers. He wasn't doing it for anyone other than her, wasn't doing it to make a point or shame the devil. He embraced her around the shoulders and held her without a word.

"This is not what I came to Arcanium for," Kitty muttered. If she was ashamed that he knew how she felt, that didn't keep her from leaning into him.

"And it's not why I made Arcanium."

"But it was beautiful."

"You're beautiful, Kitty. If their beauty has no room for yours, theirs needs to change when it's here. The rest of the world has cornered that market. This is mine, and I won't let you be lost in it. The day you cease to be the heart, this will cease to be Arcanium."

"You already think Arcanium needs to change. You've been thinking it for a while. What if it needs to change to *that*?"

"Circuses like that are a dime a dozen in our dying market. Arcanium will not be taken or absorbed by something so common. If this goes the way Fairuza intends, it's the big top performances that would change the most, but we'd still keep them Arcanium, wouldn't we? Don't worry, love." He kissed her shoulder then withdrew, stroking her loose hair. "They came here looking for shelter from their own storm. They're the ones who are desperate, not us. And just think of the costumes you'll make."

Kitty managed a smile.

"Do you think the Funhouse will scare them off or intrigue them more?" he asked.

"Probably both. They're craving weird right now because it's new. But after a while, I don't think they'll want to stay weird."

"They won't have a choice if they intend to stay with Fairuza. And if some of them slip like I think they will, they won't have a choice at all, will they?"

"I'm not sure if I want you to take my jealousy out on them by making them the very oddities they're not prepared to live as. Liz was bad enough, but I know you're looking for another Torso who isn't incapacitated, another set of conjoined twins, another Human Knot... It's one thing when it's natural, Bell, but you already have enough Skeletons, and pissing you off isn't enough to justify doing that to people. I've learned to live with it, thrive with it, as have Carlo and Okeyo—most of the time, anyway—but I wouldn't wish the process of getting to that point on anyone."

"We all have trials, Kitty. Sometimes they happen on their own, and sometimes they're chosen for us. I've given my warnings. Fairuza's warned them multiple times over. If they're still arrogant enough to think they can get away with whatever they want just because they're pretty, I think Arcanium is the perfect place for them to realize there's a limit to that superpower, don't you?"

Kitty closed her eyes, but Bell heard enough in what she didn't say. She was an empathetic woman — inevitable for someone who made it their business to take care of people behind the scenes, someone who had suffered needlessly from people's cruelties long before jinn or demons got their hands on her. It hurt her when he brought people into Arcanium against their will by turning them into something else — even when they came in because of something they did to her — because it made what she was a punishment.

But it hurt her, too, that the people he brought in often considered being an oddity worse than death when it was her life. Revulsion was part of the process, but that didn't make it easier for Kitty to handle or prevent her from taking it personally.

"If you wanted to be a part of the Funhouse tomorrow, they would flock to you, and they don't even know that they want to, the narrow-minded pricks. They don't deserve what you would gift them." He pressed his forehead to hers. "I'm trying, Kitty. I don't know if I can keep her from the truth. It's painful, seeing her happy and knowing that it's…"

"An illusion." Kitty sighed. "Don't take that away from her."

"She cornered me in my tent."

"She's five-foot-nothing and human, Bell. How hard is it to refuse her?" But as Kitty raised her head, she bit her lower lip to cut off anything else she might accuse him of. "That was mean and I know better. I'm sorry."

"She's determined to know what happened, even though she knows she wanted to forget it—like waking up in a bathtub with one less kidney and no knowledge that you were the one who sold it."

"An odd but apt analogy. Can you just—I don't know—tell her? Don't show her but tell her what happened?"

Bell shook his head. "Either it will break down the walls around her memories or she'll lack the context for it to mean anything to her. Memories need emotion for them to matter, and she's looking for something that matters. The only solution is to shut her out, but I'm afraid of what she would do, who she would go to, if she can't find her answers here. So I'm caught between respecting her wishes then and respecting her wishes now."

"Which will cause the most pain?" Kitty asked.

"I can't know." That was the worst part, not being able to see what his decisions would do to her, losing the certainty that he had even for Kitty, Neve and Lizzie.

That he completely lacked Maya's future but not those of others he loved left him breathless with the kind of powerlessness he hadn't known since Arcanium had been torn from him like his own skin.

It told him all he needed to know about what Maya meant to him, even after her condemnation of his errors, after leaving him then returning a changed woman, because nothing but Arcanium's future had ever been hidden from him in this way. Without even a foundational future, possibilities from which to choose, Maya paralyzed him. He was at a loss, and that just didn't happen.

He also couldn't shake the feeling that the reason he couldn't see the impact of either decision was because there was no good decision.

To refuse her the memories she sought and shut her out from Arcanium and Illumina would lead her to search for answers among other demonic and jinn enclaves, the way she'd searched for Illumina. But they wouldn't be as considerate as Illumina or even Arcanium, because she'd likely stumble onto a dungeon that was being used exactly as it had been intended. The small protections Bell had given her when she'd left would save her from demons and jinn searching for her. He could do nothing to protect her if she walked straight into a pit of vipers.

But if he gave her the memories, she'd have to relive them a second time, and Bell didn't know if she could live with herself—which was why she'd had them removed in the first place.

He'd turned the dilemma every angle to find an escape route. Locke had been a conquerable enemy, straightforward. What he'd left behind was more diffuse, an enemy Bell couldn't fight for those who had buckled under the demon's private and marketed torture. He could combat shame, but by its definition, he couldn't combat defeat, nor his contribution to it.

"If there are no good answers," Kitty said, "you have to trust your instincts."

"The same instincts you beg me to resist at every turn as inhumane and borderline sadistic?"

"The instincts to get her out of here."

"I have a shot tomorrow—if the Funhouse is too much for her."

"Bell, you can't…"

"I'm getting such mixed messages, Kitty Cat." He had to laugh, though, because he wasn't confused. "I'm not going to touch her, and I'm not going to put her up on stage. But I might have to lift the moratorium on the others' flirtation. As long as they keep their accounts of the past to themselves, she's going to have beat them off with a stick. Or theirs, if that's her preference. Then she'll have to decide if she's willing to confess to the nearest priest as often as Arcanium would demand of her."

Kitty wrinkled her nose. "She's back to that, is she? She's sleeping with Fairuza, and she's still back to that?"

"She never left. She merely changed her justifications. And what kind of priest she confessed to." Bell stared across the ring at where the Ringmaster glowered at him—not out of misplaced jealousy, just because he could. "Will you help?"

"I'm not sure what I can do. She doesn't see me anymore. She's back to feeling sorry for me but not really seeing me—which doesn't make my heart break at all, Bell."

"Speak with the others and let them know that, although she's not as she was, Maya's fair game, like the rest."

It wouldn't be dangerous to her by any means, because all the usual rules applied. But she would find herself a lot more popular in a different way than she'd prepared for, while also under the sex demons' increased influence.

He wanted to scare her. He wanted her to scare herself. Saving her would only work if it were her decision, if she relinquished her ties to the supernatural circus world on her own.

"The demons have more people to play with than before," Kitty said, "and they're still enough of a novelty that they'll have their hands, laps and everything else full."

"None of them will be like her."

Kitty nodded slowly, because it had never just been that Maya was beautiful. She was a demon's dream as well as man's. She always had been. "I don't like it."

"Neither do I."

Chapter Eight

Bell preferred warehouses for his Funhouse events. If he thought he could get away with it, he'd do his whole circus in a warehouse like this all the time—just one big, haunted funhouse followed by a big top performance in a more open area.

He could manipulate any blueprints, but parking would always be a problem in the city, as would noise complaints and increased harassment of his oddities by delinquents and nimbies alike. He managed to muffle the noise and keep anyone from seeing inside during his Funhouse, but only for a night. After that, people started getting suspicious when they saw such a motley crew entering and exiting at all hours of the day, people who ironically didn't make *enough* noise for the number of people.

For those in Illumina who didn't have a wardrobe designed for the venue, Kitty brought out several racks of options that Sera would adjust as needed. They could choose from evening wear to lingerie, from elegance to the kind of thing that Sasha loved to make for Arcanium's cast—intricate SM costumes, leather with a sharp metal edge, practical or ornamental, depending on the wearer. She, too, could make quick adjustments with her own magic, which saved Kitty time and pins so that she could focus on picking the right outfits and doing the hair and makeup for anyone who asked.

However, most of Illumina kept themselves separate, discomfort as palpable as the rasp of sandpaper. It was one thing to fantasize about the Arcanium cast at their sexiest, making themselves potentially more available with each other and with strangers. It was another to see it actually about to happen, to see circus folk like themselves deliberately made into cravable objects, well into the murky realm of sex work, although everyone participating on the floor was there voluntarily and Bell didn't need the money he earned for these events—not that he denied the cover cost for their presence. He never undervalued his people.

Bell perched in the recess of a brick column and peered down at the crowd. He held fewer Funhouse events than before, not least because Locke had taken advantage of their more relaxed security. When no one would have dared to take Arcanium, Bell had considered the lapse in security an acceptable risk. Now, nothing was worth letting down his guard. Bell pulled all his circus with him during the events, including the golems. He left behind only the clowns and a few spells to protect the caravan and the tents from common thieves. The place wasn't the real circus and didn't need the bulk of his magic to protect it.

Demons wouldn't go after mere tents, even enchanted ones.

No one would slip Arcanium out from under him ever again. If they wanted it, they would have to wrest it from the jinni who kept it cuffed and chained within his own power, even if that took more energy from him, especially outside its usual borders.

Bell put his fingers in his mouth and whistled. The already subdued conversations quieted into uneasy silence.

"As blurred as the lines can be within Arcanium, they're not going to get any clearer here, which is why *you* need to be absolutely clear about Arcanium's rules. No one can be forced into doing anything they don't want. Just because they're naked and simulating or actually having sex doesn't mean they'll say yes to anyone who comes up to them, nor that they should. With Lady Sasha and Lord Mikhail acting as social lubricant even more than usual tonight, you're going to be sorely tempted to simply take what you want. But the Ringmaster will be waiting in the wings, just in case you somehow believe that your urgency supersedes their agency. It doesn't matter if one of my people has had six cocks in them. You're not entitled to be one of them. You are not going into this with a vague disclaimer. No one can claim that they didn't know."

Bell crossed his legs in the nook and leaned forward to rest his elbows on his knees. "Now, Illumina is welcome to enter the Funhouse as guests or as cast. Guests should glam themselves up accordingly. Cast should dress down. You are also welcome to stay out here in the green room if you don't want to be approached by rich strangers being less subtle about what they want from you. Make no mistake about what we are offering. It's a heady, sybaritic experience, but it's not for everyone, especially not for anyone under the age of eighteen. Tara, Malcolm, Jasper, please go back to the cots now. There are tablets for you to watch movies with noise-canceling headphones, and we do have chaperones to make sure you use them."

"Why bring them at all if they're not even allowed to hear anything?" Canton asked.

"Because I'd rather they hear a stray moan than get kidnapped by demons because all of my focus is here. And the clowns will eat anything under the age of eighteen without oversight."

"How on earth would they possibly know that they're under eighteen? Do they have a direct line to the MPAA?"

"Do *you* have trouble telling if someone is under eighteen, Canton?" The truth was that the scent of anything over fifteen started to seem old to the clowns, but since Bell gave them license for under eighteen, they didn't say no to it. Really, they wouldn't say no to anything that trespassed, but cured meat was on their menu only by necessity.

His final warning concluded, Bell jumped down from the column to enter the Funhouse.

This warehouse was set up like a maze that started on the third floor and ended on the first, where the partitioned rooms opened into a three-story-tall open factory, with privacy booths, exhibitionist platforms and various cushioned furniture peppered throughout, the catwalks ideal for looking down from above.

To one side, Shane had taken her place by the open bar and feast tables, where she could be fed in her meat bed like an exotic pet. Not a few fingers had been nipped since they'd started offering her in the

Funhouse events, but it only had to happen a few times before word got around to be more considerate, and Shane was a lot better fed than she had once been — enough that she could take lovers willing to risk their cock in her cunt-mouth. In Bell's experience, men loved to stick their dick into something potentially dangerous if they thought it would feel good. He hadn't always been immune to that foolishness, either, although he could always regrow his.

The rest of the exhibits took their places in the rooms, which were interspersed with the more experiential elements of his haunted funhouse as well as the usual Funhouse tableaus designed to whet appetites — and in isolated cases, satisfy them.

Bell no longer put most of his cast in closed glass cases like before. The rooms were open with low lighting — dim chandeliers, candelabra, churning lights to disorient, lanterns, moonlight — no closed doors or blacked-out windows.

Of his old cast, Caroline, Seth and Riley didn't participate anymore, but Colm had taken on his more demonic guise to hide on his own among the rest. And as long as Neve stayed with the incubus and succubus, they could protect her from anyone who threatened to invite themselves into her tableau.

The Spider had also resumed her place at the beginning of the Funhouse, the sight of her multi-limbed body in nothing but black body paint their introduction, but she didn't play with anyone a vast majority of the time. She was still protective of Neve, and sometimes they played for others' pleasure, but they preferred to do that for Arcanium dinner parties rather than to entertain strangers who hadn't a clue what they were truly seeing.

Fairuza gamely took a place opposite Dez, who was tended by his golem nurse during Funhouse events. In spite of the torture he'd suffered with the rest, Dez remained physically helpless against what the succubus did to him and helpless in general to do anything about it. He took what Bell permitted him to receive with mixed feelings, but no one except Bell ever heard his agony. Bell would only remove the skin covering Dez's mouth on the day that he stopped blaming Elizabeth for getting him into this situation, for his thousand humiliations a day, for the torture that had yet to create any sense of self-awareness.

It was only appropriate that Dez also not be able to see through the skin growths over his eyes across the room to the candelabra flickering around a marble bathtub filled with real human blood. Monsters and demons — and Bell — alone would know Fairuza's commitment to craft as she submerged herself completely then raised herself up to recline against the back, thick hair clotted maroon, white eyes wide and her breasts bare and dripping with the blood of her enemies.

Bell approached the tub. Fairuza followed him with her eerie gaze.

"That is not *taharah*," he said.

"I haven't been pure in a very long time." She'd already entered into her character, her voice deep and hypnotic with a faint reptilian menace. "You have a way with corruption."

"And where is the next subject of ours?"

"She hasn't decided whether to be a part of this yet."

"Fai, we're not going to have another Funhouse in a long time. This is our best chance to convince her to leave of her own volition."

"Then you'd better convince her. I'm sure bloody footprints are atmospheric, but you try explaining that to the first person who gets it on their shoes."

"Damn it." He swept from Fairuza's room without pretending he wasn't irritated that she'd once again left him to become the only villain in Maya's story. He'd already destroyed Maya's life enough without Fairuza giving him more ways to have to do it, at no expense to her own relationship.

He ran through the antler room, where his one and only faerie, Sera, reclined at the feet of the Horned God, his one and only god, who had spread his antlers to fill his side of the room. More antlers sprouted from the brick walls and the concrete floors like fungus, but Sera rested on a bed of flowers.

Salem, who had entered the circus after Sera — because he'd been the one to chase her into the circus in the first place — had situated himself elsewhere. The Bearskin posed in his Ursal form in the darkness, appearing taxidermized in a room with the funhouse werewolf, the gargoylian Creature, the Sphynx and Skinless, with her flayed body like a Body World dummy. What initially seemed like a trophy room came to life when someone walked into the room, where the eerily still bodies invited closer inspection.

Lazarus, Magda, Seth, the Albino Triplets and Carlo had taken over one side of another room, creating a tableau with their beautiful, strong, strange bodies that recalled a gruesome chiaroscuro painting. Carlo's false legs rested on the floor at Lazarus' feet as Magda and the Albino Triplets surrounded Carlo's agonized, naked body. They bore silent witness to the Christ figure dying and hard under their hands. They would move subtly over the course of the evening, the religious elements of the tableau shifting to blasphemously pornographic. Marina, the one demon in the room, could make time move much more slowly for them so that they didn't have to strain their bodies too much to stay still. It could take them hours to complete the inevitable orgy, hours of pleasure that all of them had willingly volunteered themselves for, because an orgasm alone could last fifteen minutes.

In the Skeleton Room, all his Skeletons but Shane had taken an ottoman at various points of the room. The machines seemed all-the-more appropriate in an abandoned factory, as though they'd been repurposed for more lascivious intent. None of the machines followed the same rhythm. The mechanical creaks and whines left no second unstimulated as the machines slowly pumped thick dildos of supernatural and extraterrestrial cocks into the Skeletons' pussies.

The Skellies who had been changed into actual human shadows had been body-painted much like the Spider. Lily had chosen green, Alicia red, while Vivian was her usual sugar-skull from head to toe. She was also high as a kite on literal Ecstasy, which the odd chef gave her to make the Funhouses easier to endure for its pleasure rather than any destruction she might be inclined to wreak if given the chance.

Nasreen, the only Skelly who hadn't been emaciated, had donned a body glove in an elaborate skeletal design, utterly sheer where there wasn't any lace in the shape of bone. She sat astride a Sybian. Her sinuous hips, trained by years of belly-dancing, moved in an otherworldly rhythm over the tentacle attached to the machine.

Neve, Mikhail and Sasha took up their own room, because the combined effect of all three would be too much for anyone else to share. Torches illuminated the biggest of Sasha's serpents — boas, pythons and her king cobras — wrapped around and slithering over the three where they reclined together. Mikhail and Sasha had donned their usual leather and spikes that discouraged anyone from touching them or trying to fuck them, but Neve had eschewed all but her jewel-encrusted eyepatch and the necklace that Lady Sasha had loaned her and never retrieved.

Already, Sasha and Mikhail worked their magic on her, and in doing so, worked the magic through the transplanted circus, turning the cold, impersonal factory warm with raised body heat. Early moans rose through the echoing chambers like the soundtrack he used in the haunted funhouse. The red diamond on Neve's finger sparkled as she stroked over the raised scars that jigsawed her body.

Bell found Maya sitting near Kitty and the costumes in the green room, still woefully underdressed for a guest in her leggings and woefully overdressed for entertainment in a summery cotton dress.

"You're not attending?" he asked.

Maya squirmed where she sat, visibly uncomfortable, and not because of what the sex demons were doing — or not only because of that. "It's not really my scene. I thought it was voluntary, not mandatory."

"You won't know whether you want to be a part of it until you witness it for yourself. You don't have to do anything with anyone, but I would prefer if everyone at least sees what we do."

"I'm not going to want to be a part of it. Look... I know that the arts and sex work have historically gone hand and hand, but I'm not interested in being the prima donna pleasuring my patron."

"*I'm* your patron. You'll not be pleasuring me."

Kitty rolled her eyes where Maya couldn't see.

"I just don't want to do it, okay?"

"Far be it from me to pressure you, love, but I don't understand why you refuse. You'll never find a safer place to do these things, safer people with whom to do them. There's no risk, and everyone fully consents."

"It's…" She stopped short of saying 'wrong', clearly cognizant of all the people around her who would take grave offense.

"You had sex before Arcanium or Illumina, Maya. You jerked off your boyfriend during the big top performance when you first came to us—no pun intended, because he didn't bother returning the favor."

Without makeup, she couldn't hide her blush, florid in her cheeks and darkening her ears.

"I know it seems like I'm the biggest hypocrite, but it's not…" She squirmed again, lowering her eyes and gripping her knees. "I'm human, okay? And being human, I will make mistakes. That's why confession is such an important sacrament. I made mistakes, and they didn't feel like a big deal when they were with other imperfect human beings. But when I joined Illumina, it was different."

"Because Fairuza is a woman?"

Kitty paused as she went through the evening dresses for one of the Illumina tumblers standing behind her.

Maya had been insistent, unequivocal, in his tent, but discomfort made her awkward and uncertain. "That's less important than the fact she's jinn."

"But now you know that she's only jinn because I made her that way."

"I didn't know that before, and I don't think it makes a difference. It's one thing to screw another fallible human. The fallibility seems a lot more intentional when someone who shares fire with demons does it."

"You think I made her the devil on your shoulder." It almost amused him that that was precisely the role he'd decided to embrace for the purpose of saving her—perhaps even saving her soul, whatever that meant. He and Fairuza had joked that they would play the corruptors, but Maya had clearly seen that tactic coming. The memory of his chest under her hand had played in her head over and over since she'd left the tent, a reeling, lustful cycle that left her deliberately distant, more and more uncomfortable as he continued to approach her, although he was more clothed than before.

Uncomfortable, because she still wore the bracelet under the loose sleeve of her dress and hadn't tried to remove it. And he knew all too well what dreams had woken her in the middle of the night.

"They warned us about evil. They taught us about exorcisms, demons in the pigs, the devil in the desert, but it all seems symbolic, like wrestling with God— until you walk into a demonic circus, and everything becomes completely real. Then I meet you, face to face, and it seems…"

"Tempting." Bell stopped a good six feet away from her, a stark contrast to when she'd first entered Arcanium and he'd been unable to keep his hands off her. He relished the sensory, connected through scent, sound and touch, craved the intimacy of the physical to match that which he experienced through the thoughts and emotions that swirled around him—an alluring tangle reminiscent of what he could do with his burning body underneath cool sheets. He wanted to hold what was his, and she'd been his with the wish that had first bound her to Arcanium.

Her uncertainty compelled him more than her confidence, because it made her more the human she'd been at the beginning, the human he'd coaxed into discovering pleasure and the value of her sexual desire, the power she carried within it that she would have denied herself by offering it to the unworthy.

And here she was again, with all her lessons unlearned. He desperately wanted to teach her again. By her reckoning, corruption. By his own, enlightenment. Perhaps only one of them could be right.

"The devil was once an angel of light. Sometimes he still seems to be." It was something she couldn't say out loud—religiosity of her sort wasn't common among carnies—but she'd interacted psychically like this with Fairuza before, so she knew she could.

"I'm no angel of light, nor am I a demon."

"What makes a demon and what makes a jinni, if they come from the same fire?"

"The same thing that makes a monster or a saint of a man. It's in the choices that I make, in the form I choose, my intentions and my actions. I am not a demon or the devil incarnate, Maya. It simply pains me when I encounter such self-denial. The Creator gave you an earth full of tastes, textures and sounds, and he gave you a body with which to enjoy them. I cannot understand why you do not taste the juice of the fruit right in front of you."

"There's a whole story about why that's a bad idea. We presented it to you in the form of interpretative dance."

Bell smiled. "You're far from a nun, Maya DeLuca, but you don't have to participate. You can have a glass of champagne, avail yourself of the odd chef's feast and do nothing but observe. Illumina was invited so that they could better understand what they would agree to become a part of. If you insist on remaining a part of Illumina seeking a place in Arcanium, the Funhouse is an integral part of that."

"Not if participation isn't mandatory."

"But your presence is, and the sex demons don't discriminate. You're going to want something tonight."

"I can't."

Bell asked with a gesture whether he could join her. "We both know that's untrue."

Maya licked her lips as she considered denying him. But she moved over on the ottoman for him to sit next to her. "Semantics. I *won't*."

Bell touched her hair, the curly mass that had knotted around his fingers so many times before, that held the scent of her in its dense locks. He tucked it behind her ear with gentleness that her expression showed warmed through her in spite of herself, contact with no expectation of sex to accompany it. "Are you afraid that you'll sink head-first into oblivion, reveling in the best of what your world has to offer, then suffer for the rest of eternity because you enjoyed yourself?"

"It's like you know the Bible or something."

"I pre-date any version of the Bible, Maya. I don't exist in a world where your version of truth is a foregone conclusion. None of the demons, not even the hellborn, reel at the sight of a cross or burn under holy water. The earthside hells I've encountered are senseless, hopeless places of the captured, not the unclean. And demons are not the only ones who create them. There are plenty under the auspices of man. I never had any intention of creating a hell myself, nor in replicating an ascetic's life. I do not value virtue, although it can be a lovely thing in the right heart."

"You don't believe that my heart is virtuous."

"I believe you are made for something else." He withdrew his touch so she wouldn't assume that purr in his voice was a proposition. He didn't need her to succumb to him. He only needed her to succumb to someone. "You are capable of *all* kinds of passions. If you do nothing but sit in the open room and express how good the food is, I will feel as though I have succeeded at encouraging you indulgence."

"You're taking the lead from the Seven Deadly Sins, aren't you?"

"They aren't even biblical, love, and I can't believe that simply enjoying what has been provided with such consideration for you—the whole sensory world—is corruption. How cruel a Creator would have to be to condemn those whom he created innately evil for the evil he created in them."

"I can think of a few theologians who would disagree with you."

"They can bite me."

It was Maya's turn to smile, likely from the image of John Calvin taking a bite out of his ass.

"There is plenty of room for salvation without making *everything* a sin. Condemnation of flesh foments shame, which brings flocks in droves to the slaughterhouse for sacrifices. One might argue that they're the greatest hucksters of all time, creating the problem to offer a solution. I've no patience for it. I *have* been known to like a decent holy man or woman, you know." He nudged her shoulder with his own. "The Spider's father is a prophet. Although we're not on the best of terms, I respect him greatly. I met Francis of Assisi and was quite fond of him, as well. Like I said, I value virtue, but I don't value it above all other things, and not everyone has such a calling. Sometimes, a calling pulls them in the other direction."

"This feels very much like a call to apostasy, Bell. You're trying to convince me out of my faith and into the fire—an awful lot like the temptation I was afraid of here in the first place."

"I'm not trying to convince you out of your faith, only pointing out flaws in some of the tenets. Who am I to tell you that some version of your faith is wrong? I've only been here since the beginning. Not the beginning you know but *a* beginning." He stared out at the shifting colors of the sunset out of the window, shadows of the cityscape breaking and darkening the light. Living in fields had its issues, but he could always see sunrise or sunset in every direction, with no obstruction to keep him from its glory. That was his cathedral and stained-glass windows, the moaning of his cast his version of a choir. Maya would consider that sacrilegious, but he could think of nothing more beautiful, even if it wasn't holy. "You confound me, Maya. You always have."

"I wasn't just another one of your people, was I? I was significant to you."

"Most of my cast is significant to me. Even the prisoners were significant in my disgust for them."

"I didn't disgust you."

"No." He lowered his elbows to his knees, hanging his head above slack hands. "I do not seek your destruction. That is what makes me jinn instead of demon. For all its troubles, the earth is a good place to be. I don't concern myself with heaven or hell. I wouldn't want either. We make enough of both here."

"Is this heaven or hell?"

"Yes." He handed her a plate that he conjured from nothing, with food that he stole from the odd chef's arrangement. "Tell me these are not the sweetest, juiciest strawberries that you've ever tasted."

Maya hesitated.

"They're not spiked. Really, Maya. I have an incubus and a succubus. What use have I for drugs? Although if you have a recreational interest, I do have the means."

"I don't." She took the plate. "They're just normal strawberries, though?"

"I procure only the best for the odd chef, and he has an exceptional effect on any food within his vicinity." He didn't tell her that the reason for that was because Jonas was a hellborn gluttony demon who used his powers simply to serve good food. He kept his demons' secrets, and Jonas deserved the benefit of any doubt, far more than the woman he'd chosen for a lover.

Maya bit into one of the strawberries, deep red and almost as big as her fist. The dark juice swelled around the broken skin. Bell had to turn away, his own mouth watering.

It didn't help that Maya groaned in surprised delight. "God, that *is* good."

"There's more where that came from." He took a breath then stood. "I do hope you'll join us, Maya. There's not much to be done with sex demon influence but satisfy it, otherwise it only gets worse. If Illumina remains, that's what you can expect from Arcanium — constant temptation, intensifying each night until the desire is met. Only then will you sleep more soundly."

Maya grabbed his arm before he could leave. Even though it wasn't bare, she released him quickly, as though just touching him had been hot enough to burn. "What the fuck do you know about my sleep?"

"I can't sleep when you're frustrated. You pull me in. I know you don't want me there, and I know why, so I don't sleep. It's a good thing I don't need to." He offered her a smile while she tried to figure out how to call him a pervert if he was deliberately trying not to be. "Food's on the open floor. If you want to go through the haunted funhouse, slip out the back and enter through the front. It'll give you a better experience. But if you'd like to get some sleep while I'm otherwise distracted, feel free to join the underaged in the temporary rooms. Good night, Maya."

"You're soft on her," Fairuza thought to him without ire as he stepped out onto the open floor.

"If it were anyone else, I'd be the unrepentant sinner she believes me to be. But I can't go about this in the same way I did before if I want her to leave rather than to stay. As long as I'm handicapped in how I handle this, I'm afraid the kid gloves are necessary."

There was always another way. She feared him because she was afraid of what she would do with him, but he could give her something to truly fear.

He had taken many guises over the centuries. A demon had never been one of them. That didn't mean he didn't have a demon face that he could become, demonic impulses to exploit that Maya had tapped into once before, when those impulses had been mutually beneficial. But that would be the very cruelty humans were so quick to accuse him of.

And he feared it himself. He feared what would happen if he let himself lose what humanity he had claimed. Jonas kept his locked home of many indulgences to stop himself from backsliding. The Ringmaster tempered his evil with Kitty. Kitty had always been a tempering influence to Bell, too, but not enough to stop him from doing whatever he liked.

As he'd said, the difference between demons and jinn was in the choices they made. He'd used a dungeon as a template to make Arcanium whatever he wanted it to be, but Locke had shown how easily it could become a dungeon again. There was little to keep Bell in check, little that could stop him if he decided to change. Like wishes, like promises, his decisions carried significance that humans couldn't understand.

The last thing Arcanium needed was another demon at the helm.

He would find another way to save Maya. Something that didn't damn the rest of Arcanium, and Illumina with it.

* * * *

Champagne flowed as rich patrons walked through each Funhouse room to find the tableau that suited their fancy.

The Illumina cast who had decided to participate in the tableaus struggled without Bell's or Fairuza's direction. The only three who had figured out what to do for themselves were the five dancers who had represented Adam, Eve and the serpent, whose routine lent itself to sexual interpretation—not to mention

Adam, Eve and the head of the serpent had been a triad ever since Fairuza had choreographed the dance, suggesting she'd choreographed more than the dance at the time. The contortionists who made up the serpent had also experimented with each other a few times, enough to be familiar with each other's bodies. Fairuza set the ambience of the empty room they chose into something resembling the set of the performance, and Sasha and Mikhail, in the room next door to play off the theme, charged the already existing sexual tension between them to a breaking point.

The rest of the cast sprinkled themselves through the haunted funhouse and tried to play by ear, but ultimately, the effect of the sex demons on their displayed bodies drove them to play by something else.

Insulated societies like Illumina always had untapped potential between unexpected pairs or groups. Between the free champagne and the sex magic, restraints and inhibitions floated away like red balloons in the hormonal storm that raged through the Funhouse. Illumina cast who had never allowed themselves to consider each other bloomed together like dark roses in Bell's garden. There was nothing like Arcanium to make people realize what their secret kinks were. And while many people still had plenty of it, there was no room within this particular funhouse for shame.

It might not have been artful, but a bunch of artless pretty things in leather and lingerie finding corners and empty rooms of their own acted as inspiration for his patrons nevertheless — unnecessary ringers. There would be repercussions the next morning, of course, but Bell didn't foresee any lasting damage to existing relationships — only an evolution after the initial, inevitable conflicts. Illumina would survive intact and, in many ways, grow stronger, because these kinds of attachments—forged through shared strangeness—made it more difficult for people to leave. It had certainly kept people in Arcanium longer than they would have stayed otherwise.

Bell, on the other hand, kept to himself in the dark corner of the serpent room.

Sweat plastered the Henley to the small of his back, and his leather pants couldn't hope to contain his erection from watching Neve. Willing the erection away wouldn't end the arousal that coursed through him like molten rock. It had only been a week since he'd been with Fairuza, but the Funhouse made abstinence like this excruciating without any of the thrill, because there was no anticipation of relief.

In watching Neve, he remembered every wicked thing Maya had done, first for him then for herself. The punishment she'd taken on for allowing herself that wickedness hadn't hoped to match the breadth and depth of what she'd been willing to do. The more she'd wanted, the more he'd developed a taste for those things that he'd never desired before. One could argue that his affair with Elspeth had been more sordid, but one expected that of a demon. To find it in a human—vulnerable, fierce and with the urgency of the mortal—was far rarer.

He'd modeled Neve after the Spider, in that their easy arousal swept them along like driftwood in a raging river. But Maya had cut her own path with a machete, slicing through herself as much as the foliage to find someplace deeper, more dangerous, uncharted. The potential had always been there, and he sensed it within her still. His only hope was that she didn't cut herself too deeply on her path back into that dark forest, that she only went just deep enough to leave, lest she find herself so deep in that darkness that only Arcanium could hope to ever satisfy her again.

Rather than watch Maya from afar, Bell poured all of his attention into watching Neve in the serpent room — the most popular by far, and the one in which patrons, cast and guests alike had to stop to relieve the unbearable arousal that proximity to the sex demons caused.

Not to discount the effect Neve had on her own. Scarification had marred none of her appeal.

The serpents forced the spectators to keep their distance. Neve had always been ambivalent about audience participation, but ambivalence had settled into certainty that she didn't want anyone but Mikhail and Sasha touching her, not even the disembodied hands that Bell had once given her. The golems had to clean up after multiple spendings all over the room, but as long as no one tried to join in, Neve accepted their voyeurism and submitted herself to the incubus and succubus. They couldn't take her — couldn't fully satisfy her — while in their present leather regalia, but they could give her orgasm after orgasm in other ways until later that night when they would remove the spikes from between their legs.

The haunted funhouse could go on indefinitely, a steady rotation of rooms, each one a new depravity, a cycle of arousal for men and women alike until they'd seen everything — come to everything — before leaving for the evening. *Come to leave.*

But transitioning to the main floor gave those who weren't part of the haunted funhouse a chance to interact with patrons as well. And it gave those who wanted to quit for the night an opportunity to bow out gracefully and finish what they started in private, away from strangers and unwelcome eyes. Many of his cast accepted being seen as an extension of what they already did in the circus when it was open, but they drew the line at sharing themselves with strangers — whereas others eagerly stepped over socially acceptable lines in the one place where doing so was safe, even if the guests and patrons didn't know how safe they were.

Eventually, at the golems' urging, the crowd thinned then cleared out completely as people headed to the bar for something more substantial than champagne and to replenish the energy that they'd lost in the ungodly number of climaxes that the haunted funhouse fostered. Those who had entered with pharmacological aid — prescribed or recreational — were still often stunned at how effective Arcanium was in conjunction.

Bell could only imagine — sometimes with real consideration and other times with a twinge of delicious horror — what might happen if he let Jonas diffuse his vice oils into the HVAC systems. How liberating it would be to strip away the absolute last of anyone and everyone's fears so that they could just *feel*. It was against Bell's law to force the issue more than he already did with the sex demons' influence, but that didn't stop him from remembering the scent of incense at his altars, a hundred limbs entwined around his jinni form the dawn after a feast day, headiest oblivion and fragrant oil slick on skin and tongue.

Wrapping a thin robe around her body, Neve emerged from the serpent pit, her thighs glistening. With the Wheel of Chance performances removed from the main floor these days, she didn't have any more official work she had to do that night.

But she paused at the entrance to the room, turning back to him, although no one else who'd entered the room had noticed he was there, by design. "You seem disappointed."

"Nothing you've done, love."

"You always watch. Not just me. Everyone. You've always liked to watch, more than the rest of us know or want to know, but…"

She came toward him in the darkness. Her pale skin reflected the light with a glow, and it lit her hair with fire. Every shift of her thighs resurrected the scent of her arousal — pure, without anything else to muddle it. She couldn't see what seethed beneath his almost dispassionate expression, but she could tell something was wrong as she took in the sight of him still clothed — for him, practically armor — his cock still trapped in his pants, with no effort made to free himself.

When masturbation was invited in an exchange of exhibitionism and voyeurism, satisfaction could be had. Neve had known he was there from the beginning. He could have stroked himself off to her at any time and broken through at least some of the sex demons' magic, although it would have returned just as strong later that evening when they could finally feed and feed and feed off Neve, which of course only gave them more to feed from. Providing the sexual batteries of Arcanium with an endless charge had been one of his better ideas. If he'd brought Neve in for that alone, he could claim such good intentions.

Neve couldn't read him, but he couldn't hide everything, even in the dark. His cock could be flaccid and she'd still be able to look into his eyes and know how much he wanted her, wanted *something*.

He'd been there for every hour while Sasha and Mikhail had played her like an instrument. It had tied him to her, strand by strand, until it felt like their mutual desire could never be untangled. He wanted nothing more than to grab her by the hair to pull her against him, trace the lines of scars that he'd given her, relive their blood and stinging heat.

Still leaning against the wall, Bell placed a hand on her shoulder to keep her at arm's length.

"You can have what you want. I've been...healing. You've been patient." Neve led his hand across the robe to shift the fabric to the side. It was only invitation. When he withdrew his hand, she didn't pursue.

"I know why I didn't want anyone to touch me. I know why the others left and why it took the rest of us so long before we could do this again—and if it had been anywhere without sex demons, it would have taken longer. With them, we just *couldn't* wait, and it wasn't like it could screw up our brains any more than they already were." She joined him in his corner, leaning against the other wall, her arms crossed. "The demons bounced back like rubber. What's keeping you? Because it's not just Maya. You were like this before Illumina showed up."

"Let's just say the pursuit has lost some of its joy."

"You aren't as subtle as you think you are. You still want me."

"Always, love." He stretched across the distance and caressed her cheek, nudged the fall of hair down the side of her face. "Just not tonight."

"Kiss me?"

It broke ribs to refuse. Lust pulsed from her as though she were a heart and sex the blood that rushed in and out of her. He'd desired her from the moment she had entered his tent, and all he'd ever done was kiss her, destroy her then cut her apart. He would show her one night that it could be as sweet as that first kiss. He felt as though he were bleeding from the mouth, to deny himself her kiss, her body, the deep pool of her desire. But he shook his head.

"And that *is* Maya, isn't it?"

"Not in the way you might think."

"But it is in the way I think. You put yourself in my room to torture yourself. You don't *do* that, Bell, not when there isn't an end to it."

He didn't respond, just pushed off the wall and, with a wince as his leather pants tugged against his cock, left the room. Mikhail and Sasha didn't have anything to add as they waited for their woman, the blades removed from the costumes, but their gazes followed him with the same quiet concern.

On the open floor, the party had started without him. Some patrons gathered on couches with Illumina and Arcanium cast, cozying up with each other over plates of food. Even the slightest of acrobats had learned that they could eat whatever they wanted while under Arcanium's umbrella, and after the evening they'd had, everyone was famished.

Bell walked through the winding paths created by obsolete machinery, opulent furniture and curtained-off rooms where those who preferred privacy had already taken residence.

Behind one, Selena had encouraged one of the patrons wearing special-occasion pearls to bed with Victor. Behind another, Rebekah had been chained to the bedposts—loosely, so that she could top the man brave enough to take a woman who wore a protective cage around her head. Bell couldn't remember anyone who had regretted the claw marks for their troubles.

He wound around back toward the center, where Mayumi had scared herself up a lover—which wasn't a turn of phrase. Profound dread had sent Canton stumbling through the room until he'd fallen onto the bed she'd chosen. Arcanium's onryo climbed onto the foot of the bed and crawled over him to take his cock into her mouth.

Her long, black hair covered the bed like a fungus and tangled around his limbs, although they didn't bind him down. Canton shouted, even screamed, when she forced every ounce of the dread she carried within her into him, yet his cock remained full and hard as she continued to wetly suck him in—a full-on water-drenched vengeance demon for her rapt audience and subject. No one could blend terror and lust like May, and no one realized how much they wanted to be terrified until she had them under her spell. She couldn't kill them, but when she'd finished with them, they thought they were dead. It appeared that every time she took him in he was certain she'd bite down and swallow him up, balls and all, yet he pressed down on her head to encourage her to take more, his slender, slightly furry dancer's body taut and dripping from the moisture that saturated her hair and the sheets.

Dom and Vivian were making out on a couch while Illumina's Cecilia, a small woman even by Arcanium standards, rode Del, who would be a giant without the comparison of actual giants.

George—not the most popular oddity of Arcanium on a good day—usually found himself the object of more attention than usual during Funhouse events, because he could pleasure two women at once. After months of potential partners preferring the demon face, the demon had agreed to share his secrets with George, not to mention the length and dexterity of his tongue. When both George and his other face could satisfy, demon and man often earned more for the body they shared.

The Sphynx had never dreamed that he, too, would be an object of intrigue, his micropenis the subject of frantic devotion by one of the patrons while she straddled his face.

The Parrot was making one of the patrons laugh as he took her from behind, imitating the voices of men she dreamed about. Humor could be a wonderful thing in the bedroom, although it marred the mood for some. Not for this woman, with her silk gown loose over her midsection and the skirt hiked up for the Parrot to fuck her.

Fairuza had found herself the center of five men's attention—two from Illumina and three patrons, men ranging from twenty-one to seventy-two. She showed none favor but smeared the unclotting blood from her body over all.

There was almost literally something for everyone, including what they hadn't known they wanted or needed.

Bell walked the room alone.

Chapter Nine

Bell finally settled on the other side of the bar from Shane. Jonas wasn't the best buffer, considering his own suppressed appetites had found an outlet as of late, but his self-control was better than anyone else's in the circus.

Jonas didn't say anything. He just handed Bell a Bloody Mary then otherwise ignored him. Jonas had always had an uncanny ability to know what someone needed—usually an item on a menu, but he could discern other needs among a subject's various hungers.

Bell drank three Bloody Marys in succession. He didn't drink to get drunk. He'd need a barrel before anything short of absinthe could give him the barest buzz. He also wouldn't slow himself with oblivion wine when he had to keep track of so many people. Patrons of Arcanium rarely stepped over the lines he drew anymore. There had been too many 'mysterious disappearances' of those who had, regardless of how many zeroes one could tack on to their net worth. But Illumina was still adjusting.

In most of the cases that popped up in the warehouse, the people around those who broke his law policed the individual themselves or the person who had breached the boundaries struggled to rein themselves in. As long as the person listened and learned, often Bell didn't have to interfere at all. Of course, this sometimes made people believe that he wasn't paying attention. They would learn better if they tried again.

Tonight, though, Bell didn't expect he would have to enlist the Ringmaster, who had found a quiet place above the green room for him and Kitty to spend time together undisturbed. Kitty didn't participate in the Funhouse events anymore. Before, she'd been willing to engage with their patrons only in private until Maya had coaxed her into more public liaisons. Without Maya, she'd withdrawn from this kind of work entirely.

Bell chased the Bloody Marys with an Old-Fashioned then left the bar. His patrons, guests and cast were well-established with their toys for the night, some already asleep on sodden beds, tangled in hair and limbs and sheets or resting with their heads on laps or chests. It would be roughly four in the morning before the magic Sasha and Mikhail had pumped through the building would fade enough to allow erections to fully wilt and wetness to cool.

Mikhail and Sasha opened the curtains that had provided them at least visual privacy with Neve. She lay on her belly the wrong way on the bed, Sasha reclining on top of her, Mikhail next to her. Bell was the only one moving through the room rather than firmly ensconced where flesh and spirit was willing, and his cock still hadn't softened underneath the press of leather keeping him contained.

As she rested her chin on her arms, Neve visibly noted what would be plain to anyone else who caught sight of him, but she said nothing more about it, although frustration, in spite of all the attention that Mikhail and Sasha had lavished upon her, showed through the perfection of her face — perfection even though she'd removed the eyepatch. There was nothing that he or Locke could have done to make her less than she was.

That perfection beckoned him all the more to take comfort in her, which was why he turned away toward the green room. He'd put in enough of an appearance as the owner of Arcanium, procurer of oddities for unconventional tastes. Satisfaction and contentment that he could not share flooded the building. His work for the night was complete.

Maya stepped out from the green room onto the open floor.

She'd strapped herself into a dark red leather underbust corset. Nothing covered her breasts, although the accompanying harness framed them. Black lace panties and black patent leather boots completed the costume she'd chosen. She wouldn't know, but she'd worn it before.

The tall, silver, metal stilettos clicked on the concrete floor, harsh against the otherwise smooth, sensuous sounds from the beds and couches, now that intensity had conceded to intimacy. Sharp enough to make a man wince, but in spite of the knife blades under her feet, no man who winced would dare to look away.

Some of his patrons recognized her and vaguely thought that they hadn't seen her for a while. Hadn't she been sick? Hadn't she left? They didn't understand what Maya entering the Funhouse meant like the cast of Arcanium did.

Bell took a step back as she continued to walk straight toward him. His cock twitched with each sharp click of her heels. His shirt would hide some of his erection, and the tight pants would hide more. But because nothing truly bound him down and he, like other demons and jinn, was exceptionally well-endowed, he couldn't hide how much he was turned on, and it was too late to conceal his weakness from her, especially as his continued to thicken and harden the closer she came.

Her breasts trembled with each step, but he fixed his gaze on her eyes — determined and almost black in the dim room — forcing himself to be more disciplined than any other man who might have been distracted by what she offered them. And even with an orgy winding down, she offered and distracted plenty.

"You're a little late to the party," he said, "but I'm sure you can cozy up to almost anyone who takes your fancy looking like that, love."

"Almost anyone. Meaning not you." Maya stopped a table's length short of him. She didn't try to control where her gaze wandered, over the chest and arms she'd seen uncovered, over the bulge showing underneath the hem of his shirt. "What if I don't want anyone else?"

Bell held up his hands, whether to soothe or warn her unclear. "It's not that I don't want you."

"Except for the whole 'backing up like she's got the plague' thing you just did. If I was never important to you, all you need to do is fuck me and I'll be on my merry way. But the more you try to avoid me, Bell, the more important I seem, and that just opens up a world of questions. Even more after all the stories I hear about how crazy the sex parties are around here, how you're the pimp of the whole place—yet you're the most clothed here. It's not purple fur and a snakehead cane, but it's practically modest. You walk around the circus half-naked, with the rest of you requiring very little in the way of imagination, then you cover up to come to this place? You try to get me out here, then you act like I give you third-degree burns every time I touch your skin."

"Why on earth wouldn't you want anyone else? Anyone at all?" He gestured to the rest of the room. If they hadn't noticed before, cast and patrons were noticing now. Maya made no effort to stay quiet and polite, and her costume lived several counties away from both.

She scoffed, her hands on her hips. "Maybe because they've been tiptoeing around me just like you. All I want to know is what happened. Because *something* happened. I've got demons treating me like glass and a jinni treating me like Typhoid Mary."

"You know what happened, Maya." He took a step toward her then another, relaxing his body into something that didn't telegraph how wrong this was going. He might have believed Mayumi was sending another wave of her dread, but Mayumi was occupied and only emanated fear when it served her needs. Bell served none of her needs, so his dread had to be his own, although his prescience gave him no particulars on why.

"I have a *Netflix summary* of what happened. No one will give me anything more than that. I try to ask people, but they either miraculously have something they need to do or they're miraculously not there—and I *know* you're hiding something from me. You're hiding so much more than they are. You'll put your hands on anyone who comes to you, but you'll barely touch me—
"

Bell took one of her gesticulating hands. Her nails caught on his skin but didn't tear through. That he voluntarily took her hand surprised her into silence.

Bell brought her hand between both of his, cradling the loose fist, brushing his thumb over the veins in her wrist. "This doesn't make you feel better, does it?" he said gently. "This awakens what you've been chasing, but it scares you, too, because it's powerful and you don't know why. Ever since you stepped foot into Arcanium, you've felt its pull, like a haunted house telling you that you're home, and you're angry because you know you're missing something crucial. Your instincts aren't lying to you, Maya. Your dreams are. You left Arcanium for a reason. You had Fairuza remove your memories for a *reason*."

"It wasn't the torture." She stared intently where he caressed her, where he traced the lines of her palm like the reader he was, although he'd never needed the lines. "It was you. You're the reason I ran. You're the reason it was so bad I can't remember why I wanted to forget."

"Yes." He released her hand, which hovered where he'd held it. "We've been dancing around the subject, Fairuza and I, but while you are a wonderful dancer, you always fight to lead."

Bell brushed his hand over her jaw, unsettling her scent—no perfume, just her skin after marinating in the sex demons' spells for hours. He leaned toward it, breathing her in, until he'd brought his nose right against her neck, her hair a cloud of silk against his face. She clutched at his arms, perhaps to stop him at first, but he inhaled deeply, closing his eyes and gritting his teeth against the groan that threatened to escape him, and she neither let him go nor pushed him back.

"You could have *anyone*," he whispered in her ear. "You have everything you've ever wanted. Why do you seek to destroy that?"

"I don't know." She grasped the back of his neck when he started to pull away. "I just know something's wrong. And I want..." Her breasts pressed against his chest, and he cursed the fabric that dared impede them, cursed himself that he had chosen to cover himself tonight of all nights.

She wore his gold bracelet. He squeezed her arm through the warm metal then along bare skin interrupted by leather. He infrequently resented Sasha's leather work, but now all he wanted was smooth and hot, hotter every second he touched her, triggering the magic that had both of them nearly staggering against each other.

"You need to go." He drank in her scent as though to trap it inside him forever. "You need to leave Arcanium and Illumina. You need to run far, far away from us. It's not safe here for you. *I* am not safe."

Maya made fists in his shirt to pull herself flush against his body. She wrapped a leg around his, the sharp heel stroking a line up his calf. "You think I put this on to be safe?"

Then she planted her feet and abruptly shoved him back.

Curious, how clumsy he became when he couldn't see what to prepare himself for. He stumbled just as awkwardly as any man. She shoved him again before he could get his full footing. His back slammed against the husk of some machine, the purpose of which was irrelevant. What mattered was that Maya brought herself against him again, her red nails stark against his white shirt as she smoothed her hands up his chest, *feeling* him so much more firmly than before, as though if she pressed harder, she would recall the last time she'd done the same.

Maya raised her head to him, her lips so close that they brushed his as she spoke. "Do you want me to leave?"

"*No.*" More moan than reply, because he couldn't hold back anymore. The *wanting* that came from her entwined all too well with his own, and she was *there*, against him, soft and hard and insistent and so damn innocent. He wrapped an arm around her, his hand almost between her legs as he tangled his other in her thick mass of curls.

The kiss continued the argument almost as loudly. He pulled on her scalp, forcing her head to move as he pleased, but it pleased her, too, because her little moans vibrated through his tongue every time he jerked her head to another angle. But she was far from passive, meeting his tongue between them instead of yielding to him, chasing him into his own mouth, releasing his shirt to grasp the cock straining the leather covering it.

When she realized how big he was, her breath caught with a gasp that might have seemed melodramatic under normal circumstances, but she had no memory of other cocks she had taken, and she hadn't yet made the rounds to inspect what other demons had to offer. He would impress her in comparison to men she was used to over the years. Whether he was the biggest of the pack didn't matter when he was just *big* in her hand, although the leather made it impossible to get a good grip.

Fear and fascination. He'd made himself small in this form in comparison to the truth, and there had been times he'd made himself even smaller, because he was all too aware that size wasn't nearly as important as what a man was capable of. But there was nothing like that moment of shock, immediately followed by intrigue, knowing that he would be too much if it weren't for the magic that made any body accept him with both ease and ecstasy.

Not one of his women or men had ever complained about his body. They'd complained about Bell himself, but any form he'd chosen endlessly pleased when he put it to use, even just to display. He'd been less attractive, he'd been a woman and he'd been an old man. This was the form that felt most like himself, even though it looked nothing like what he really was. A shapeshifter could never truly be trusted, but they did have their preferences, and the fact that their form could change didn't make those preferences less true.

Right now, he wanted to shed everything—his clothing, hers, his skin, his form, until there was nowhere left to stretch, nothing left to tear through, and she could take *all* of him, all of what he was. But there were still the walls that Fairuza had erected in Maya's mind. He could never reach all of her. What she felt, what he did to her, would never be complete. But it was almost enough.

She jerked at the button and the zipper on his pants, pushed up his shirt until he had to break the kiss to help her pull it over his head. Warning lights swirled and sirens howled in his mind, but they were nowhere near as bright and loud as the need that the incubus and succubus demanded from them. Bell could control himself, but God, he didn't want to. He threw his shirt to the side, and she lunged forward to kiss him again.

Everything they did was so exquisitely and perfectly familiar to him, but it tasted new to her, reminding him of the first time he had asked her to beg and she had, the first time he'd thrown her onto a platform to conjure her pleasure in ways she'd never thought she could have and had never asked for.

This Maya was an older Maya, with at least one jinni under her belt within the reach of her memory, but being with Fairuza wasn't the same. For all the fire that burned in Fai's spirit, her potential was still untapped, her indulgences varied but not yet to the intensity that she was capable of. New jinn harbored fear—fear of heights, fear of falling. Bell had long since embraced falling, knowing that he could hit the ground without repercussions and that he could hold whoever warmed his bed close to keep them from hurting more than they pleaded him for. Maya had sampled the divine in Fairuza but not even close to what she was capable of matching.

He loved her spirit, the fight, the unwillingness to submit without him earning it, which meant Fairuza had already retaught her the worth of her own pleasure.

He lifted her effortlessly. With Bell bearing the burden of her weight, she didn't have to brace herself and could reach down between them into the open leather and draw him out. Her breath hitched as she stroked up his unconfined length, twisted her hand because she couldn't wrap it all the way around his girth. She released him, though, to bring her hips flush against his, to use their rhythm to stroke him — not enough, just enough — as she instead mapped the terrain of his abdomen and chest.

He hitched her up higher, kissing away from her mouth to her neck again, leaving dents where his teeth worried bruises that would bloom by morning, although she'd never bruised easily. He bit at the straps that he would tear away if they weren't Sasha's creation then dipped down to breathe on the broad but tightened nipple, flushed from the stimulation against his chest, begging him on its own until Maya grasped his hair to guide him in. He parted his lips, his breath hotter and hotter to her the closer he came, even when inside his open mouth, but still he didn't give her what she tried to force him to take.

She canted hard against his cock, the fabric of her panties undeniably damp from her arousal, then arched to push her breast into his mouth. He avoided her without effort, making himself wait as well as her as arousal tightly coiled in his abdomen, within his erection.

Maya slid her hand up to his neck then shoved him against the metal machine again, the back of his head striking it with a sound that resonated through the entire room. She didn't try to protect him from pain, nor did she apologize.

That's my girl.

Tightening her strong thighs over his hips, she raised herself up on her own to press her breasts to his face. He would happily smother himself anywhere on her body, and that was a particularly pleasant place to do so. He soaked in her cries with something like desperation as he kissed and licked to the peak of the breast he'd refused. This time, he couldn't. He trapped her nipple in the hot wetness of his mouth, suction tight and nearly unbearable, until his teeth showed her all that she could bear. She lost the strength in her thighs, ground against him as he gathered her up again.

"God, if you knew how long..." he groaned as he worked his way back up to the protrusion of her collarbone.

Maya didn't stop pressing herself against his cock, but she placed a hand on his chest to push herself away. "Then we *have* done this before."

Bell didn't say anything. As the entire room evidenced, having sex before didn't make her important. She couldn't know that the number of his people he'd fucked had been comparatively low — comparatively when compared to her, in fact. She'd been one of his most prolific companions, a fact that had made him love her even more, because a voyeur deity always liked to watch, and being able to watch firsthand was that much better than watching where he wasn't invited.

He didn't tell her that she could have anyone in Arcanium because she'd *had* almost everyone who liked women, and quite a few of his newer cast would just as enthusiastically consent to a night or more themselves. She wasn't as uniquely universal as Neve seemed to be, but much could be said for charisma. In spite of her abrasiveness, Maya had always possessed that magnetic quality, the kind that men earlier in her life had tried to quell and belittle to make themselves feel more powerful, not realizing that it only showed how weak they were.

She caressed the line of his cheekbones, peered into him and found nothing. Her irritation couldn't diminish the desire boiling over, threatening to set fire to everything it touched, but he could survive any fire she set to him. "Tell me I didn't mean anything to you."

Bell had lied before. He *could* lie. He didn't like to lie to his people, not when the truth could be used more effectively and because, with all the things he did to the cast, truth fostered the trust he needed to care for them properly.

It would be so easy to lie to her. To give her not the answer she wanted but the one she needed, to fuck her and leave her bereft in the morning, show her in deed rather than tale that she meant nothing and that he could cause her pain that wasn't worth staying for.

"You were significant to me." Bell tried to undo some of the damage he'd done to her hair. It was wild at the best of times, but now she appeared feral, although she'd gone still. "Many of mine are. But who you were to me is immaterial."

"No, it isn't. Do you know what I feel when I see you? When I'm around you? The moment we stepped into your circus, into the ring? It was like I'd known you forever, but I didn't know *why*. I didn't know why the only thing I've wanted to do since we all came here is this."

She insinuated her hand between them, pushed her panties aside and raised herself up to bring the head of his cock to her pussy. Without hesitation or pause, she sank herself over him. Her entire body clenched in fear that the stretch would be too painful for her to withstand, but nothing impeded her descent. Her arousal slid her down faster than she expected. Her cry climbed, but she muffled it by taking his mouth again, abandoning any semblance of control or dignity. Thought fled from her mind. All that was left were the sensations that he gave her.

He could lose himself in Maya when she herself was lost, could shut off his mind to everything that wasn't the maelstrom of lust that moved her body over and around him, bringing him deep every time. He held her by her thighs and rolled his hips forward to meet her, his groans discordant with hers, because he knew this couldn't last, shouldn't last. He *shouldn't* be doing this. But like her, this was all he'd wanted since she'd walked back into his circus. He had her in his arms, around his cock, had her taste in his mouth, her pleasure fogging his head. The last thing he wanted was lose everything he'd craved since he'd pulled her into Arcanium in the first place.

"I shouldn't want this." She hooked her arm around his neck and quickened her pace, shivering as she moved. Blood flushed her cheeks and heated between her legs, lighting up her desire around him. Her sensations were as much a part of his pleasure as his own. "I shouldn't do this at all, especially with you. But I've never been very good at...not doing this. I don't think I've ever wanted anything as much as this, and it's never been this fucking *good*."

It had, though. A thousand times, it had been this good. He remembered every gasp, every cry, every time she'd tightened around his cock, his tongue, his fingers, his fist. But for her, this was her first and only. Nothing but unimportant, pathetic men before, hardly worth the mention for the pitiful attempts to give her orgasms, so much so that she'd had to become far more proficient at giving them to herself or faking them to keep her boyfriends from knowing how inadequate they were.

For her, Bell was a revelation.

If he kept going, he would bring her to the point of addiction once more. She would believe that he was the only one from whom she could derive this kind of pleasure — from him and Arcanium. And she'd be right. The rest of the world fell woefully short of what she deserved.

But in Arcanium, she would be constantly reminded of what she didn't know, and he would be constantly reminded of what he kept from her — the only reason that she was with him now at all. If she had all the information he did, she would hate him for this, hate him for touching her, for taking what he wanted while she was unable to tell him no, and he was taking advantage of it, even though she'd been the one to literally jump on him.

This — *this* — was exactly what he'd hoped to avoid doing to her, even if she didn't realize she was doing it.

They rode within reach of their climax, cold-hot density gathering between their legs together.

Bell grabbed her arms so hard that she whimpered, not entirely from pain. Panting, he lifted her from his cock and threw her to the floor.

"No. I can't do this. I can't do this to you." He held up his hands again, this time to keep her back as he edged around her. He stumbled away from the stunned, lust-stoned audience who had been hanging on the tenterhooks of their rising pleasure, but he didn't care about the rumors this would foster among his patrons or among Illumina. Those who'd known him long enough would only question why he hadn't done it sooner. But given how Maya had walked out onto the open floor, perhaps they would forgive his temporary insanity.

Bell slammed the door to the green room behind him. The force of it shuddered through the walls and the partitions that the golems had set up to create makeshift rooms for the cast who wanted to sleep in more privacy than the open floor afforded.

He stepped to the side and leaned on the smooth, painted cinderblock wall then grasped his erection and stroked himself furiously, knowing that his efforts would be inadequate.

Maya burst through the door just as he brought himself over, spilled onto his hand and spattered the ground. Bell didn't mind a mess, but the one he created because he *hadn't* finished her off or himself within her seemed sordid, cheap, the kind of desperation associated with not being able to attract a partner rather than refusing to harm her.

He jerked himself off until his orgasm was complete, although he could have spent a dozen times without reaching the end of his need.

"Goddammit!" Maya slapped the wall then shook her hand from the pain. "Why are you doing this to me?"

"It is my decision to say no, to refuse whomever I choose. And you must abide by that decision." He fought against loosing his own string of curses with more weight than hers, although she'd occasionally amused him with her creativity. "That is the law."

"And what am I supposed to do with this? I was almost there. You were there with me. And...I can't finish myself off. That's what they all tell me. But *you* can? How is that fair to anyone?"

"I can finish. You can finish. It does nothing." He cleaned off his cock and his hand but not the floor. Let it be a testament to his moment of weakness, loss of control that he shouldn't have been able to lose—not like this.

"You don't look as bad off as me."

"Looks are deceiving, love. If you haven't learned that by now…" He forced his cock down, tucking himself back into the leather. "I already told you that there are countless partners out there who would give you what you need. I have nothing for you."

He ascended the stairs toward the abandoned spaces above the green room, where broken glass, debris and stains from squatters discouraged anyone without magic from sneaking off.

Maya tried to follow him, but Bell threw up an invisible wall that kept her back.

"You did once," she called up after him. "You almost did again. We were almost there. I know what you were feeling. I know your emotions, the physical sensations. We were practically one mind. You have everything for me, but you're keeping it away, and I don't understand why."

"You don't need to understand." He paused on the landing. "If you don't leave on your own, I'll find a way to force you. And I don't want to have to do that."

"If you don't want to hurt me, then don't hurt me. Just tell me why."

He looked back at her. "You were the one who decided you didn't want to know why. What part of a demon's torture do you want to remember?"

"I don't know." She pressed her hands on the invisible wall, her voice small. Even in her outfit, she seemed like a lost little girl. "All I know is that there's something important and you're a part of it."

"If you knew what you want to know, you'd leave Arcanium. You'd walk out and never come back. That's what you did before. That's all you *need* to know. Trust yourself."

"I don't. I shouldn't trust myself, because trusting myself puts me in the middle of an open room, fucking you while you fuck me back, with you kissing me like a demon and making me feel like a whore in all the worst and best ways. I've done a lot of bad things. Why do I feel like you're the worst?"

"You need to figure out what you're willing to accept. I'm tired of you pursuing and condemning me in the same breath. I know you're conflicted about what your body tells you and what the Holy Writ impossibly demands. You don't trust me. You should. You don't trust yourself. You should. But if you decide to wrap yourself in the purity of your religion, then Arcanium is not the place for you either way. There's only so much that absolution can accomplish when you know you're going to do what you shouldn't, and although a circus-themed dungeon can help you recreate whatever element of the crucifixion you personally prefer, it is not designed to prevent you from pursuing that which you desire. If desire itself is your sin, love, then why are you still here?"

Maya lowered her hands from the invisible wall, her eyes wide as though she'd been struck backhand.

"There are worse things than never having the closure you seek. There are worse things than going out there and having a normal life with a piece of your memory missing. People do it all the time. I don't understand how, because I remember what was, what will be, what could have been and what will never be. I see what other people forget. The memories are there, but they've let the paths grow over until vines climb the trees and leaves cover where paths once were, and you don't even remember what you've forgotten. Yet many of you live perfectly well without perfect memory. I suggest you use the insomnia your frustration will cause to make some important decisions rather than stumbling through the funhouse over and over again, trying to make it make sense and acting affronted when it deceives. But *I* will never lie to you, Maya."

"All I want is for the ride to stop, because I want to get off—in more ways than one." She tried to laugh, but it died. She covered her breasts with her arms as she rubbed the back of her neck. "I can't go home. I don't know why, but I know I can't go home."

"There are many places other than home to go." Bell descended the stairs again. He sat so that he was almost level with her. "There are places to make a home. You have all the money you could need to put down roots anywhere—or to become a nomad, if home is something less defined to you. Do what Fairuza did and make your own circus or join another with a less supernatural bent. You could become a fortune teller. You have the means. I just need to remind you how to reach them as soon as you're well out of reach of Arcanium, because I can't have you reading minds here, now, can I?"

"I read yours. Not in words or images but…I felt what you were feeling. And I've…" Maya swallowed. "I've *been* feeling what you're feeling. Not as much as I did a few minutes ago. It's like electrical wires buzzing. I can feel it in the back of my skull, more intense the closer we are. You've been calling me."

He sighed, lowering himself to brace against his thighs. "I really didn't mean to."

"You don't strike me as someone who does things like that by accident. You strike me as someone who gets in trouble for what he does on purpose."

"More often than not. But sometimes things tend to make themselves known. I'm sorry, Maya."

"I can't blame you for that. I've been transmitting, too, haven't I? You mentioned my dreams."

He smiled. "That's not unusual. Jinn don't dream on their own. We have yours." He'd told her before, but it pleased him to tell her again. "Don't worry. In Arcanium, I'm quite accustomed to being pulled into all manner of dreams. Now, go on out there, love. Have a drink, have some chocolate cake and take your pleasure with better company than mine. I'm tired."

"You're not tired," she said softly. "You're immortal."

"There are all kinds of tired, and I am several of them. Good night, Maya." Keeping the bottom of the stairs locked against her, he raised himself to his feet and ascended once more.

Amid the debris, only one room was occupied. The Ringmaster had taken Kitty to the top floor. Bell had four other floors to himself, but instead he climbed to the roof.

The city smelled of exhaust, oil, grease and smoke, not enough trees and space to filter the air, too much metal and glass between him and the sky. But the roof afforded him some quiet from the psychic cacophony below. He couldn't tune everyone out entirely. The Funhouse could too quickly turn into something for which he would have to pull the Ringmaster away from Kitty, which would be all the more reason for the

Ringmaster to put all his strength and skill into the lashes, if circumstances led to them. But Bell could put some space and many feet of concrete between himself and the rest.

The skylight windows made temple shapes behind him, although skyscrapers dwarfed them. A god could feel small in a place like this, where man built structures to feel less small. He couldn't even see the stars, no matter how intently he peered into the obscured atmosphere.

The city was neither quiet nor peaceful, but he closed his eyes and breathed. He wouldn't sleep.

Chapter Ten

While his people rehearsed for the weekend, as well as all the things that they did during the week without his guidance, Bell remained cloistered in his fortune teller tent.

He stared without blinking at a prism of rutilated quartz. Within the crystal, he'd imprisoned an inconsequential demon. He merely searched through the golden rutile and imperfections because it was a lovely thing and gave him something to focus on that wasn't his own mind.

"I don't think you'll find the answers to the universe in there if you haven't already."

Maya let the tent flap fall behind her. She was back in normal clothing, not that it made as much of a difference to him as she might have believed. A good piece of leather could render her absolutely stunning, but she could wear sweatpants and a unisex T-shirt three sizes too big for her and he'd still see who she was underneath the clothes, underneath the skin. A pair of loose jeans and a tank top made her fit in better at a shopping center, but only if people weren't paying attention, and she was the kind of woman who other people paid attention to — the way she walked, the way she tossed her hair, the dark beauty in her eyes. The carriage of a dancer and acrobat only enhanced what had already turned heads.

The trouble was that he'd hoped she'd learned last night not to try to turn *his* head.

Bell set the prism back into the chest with the others. "There is no answer to the universe. The questions are the answers."

"Spoken like a true charlatan." Maya peered into the chest. "Are those all demons you sucked out of his Arcanium? All of them?"

"The ones still living." He closed the lid and slid the padlock back into place. The lock was pickable. The spells that protected it were not.

"There are an awful lot of them."

"A whole stadium full. Would you like one? They're harmless, and nothing will free them. If you smashed the crystals into a thousand pieces, the prisoners would simply reside in progressively smaller fragments."

"Maybe another time. I've just been dying for a demon to put on my shelf." She sat across from him at the table, this time taking up the tarot cards herself. "I've been thinking about what you said."

"Not long enough."

If she'd been thinking more clearly, she would have chosen to leave, but she wore neither a backpack of all her belongings nor sensible shoes.

Nor had she found a lover at the Funhouse after he'd left her behind. She'd found the drink and the chocolate cake. She'd drawn the line at jumping anyone else's bones, although after her display, Illumina cast who'd been too cowed by her before had approached with the courage of the moment—or rather, with other decidedly pointed variables scrambling their fear of rejection.

She'd gone to sleep frustrated, dreamed strong enough that he'd sensed it, but because he hadn't slept himself, she hadn't been able to pull him in.

Maya shuffled the tarot cards then placed three face-down in succession before her. She'd told tarot to customers of Illumina before, but it was different with an enchanted deck that wasn't her own, just like it was a lot easier to write up a horoscope when one didn't believe that the position of the stars and planets had any effect on one's life. When she set the unused portion of the deck down, her hand trembled. Before she changed her mind, she turned each card over, the indecision showing on her face, even to him.

The Golden Scissors. The Lock. The Bell.

His tent was warm because he hadn't made any attempt to keep it more tolerable for human customers, but Bell's gut went cold. The chill stretched all the way to his fingers, the opposite of tugged heartstrings, although they were involved nonetheless.

She'd chosen and presented the cards for herself. They were meant for her. And their meaning was abundantly clear.

"No." Bell stood from the table, although he didn't disturb the cards. He didn't dare impart them more power.

Maya gathered the three cards together and put them back in the deck at random. "The enchanted deck has spoken."

"No."

"If I'm going to leave, Bell, I should understand why I'm leaving. Do I have good reason to leave? Did you give me good reason to hate you?"

Bell grasped the edge of the sideboard. The crystal skulls stared with empty eyes back at him. "Yes."

"Is that the reason you're not going to give me my memories back?"

"No. You sought Fairuza to have them removed because of you, not me. I can live with you hating me, Maya, but I am not the only one you will hate. I offered to remove your memories and she did remove them to *protect* you."

"I'm a big girl. It's time to take off the training wheels. It's time for me to know."

Bell pushed off the sideboard, clenching his jaw so hard that it hurt even him. He didn't have to do this. He could create a barrier twenty feet on every side of him to keep Maya away indefinitely. Then Fairuza would have to deal with Maya's insistence, since he doubted Fairuza would apply the same distancing magic on the woman she'd taken such a personal interest in teaching. Maya had walked away from Arcanium, which had removed responsibility from him—not by his choice but by hers—and given it to Fairuza as soon as she'd joined Illumina.

Bell could tolerate her presence in Arcanium indefinitely. He could find another lover or avail himself of strangers to wash away the taste of her, the feel of her, by sheer quantity. Perhaps he would finally allow Neve to coax him into her bed.

He didn't have to do this.

"Bell, don't you dare," Fairuza whispered in his mind.

Bell locked his tent tighter than a prison. Air flowed through, but not even an insect could cross his barrier.

"Do you understand that you cannot have your memories removed again? To do so would bring you right back to me, and I won't do this to you a second time, or a third, or a fourth. It will hurt enough without doing it to you over and over again, like some twisted form of karmic rebirth."

"The others aren't doing well, but they're still here. They may be screwed up, but recovery is possible. I'll know that."

"It won't help you." His insides twisted into a tighter knot, threatening to fuse together. He conjured a mug of tea. "Drink this."

"Will it—"

"It's just tea. Hopefully, it'll settle your stomach."

Her own tension drew from what she saw in him. When she took the mug, it was as though she were several decades older, with the rusty joints of someone who wasn't a magically enhanced acrobat. Wary, she sipped from it. "Cinnamon spice."

Bell sat across from her again, memorized the woman that she was now, lit from within, golden skin, a smile in her eyes if not on her face, despite the shadows underneath. A face that knew how to smile.

"There is a solution that we haven't discussed. I could offer you the same choice I gave to the rest of my cast—what Fairuza should have done in the first place. I could release your memories of my Arcanium alone. There's enough heaven and hell there without releasing Locke's Arcanium along with them. You wouldn't be alone in that loss. You will know me. You will know Arcanium. You don't need to remember everything to remember enough."

Maya sipped her tea, but even if Bell couldn't read the thoughts and feelings on the surface of her mind, he would already sense her resistance. Maya didn't do things by halves. She'd asked for all her memories of both versions of Arcanium removed, and she wouldn't be content with only part of her memories restored. It didn't matter that Locke's Arcanium was all hell, no trace of the heaven that she'd tasted with Bell.

She thought she needed hell.

"This is your last chance. Please, Maya."

Maya set down the tea, grabbed another tarot card and slapped it down.

The Plague Doctor.

"That didn't have quite the impact I intended it to," Maya said, inspecting the card more closely.

"No, I believe it had the desired effect." Bell turned the Plague Doctor over again and put it back in the deck without further comment. Bell hadn't written explanations on the cards. He was the only one who needed to know how to interpret. To tell her the meaning would be less than encouraging, but it wouldn't alter her choice, and it wouldn't change what he had to do.

Bell gestured for Maya to lean in closer then pressed his fingers to her temple. He could do this without contact, but contact made magic so much easier.

"Bell!"

If he left it to Fairuza alone to handle the matter, they would reach this point eventually, because if Maya didn't get what she wanted here, she get it out on the streets with much less scrupulous characters, most of whom would recognize her and relish the fact that they'd restored her memories right before stealing her away for themselves—and they wouldn't even have to pay for the pleasure.

He could refuse. He could punt the responsibility to Fairuza, the way she had to him. But Maya always got what she wanted, one way or another.

Like he'd told her, he could live with her hating him.

"It's time." It was all he had to say.

Within Maya's mind, he pulled down the walls, one by one.

Memories spilled from containment like a river over a floodplain. It wasn't a disaster. They didn't crash down, sending her reeling, drowning, gasping for breath and grasping onto anything that would hold her steady. They spread over her mind, seeping into earth. She drank them in as they came to her all at once, although she could only process them one at a time. Shock hit her before the full extent of what she'd hidden from herself finished sinking in.

He broke skin contact and sat back. The steam from her mug of tea formed a veil between him, but through it, he watched the light in her eyes die. The gold of her skin from sun and from the natural glow that called everyone around her like flame dampened, guttered, snuffed out, luster flat and lifeless.

The miraculous resurrection of Maya DeLuca was over. Reality, an unwelcome guest in Arcanium at the best of times, returned unglamorous, ugly, sapping her of what illusion she had created of life — a disease that could not be treated, only managed, and that rarely well.

Maya's shoulders twitched slightly with every blow of remembrance, something she would flee from if she could, except the demons were in her own mind, and there was nothing left to cage them but herself.

When it was over, neither Bell nor Maya moved, but the parlor table became a canyon both too vast and too close, depending on which side they were on. Above the paleness that undercut her darker skin, she looked up at him, the black of her eyes like cold obsidian glass instead of warm coal. Were it not for the flecks of brown, she could have been a young demon herself.

"So I don't get to lose that again, huh?" The corners of her mouth almost imperceptibly turned down, and the whites of her eyes and edges of her nostrils reddened. But she only blinked once, and the moment when it could have spilled over ended. She was dry and cold, empty and full, all at the same time.

"No."

"You're a wordy fucker today, aren't you?"

"I don't have much to say for myself."

"No, you don't, do you?"

As she stood, Maya picked up the mug of tea and tossed the rest of the steaming liquid onto his face and chest.

He hadn't seen it coming the prescient way, but he'd seen it coming the way anyone would when a fatally angry woman had something scalding within her reach. It hurt only for a moment, and his eyes had been closed. In spite of the steam, it wasn't as hot as it had looked, and he had a much higher tolerance for temperature variance.

Bell brushed the worst of it away from his face. Throwing tea wasn't petty punishment. It was all she could do, the only thing within her reach that she hadn't already done. But whatever she did wouldn't change what had happened to her, all the things she now remembered that monsters and demons had done and made her do. And that he was responsible for it, for her pain and everyone else's, because his hubris hadn't just gotten them hurt. It had sent them to hell on earth.

When gods made mistakes, aftereffects rippled out like a devastating earthquake. He had risked that, risked *them*, believing that he could get the better of anything. He continued to do so, believing that if he could get the better of Locke and every other demon in that monstrosity of a circus, nothing else could trick Arcanium away from him again.

He wasn't wrong. Arcanium had only ever been taken once. But he wasn't quite right either, was he? Because the risk still wasn't zero. He wouldn't make the same mistakes, but there were all kinds of other mistakes he could make, and he was still putting himself in the position of making them one day.

Arcanium was worth it for him, but it wasn't worth it for her — not with what she'd gone through every day and night while under Locke's reign, not with what she'd been forced to watch happen to others, not with the revelations that time had given her.

Maya's movements lacked her usual, magic-enhanced grace. Her gait had stiffened, each step an effort as she headed for the tent flap. She stopped at the edge of the Persian rug and fell to her knees, the impact startling a cry out of her. Then she heaved with a shuddering cough. He pulled her hair out of the way as she threw up the tea and whatever she'd had for lunch.

"Don't touch me!" She struck behind her to knock his hands away, but he hadn't moved from the table. He held her hair away from the vomit with his magic.

Maya gathered her hair back herself and pulled an elastic around it. "That's not any better."

She turned to the side to cough again then spat the rest of what was in her mouth onto the grass. She stayed on her knees, turned away from him.

"What did you want me to do?" Bell stripped away any recrimination that she could have used to fling back at him. He was powerful, not perfect. Where she was concerned, his psychic power didn't always serve him well, of which she was aware — even more so now.

"You did what I asked. I understand why you did it, and it wasn't because I was a five-year-old wearing you down for a treat. You didn't see any other way to satisfy that empty space left behind by the removed memories." She leaned forward, closing her eyes against another wave of memories, another wave of nausea. "But I think you could have sat me down and just told me the worst of everything. Then I could have known without…"

She pressed her hand to her chest just above her heart, where the nerves ached so hard that she feared a heart attack. Emotional pain had its price, but she couldn't die in Arcanium. And she wasn't sure whether that was a good thing or not.

That she didn't speak her darker thoughts aloud didn't change that he could hear them. Lizzie had succumbed to the impulse once, and she hadn't been the only one, especially among his prisoners. Maya had arrived at Illumina near death. Now that she'd regained the memories, she knelt once more on the brink. He held the blame in his hands like the crystals in the chest, her torment his own. It belonged to him, and he sank within her to accept it. But he could only share. He couldn't take it away, or else she would recognize his part in it and push him out like a splinter.

"To tell you too much would have rendered the walls protecting the memories structurally unsound. To remove the memories entirely would have caused the gaping holes left behind to fill with madness. The only way this could have been avoided is if..." Bell stopped, ruminating.

Then he stood and opened the tent flap, where Fairuza had just arrived, slightly out of breath from running, although she needn't have lost oxygen.

"How?" Maya spat bile from her mouth again. "How could this have been avoided? By not letting us get taken in the first place. By not conspiring to make me cheat with another woman's husband so that you could wriggle that woman on a hook in front of a demon who you *knew* was coming to Arcanium. By not letting us out of your sight and your power, lowering your guard just to literally pimp out your circus to the highest bidder. By not seducing us into trusting you and loving your circus as though it were our own while you sewed us into the spells so that anyone taking Arcanium would take us with it. And all because one person said something wrong to a stranger, because we didn't know it didn't have to be an official wish for all of your kind."

Bell didn't respond, because they were fair accusations. He met Fairuza's gaze, but she remained impenetrable, even when he offered his hand to welcome her into his tent and she accepted it.

"Yes, it all could have been avoided were I a better proprietor. I can't change that it happened. All I could do was get Arcanium back, heal what was within my power to heal then make sure it could never happen that way again. Is it fool-proof? You and I both know I've been a fool. Is it much harder to steal Arcanium than before, an already Herculean task that only one demon managed to accomplish? Yes. And if living in Arcanium doesn't teach my children that their words have weight and significance, I don't know how much clearer I can be."

"It isn't Neve's fault that you stuck her on a line," Maya said.

"I would never dream of blaming her for being suckered into saying something she shouldn't have to someone she didn't know. I blame only myself and Locke for Arcanium being taken. I blame myself for the state you were in when Fairuza took your memories, and I blame myself for the state you are in now."

"And what do you plan to do with me and my present state?" Maya's attention shifted from Bell to Fairuza. Even without Maya using her nascent psychic abilities, the way Fairuza avoided his eyes while their powers grappled between them telegraphed their shared tension over Maya.

"Keep you here for a while," Bell said, without consulting Fairuza on the decision. "You needn't walk among the rest of the circus or participate in any performances. But the way you're thinking right now, Maya, I might as well hand you a gun if I let you leave Arcanium now."

"You can't keep me here. You gave me my freedom." Maya crossed her arms, cupping her upper arms as though cold, in spite of the day's heat. She twitched at the sensation of the gold bracelet.

"Yes, I did. Then you contracted yourself to Illumina, which is currently under my protection. And you are in need of protection, Maya…from yourself."

"Fai, help me with this." Maya held her hands out to Fairuza in imploration, but although Fairuza took them with as much warmth as she carried within her, she shook her head.

"I gave you a gift, Maya. You didn't spit on it, but you decided to return it, in spite of countless warnings not only from myself but from Bell. He didn't do this for you because he wanted to hurt you. Quite the opposite. He did this for you because he was afraid that if he didn't, something else would hurt you even worse. I can't help you now."

Fairuza stroked the line of her hair then cringed where a few drops of vomit had caught on the strands. With a thought, she cleaned Maya's hair and mouth, although she could do little for the nausea still roiling in Maya's gut. "Go back to the caravan. I'll come by in a while to give you something to help you sleep without dreams."

"You think I want to sleep?" Maya stepped closer to Fairuza, close enough to kiss, although nothing in her demeanor suggested she had that on her mind.

"No. I think you want to burn Arcanium to the ground. But you'd burn more than Arcanium down with it. Most of them suffered your same fate, and those who came after were pulled into service because of what happened, wrenched from their lives like you. Don't condemn them because you condemn him."

Murder relit Maya's deadened eyes. She considered wrapping her fingers around his throat, taking advantage of the fact that he wouldn't fight back. She contemplated impaling him with one of his quartz wands, setting fire to the tent, hitting him with the wooden idols then the parlor table, smashing his handsome face bloody, breaking his nose and teeth. But she'd done much of that already, and he'd recovered from all physical blows, including ones that would have felled lesser immortals.

She couldn't hurt him permanently, but taking Arcanium from him... That would break his nigh-unbreakable heart. Normal fire wouldn't be enough, but with her psychokinetic abilities electric through her furious blood, she could do quite a bit of damage before he stopped her. Only Fairuza's warning that people would get hurt in the process kept her from doing it. The grass was dry, easy kindling. To burn down the tent would risk the others as well.

Maya pointed to him then herself. "We're not done."

"No. I suppose we aren't." Bell bowed to her, briefly lowering his eyes in a gesture of respect that she wouldn't realize he showed her.

Maya struck at the tent flap to open it then stalked out.

"Why would you—?" Fairuza began.

"Are you really going to ask me why I did what you forced me to do? I am convenient and I'm willing to play this role, whereas you like to be seen as the benevolent, white-gowned saint who escaped Arcanium to create something more palatable—less seedy underbelly, more spiritual transcendence."

With a gesture, Fairuza's feet dragged on the ground then the rug, until she was right before him, where averting her eyes would be a sign of weakness. He took her chin between fingers considerably less gentle than the last time they'd been in this position. Fairuza made no attempt to shake him off.

"This is about more than your poor financial choices, Fairuza. And because you won't let me see what it is, I can't help but think it's nothing good."

"Do I strike you as the villain in this piece?" Fairuza straightened her demure sundress, lifting her chin out of his hold. "At my worst, do you think I would ever put your people in danger again, after knowing what that does to them?"

"I don't know." His breath scorched as it came back to him from Fairuza's skin.

"I only want what's best for Maya."

"And what's best for you."

"Can you claim that the same isn't true for you as well?" Fairuza inhaled then brushed her hand over the sticky residue of the tea. "You smell good."

Bell knocked her hand away. "I want you gone by morning. You have the evening to pack everything you need. That is my gift to you, for the sake of what we used to be. Take Maya with you, and don't let her out of your sphere until she's strong enough. But anything left you want to do to her that you'd rather she hate me for, you'll have to do it yourself. Arcanium will survive without Illumina. I don't care if Illumina survives without Arcanium. That's on your head and in your heart, Fairuza, not mine."

Fairuza tilted her head, so still and quiet that he heard her heart beat, slow and strong. "Very well. Tomorrow morning, we'll be gone."

Chapter Eleven

When Bell returned to the caravan that evening, Maya was sitting on his front steps.

She'd changed into a loose T-shirt and cotton pants, something shapeless and comfortable. The line of her sleeve was seamless. She'd removed the gold bracelet from her upper arm. Her lips were almost the color of the skin around them.

The nausea had persisted and so had the vomiting until all she'd managed were dry heaves, but then she'd gone to the edge of Arcanium before finally letting loose. He'd heard her screaming, living her nightmares over again while perfectly awake. It had taken every ounce of power within him not to go to her.

Yet here she was. To make matters more bewildering, the Ringmaster sat at the picnic table in the center of the caravan a few feet away. The Ringmaster never fraternized with the rest of the circus except Kitty. Maya distracted Bell too much to put his finger on why the Ringmaster had joined her.

Maya held her legs as though she'd shudder apart if she let go. "I don't understand how you can go on as though nothing happened, as though nothing could ever go wrong again."

"I don't. Things have changed."

"The faces change. Arcanium doesn't."

"Arcanium has changed. I've changed. You know better, Maya. You know that what you see isn't always what is. You weren't the only one I lost."

"And I wasn't the only one who came back. How could they come back? How could the others stay? *Knowing* that it could happen to them again, that the vultures are silently circling Arcanium, looking for revenge, and they're all the more likely to get it now? They'll start attacking. They'll coordinate. An army of fae is one thing. An army of demons is another."

"It's not the demons I'm worried about." Bell stepped toward his RV then stepped back again. He could disappear and reappear in his home, but that was a coward's way out, and although he didn't care who called him one, he held himself to a higher standard.

"Then what do you worry about?"

"Right now? You."

She smiled with her lips turned downward. "Don't worry about me. I'm like a cockroach, too, Bell. It takes a lot to destroy me."

"You've been through a lot."

"Which you know because of your glorious omniscience. You know just what I went through."

"Yes."

"Then you know what I'm here for." She clenched herself so tightly that her knuckles and elbows went pale.

Bell shifted on his feet, glanced at the Ringmaster. "Do tell."

"Reparations."

"You were paid for pain and suffering."

"I don't care about money!" She closed her eyes, swallowing back the rage barely contained within her human body. "I don't care about what you paid me to be your whore, Bell."

"Bite your tongue." If she winced at the tone in his voice, he didn't let that matter to him. She wouldn't insult what she'd never been to him.

"And everyone else's. Human. Demon. Monster. Weird slimy thing. You owe me so much more than money. You owe all of us."

Bell raised his chin as the Ringmaster finally met his eyes, the blackness there far darker and deeper than Maya's could ever hope to be, even if he'd taken her all the way into the fire and made her jinn like Fairuza.

"I have paid with the Ringmaster's lash, before the entire circus and every week alone since." It was the first time he'd admitted out loud to the sessions he took with the Ringmaster, as Maya had taken them before him. She, more than the rest, would understand the impulse. "The single public session wasn't enough. I heal too quickly for the same blows to hold the same value."

The hard line of her lips eased—but only slightly. Her absolution had become something else over time, but it had still stripped lines from her back, sometimes struck bone. Although the initial blows reached just as deep in him, he could heal much faster and his absolution had never become what hers had been.

"How many?" she asked.

"For the whole circus, a hundred lashes. For the demons, then alone, I stopped counting."

"I didn't," the Ringmaster said, but he didn't offer that number any more than the others he'd been responsible for over the decades. To him, the numbers were gold coins to a dragon.

Maya flexed her fingers to loosen the stiff muscles as she stood from the stoop. "The Ringmaster wouldn't be giving you the lashes. This isn't for the circus, although if you really regretted what happened to Arcanium, you would never have reopened at all. You would have set everyone free."

"Is that so?" Other people milled through the caravan and the tent city of Illumina, and Bell was aware that more than the Ringmaster were listening in. He didn't have to justify himself to Illumina or Arcanium. But Maya was still adjusting to the woman she'd become, with both the horror-filled memories and the blissful ignorance overlapping in a disorienting blend, struggling for dominance. *"This is a haven even now for those who went through the same torture as you. Would you deny them their haven simply because it doesn't feel safe to you anymore?"*

"Just because you fooled them into trusting you doesn't mean this is a safe haven."

"And of course the only one who realizes it is you, Maya. You've set yourself free from my influence, and you can see all things clearly now, while the rest of my people are brainwashed members of a circus cult, helpless to my charms and unable to make their own decisions."

Maya stood unnaturally straight, struggling to expand her lungs beyond the constriction around her ribs that also tightened around her throat.

Bell stepped closer. "If you want to punish me for what I've done to you, then all you need to do is ask. That is all you've ever needed to do. But don't presume to speak for the people of Arcanium who stayed. Many of them you respect too much to dismiss their feelings so quickly."

"Then don't pretend that you don't tie people here in other ways, through the relationships that you curate, enhanced by the influence of the sex demons."

"No, Maya, I naturally try to make being here harder than it already is by denying them necessary intimacy." He shook his head. "I even gave the prisoners a chance to hate me in solidarity."

"Not all of them."

"You never had a problem with how I treated them before." Bell held up a hand. "I have made my peace with the rest of my cast. You aren't doing this for them. Tell me what *you* want."

"I want what you owe me. As well as you can, I want you to understand what we went through. Because you don't. You think you do, but you don't, or else you would have let us all go when you took Arcanium back, when you saw what someone could make of it. And sometimes, that someone is you."

Hands on his hips, he stared her down, although they were on the same level, with her on the bottom step. She thought he didn't understand, that he couldn't understand, because he wasn't human. But she was the one who couldn't understand, and he had to forgive her ignorance.

"Are you going to torture me, Maya?"

"Yes." To her credit, she didn't try to fool herself she was going to do anything other than what passed through the stormy surface of her brain. "Are you going to claim you don't owe me that?"

"No."

Maya blinked, as though she'd expected him to try to charm his way out of it.

The Ringmaster had been entirely inadequate to him for the kind of guilt he'd been trying to assuage. There was no balancing the scales for what he had done, for the steps that had led to hell for his children. There was no balancing what he knew had happened to Neve, to the Spider, to Caroline, to Joanne, to Christina, to Troy, to Seth and Lars, to his prisoners and his voluntaries alike, to his demons and his humans, even though the demons had recovered more quickly. And there was no balancing what he'd done to Maya, a woman he loved more deeply than anyone he'd ever brought into the circus—for the exact reason she stood in front of him and demanded that he submit himself to torture at her own hands.

"Where do you want me?" he asked.

She blinked again. "The ring."

"Now?"

Maya nodded. "Just you, me and the Ringmaster. No one else needs to see this."

She stepped to the ground and strode past him toward the big top tent. The Ringmaster stretched his long legs, the muscles under the fitted jeans becoming more pronounced with the tension. Then he pushed himself to his feet with a smile.

He sometimes smiled for the guests, but that was a mask. The rest of the time, he only smiled if there was something for a hellborn demon to smile at, which wasn't often. He rarely even smiled with Kitty. Their affection went beyond the surface niceties expected of his human expression, given that he very much wasn't human. The grace he gave her came in the form of peace that the hellborn were rarely capable of, the cooling of the coal fire in his eyes when she doused his flame. But that was for Kitty alone.

The Ringmaster had forgiven him a multitude of sins but still held a few against him. The coals always burned for Bell.

Bell trailed them, some distance between each, but the Arcanium cast noticed him following Maya and the Ringmaster. If they hadn't yet heard that Maya was her old self, they would see at the very least that Maya or Bell was slated for punishment, and with the determination in her step, it appeared unlikely to be Maya.

Trying to control the gossip mill in a small world like Arcanium was harder than screaming at the wind to cease. Bell could stop storms, and he could technically stop the rumors, but rumors were harmless—just another facet of what allowed his people some control in a world that sometimes made it seem that they had precious little in their control. It was irrelevant what people said about him, as long as they remembered his laws and that he would protect them from any who would break them.

Bell entered the cool darkness of the big top tent. As soon as they reached the ring, he switched on the spotlights.

He didn't need Maya to tell him to remove his clothing. He did it on his own, stripping off his pants as he conjured the bench that they used for almost all the punishments. It had soaked in enough blood to fill an army of souls, but one wouldn't know that to look at it.

It was a simple bench, just three planks of weathered gray wood.

Bell straddled it without a word, smoothing his palms over the grain. Even healed and cleansed wood held memories when they were transferred by blood and tears. Within this wood's memory, Bell's own bloodiness was most recent, but it also recalled Vivian for the severity and Maya for the frequency.

Maya tensed at seeing him naked again. She looked away until he'd leaned forward to wrap his arms around the plank, presenting his back.

"Do you know what you want to do?" Bell asked quietly.

"That's why I brought him."

The Ringmaster pulled his whip from the strap that held it to his belt. He shook the tail out then handed the leather-wrapped handle to Maya.

"Having taken the lash doesn't mean you know how to use it." Bell shifted uncomfortably on the plank. "It's easy to hurt yourself trying to hurt me."

"You gave Kitty the knowledge. Give it to me now."

"What knowledge do you wish?" Bell rested his cheek on the wood to face her. Other than the awkwardness of his bare genitals on the bench, the position was oddly soporific, his eyelids heavy. If Maya had hoped he would protest, she'd underestimated the exact number of times he had already presented himself in Arcanium's name, in hers.

"All of it." Maya gripped the whip handle, clenched her teeth so hard that they ground together and she had to shake her head to convince herself to loosen her jaw. "Everything they did to me, I want to know how to do it."

Even without the power of the wish, Bell noted the nuance of what she asked for. She didn't ask for the ability to do it, only the knowledge of how. Some of what had been done to her would be out of her power to do, given biological limitations, but there were ways to improvise.

He stretched out a hand to her, gesturing lightly. If she was going to commit to this unique form of therapy, he couldn't tiptoe around her trauma. She'd seen him naked a thousand times, and even now she had no reason to believe that he would take this opportunity to retaliate, not when he had already agreed to the repayment.

"Shall we both?" The Ringmaster bared his white teeth in a beatific smile like that of any large predator. The black in his eyes widened to the edges, and the black smoke of his magic curled from his nose and from his feet. Not in an attempt to take over Arcanium as he once had. He simply couldn't contain the darkness of his hell at the promise of sharing it.

The Ringmaster stepped behind Maya far too eagerly, but of the two powerful men in the ring, Bell made her warier—as he should have, as long as the Ringmaster was still latched to Bell's leash.

Maya nodded, clasping Bell's hand with a shaky breath and covering the Ringmaster's hand behind her to take the knowledge both of them could give her—jinn and demon. Bell had never wanted to kiss her more, fought against arousal low and hot where his abdomen pressed to the wood. It was the last thing she would want him to feel when she intended to punish him for the blind spots in his love—for Arcanium and for her.

"The things I have to show you," the Ringmaster whispered in her ear, the groan in his voice undeniably sexual, although he had never expressed such blatant interest in Maya — in whipping her, yes, but never before in Maya herself.

Bell had known that the Ringmaster had developed a unique fondness for the woman who willingly subjected herself to his punishments until they weren't punishments at all, but Maya swallowed against the confirmation of what she'd only ever suspected. It wasn't like the fondness he had for Kitty, who he would hurt a hundred different ways that gave her pleasure but would never truly punish. His dark, vicious love for Kitty was a spark of humanity in his demon soul. The fondness he had for Maya was all demon, even darker and more vicious, much less protective in its possessiveness.

Bell rippled a warning in the Ringmaster's smoke, where only he and the Ringmaster could see and feel it. The Ringmaster withdrew neither his power nor his hand, but his smile lessened.

Together, they sent their collective knowledge into her, new tempests to join the ones already there — practical knowledge with the weight of centuries-old experience, so that she remembered everything done to her with the clarity of both submitting and subjecting, with the mortification of the reception and the delight of the one who tirelessly gifted the pain.

Maya gasped, groaned and wrenched under their hold, but not in torment, and neither man relented. Even without wishes, she had a wealth of memories to warn her to be careful of what she wished for. She'd still chosen this. A woman who sought such an avenue of revenge did not need to be protected like a delicate rosebud. She needed a chance to find her claws so that she would never find herself alone without knives, even if Bell wouldn't let her bleed herself dry. He could do all matter of things to her if she still needed something sharp on her skin. It wasn't like he hadn't done them before.

But hurting herself wasn't the desire rising strong and fast in the storms of her mind now.

Maya squeezed his hand until it would have crippled a lesser man, straining the integrity of her own bones. The angle meant she could do less to the Ringmaster, but whatever she did to him, he showed no pain in his reaction, just the perfectly wicked glee that came from the promise or conclusion of a good whipping. Finally, she stumbled from her crouched position to her knees — the closest thing to falling she was capable of — and broke contact with them both.

When she looked up again, Bell swore that the last vestiges of warmth in her eyes had disappeared and all that was left in her irises was black.

Humanity was a strange and resilient thing. It wasn't necessarily good, just as everything demonic wasn't necessarily evil, as evidenced by the other demons under Arcanium's domain. To assume that the cruelties he and the Ringmaster had given Maya had burned out more of her humanity by making her more evil was to ignore the pervasive, observable presence of evil within humanity.

He'd seen it within Arcanium. In the violence with which Elizabeth had succumbed to his and her shared need to render a rapist into a bloody, misshapen mass. In Kitty's love for the Ringmaster. In Valorie's willingness to mutilate and kill Maya when fear and outrage had led to a break in her psyche. In Maya's wish to tear her ex apart. In Vivian's mass murder attempt. Not to mention what had brought the prisoners of Arcanium into Arcanium in the first place. The Rotting Man, Dez, Misha, the Man-Doll, the Sphynx, John, Melanie, George... They were human and yet had done great evil, because good and evil were all part of the same coin of the soul.

Bell didn't usually concern himself with whether one was better than the other, only that he couldn't be slotted into either and that the end result justified the means it took to get there.

He couldn't say that she had become less human, but she'd lost an element of herself that had been there before.

Or an element that had been as-yet-undeveloped had finally come into full fruit.

Bell had put himself in this situation with Maya many times before, but their roles had switched to such an extreme that it left him almost lightheaded. And — dare he admit to himself — excited, which was not how a penitent should have felt.

He'd taken the submissive *role* before, but to submit in and of itself had never excited him. Most demons and jinn didn't like being submissive at all, much less actually submitting — and much less than that, to a human being.

As Maya pushed herself to her feet again, the Ringmaster stepped back into the darkness at the edge of the ring. He would prefer to be implementing the torture himself, of course, but even in the darkness, he couldn't hide his excitement.

"Let's make this all Arcanium-official, shall we?" she said. "Because this isn't a typical punishment. It's not mandatory, something you've demanded to settle a score. You agreed to this to appease me. I'm just making sure that you agree to all of it, sight unseen. Do you, Bell? Do you agree to accept whatever punishment I mete out? You just handed me all the knowledge of methods and implements that I could ever need, and you let the Ringmaster do his part. So you know what I'm capable of. Do you accept anything and everything that I do to you tonight? It's more consideration than they ever gave me."

"Yes, I accept it," Bell said without hesitation. "I accept whatever you do to me tonight. You have until dawn, although I think you'll be surprised by how exhausting it is. Even for revenge, you might not have the stamina of, say, the Ringmaster."

She kicked the sawdust, sending an almost invisible cloud into the air. He closed his eyes and wrinkled his nose against a sneeze.

"I can think of a few things I can do to you that I don't have to be actively participating in at the time." Maya sidled beside him and shoved her hands under his chest to pinch and twist his nipples—hard.

Bell shouted, jerked.

He hadn't seen it coming, and he wasn't trying to. To see her plans would allow Bell to brace himself. Neither Maya nor the rest of the cast had had that luxury. Even when the demons had told her what they were going to do, she hadn't been able to anticipate it the same way he could, able to experience himself in the future. Human memory couldn't properly anticipate pain, because it couldn't remember pain as anything more substantial than a nightmare. However, in the midst of pain, it also couldn't imagine a world without it.

Maya stepped back from him once more. "Can you give me what I need if I ask for it, Ringmaster?"

"Almost everything, with great pleasure, woman."

"Good. We'll start with the whip." She'd tucked it over her arm so she could pinch Bell, but now she took the handle again and sent the fall behind her to whisper on the grass and sawdust. "These, I expect you to count. I don't know how many I want to give you yet. The whip was one of the few things they didn't use on me, although there were any number of things that they did strike me with — switches, canes, tails, their bare hands, some of which oozed stinging liquid from their pores. So I really don't know how many of these to give you."

She swung the lash in an arc, but she didn't bring it down on him. She let the leather fall, harmless, upon his back. Bell flinched violently when it landed on him, but he shivered when she drew the braided leather across his skin.

"I'll just have to do whatever feels right. Balanced. You like balance except when you don't, isn't that right?" She let the lash fall on him again. He couldn't help his second flinch either. "I'd tell you that you can't heal yourself for this, but then I don't know how long we could actually go. Sometimes they'd give us those potions three, four times a night so that they could keep going. Maybe you heal faster than I'd like, but I'd rather let you heal so we can do this until morning."

Bell nodded, his head still pressed to the bench. If anything, the request intrigued him.

All of this intrigued him, because the question bating the breath of both him and the Ringmaster was whether she'd be able to handle doling the torture out of a powerful enough sense of revenge or whether the empathy from the shared experience would overwhelm her well before she could get into the meat of a session. People could fantasize about torture for years without repercussions beyond the ice crystals in their heart, but when given the opportunity, they balked because they weren't capable of it.

Bell had given Kitty the opportunity to whip the Ringmaster before, but that had been different, for both of them. Kitty had discovered unexpected pleasure in the power behind the whip, but she hadn't developed an affinity for sadism itself.

Bell simply didn't know whether that would be the case with Maya. The elusiveness of the answer added to the involuntary excitement that preceded the whip's blow.

This time she didn't trick him. The blow was sharp as a knife across his shoulder blades. The trick of the whip's power was in the technique rather than strength, although the Ringmaster's strength added another layer of intensity to the blows that he dealt.

Bell lurched against the bench. It would take a few strikes for him to be able to stay still, embracing the plank to steady himself, although holding too tightly would make the blows hurt more against the tensed muscles.

"One." Had this been a different kind of torture, he would have held back and waited to be reminded — but it wasn't.

* * * *

After twenty strikes of the lash, blood dripped slowly to the sawdust. He'd slowed his healing — not too much, only to give her a better understanding of the damage she wreaked. Bell had also turned his face away from her as she'd rained the blows down, because that would make it easier for her to depersonalize him. Given that she'd made it to twenty blows without hesitation, it was worth seeing how much farther she'd go.

In slowing his healing, the sting of each welt — layered on top of each other — lasted much longer than he was used to, and his body responded to that pain, even as his mind seemed to divorce from it, floating both insensate and dimly conscious. It wasn't quite subspace, or if it was, it leaned in the wrong direction. Bell sank into it with a kind of distant curiosity. He'd suffered thousands of blows from the Ringmaster. Twenty couldn't compare. But without looking at Maya, without connecting to her, the ring felt empty and he was simply in pain that tethered him to the earth so close beneath him while he floated, like a helium balloon tied to a tree root.

"Would you like me to stop?"

Bell grunted as she drew her fingers through the blood on his back, through open wounds and over swollen welts. "Would you like to stop?"

He didn't reach into her, didn't examine her mind or motivation. He listened into the silence, broken only by her breathing.

"I could continue, but I think I'm going to need something to drink. May I have a pair of clover clamps, please, Ringmaster?"

Bell turned his head back toward her as Maya held her hand behind her. Without a word, the Ringmaster gave her a pair of surgical steel clover clamps connected by a thick, heavy chain.

Maya knelt next to Bell. "Now, knowing you, you might enjoy this. But I'll do what I can."

She started with the nipple closest to her, stroking it at first. This wasn't about stimulation that made his cock twitch, although it did and he let it, because it was hidden under his hips and because he wanted her to know how she made him feel, how his body reacted to her torture — whether that reaction was what she was looking for or not. For him, the reaction was neutral, natural. What she did with it was more important to him than the reactions themselves.

After a few seconds of stroking the small piece of flesh, she pinched it again, rolling the nipple between four fingernails until it was tight, hard and an angry red. Maya attached the first clamp quickly then knocked the chain so that the other clamp swung like a pendulum, tugging at the attached clamp. The weight and swing created tension, which increased the pressure on his nipple. He grunted again, and his cock thickened, hardened. He had to adjust his hips to allow for growth.

Maya walked around the bench with no-nonsense strides and knelt to stroke the other nipple. It was obvious that from her angle, she couldn't see it very well. Feeling her way likely seemed like tenderness, but she quickly followed it up with the nearly razor-sharp edges of her nails to make him ready for the second clamp.

With the chain running underneath the wood, she'd effectively bound him to the bench.

She managed to get a grip on his hair and pulled his head up. The chain tautened across the plank and stretched his nipples away from his chest, tightening the clamps. Bell shouted, each subsequent exhale a lessening cry. He smiled, but it wasn't funny or good. Nipple clamps had never been his favorite toy. He'd always preferred to bring blood to anatomy the old-fashioned way, and if he occasionally bit, he always soothed.

"You're lucky I didn't use a dull needle, or whatever that silver ring was that pierced Neve and nearly cut off her clit. I'm sure the Ringmaster could scare me up one of those."

"I could, with some work," the Ringmaster replied.

"Would you have the imagination for it?" Bell asked through gritted teeth.

The Ringmaster glared, although not any more than he usually did. He knew invention wasn't his strong suit. One of the few things he improvised well was binding. If he could tie a knot, he could use it.

Maya released Bell, allowing him to fall back onto the plank. It didn't relieve him of the pinch, but in comparison...

"I'll be back," she said, "but I won't hurry."

After she left the tent, Bell breathed in a steady rhythm, settling into the pain as his healing finally had a chance to take hold.

"Are you enjoying yourself?" he asked the Ringmaster, who hadn't moved from his place on the partition.

"Immensely."

As flat as his deep voice became when not performing, his magic—which so few actually saw—demonstrated his emotions with far more expression, different shades of shadows, with the smolder of fire and veins of sulfur. The Ringmaster's smoky darkness resonated with glee, rippling like soundwaves of laughter.

"You've had me to yourself for over a year. That wasn't enough?"

"I can only do what you permit me, Bell, and what you permit, except in my courtship of Katharine, is the whip. I could do so much more if you let me. But you appreciate it better coming from her, and that pleases me greatly. She will not balk as you thought she might. She's only getting started. Although you have your pleasure, it is not the pleasure you would choose, and so it is unpleasant."

Without moving from where he sat, the Ringmaster pulled so hard on the chain that Bell's nipples nearly tore off. Bell screamed, wrenching up. That pulled the nubs in a different direction with the same tearing pressure, which succeeded in pulling one of them off completely.

The Ringmaster laughed, a rare and beautifully terrible sound, as everything about the Ringmaster was beautiful and terrible.

Bell scrambled to his knees, the wounds on his back temporarily lower priority to the bit of flesh that had dropped from the clamp. The Ringmaster released his pull on the other, which left Bell gasping, thick blood dripping down his chest and a piece of him shriveling to nothing on the ground. He'd regrow the part later — he'd regrown worse — but for now he left it as it was. It would heal over in a scar when his natural magic took hold.

When Maya reentered the ring, she stopped at the edge of the spotlight, because Bell was sitting up and not all of him was still there. She set down the drink caddy then handed the Ringmaster a large hot cup with a cardboard guard. The coffee inside smelled strong enough to strip paint. Caffeine wouldn't do one thing or another to a demon, so it didn't matter that it was evening. The Ringmaster didn't usually deviate from raw meat, water and anything with alcohol content, but Kitty had introduced him to coffee years before.

"You're not supposed to be upright," Maya said mildly as she put a large cup of water on the end of the bench.

Bell didn't reach for it. She hadn't yet given permission. If he'd been responsible for the torture, the water wouldn't be to refresh him.

"And you aren't supposed to be playing when I'm not here," she added to the Ringmaster.

"I couldn't resist."

"Understandable." She grabbed the dangling chain and yanked harder than the Ringmaster had, pulled until his other nipple came off so she could hear him scream as well. The clamps had succeeded where twenty lashes had not. Her cheeks and temples twitched, but she discarded the chain and the clamps on the ground. "Back on your stomach, Bell."

She took the cup she'd set down and drank from it herself. There was another large cup of water in the drink caddy, but she left that one for now.

Uneasy subspace had fled. He was dropping fast, the intrigue in his erection deflating as he lowered himself back to the bench. Oddly, that felt better to him, that he was giving her what she wanted rather than something she hadn't intended but had expected.

Maya retrieved the whip. Her breathing had shallowed and her hand trembled, but that could have been because of the unexpected effort of twenty lashes.

Bell would help keep her awake, but he wouldn't give her more strength than she had. He wanted Maya to experience torture under her own power, to take her rest when she needed it then return if she still required retribution in spite of exhaustion.

"Let's keep going, shall we?" Stepping around the bench so that she could strike him from all angles, Maya laid the lash across his back again, drawing new red lines.

Blood splattered around him like modern art, speckling her clothes, her arms, her hands, her face.

Chapter Twelve

She concluded at a hundred strokes of the whip. By the end, she'd had to stop several times to let her arm rest. She could have struck him with both arms to ease the strain, but the left wouldn't have been as accurate or strong, and she hadn't sought ambidexterity from either the Ringmaster or Bell.

After a hundred lashes, her momentum had started to fade, because anger in action didn't last anywhere near as long as anger that festered and rotted at the core. But anger like hers could rarely be exorcised without someone getting hurt in the process, and only a willing immortal could allow for such an exorcism. He'd exorcised her before – just usually from the other end of a sharp implement and with far different intent, which hadn't always been sexual, even when it had included sex.

Bell felt as though he'd been exorcised – and as though he'd been the demon removed as well. She didn't cut as deeply as the Ringmaster, but after a hundred blows of a well-braided bullwhip, his back had been stripped, his muscles flayed to shreds that he observed through the Ringmaster's eyes—which the Ringmaster would have permitted, even if he'd known that Bell was doing it, because it would delight him that Bell could experience the artistry from both sides of the whip.

It didn't matter to him now that the nipple clamps had become obsolete or that Maya hadn't given him anything to drink, although he was parched—not the least from blood loss. His world narrowed to the flesh that had been part of his back but wasn't anymore. He jerked on the bench, involuntary spasms. He kept his arms around the wood and his thighs so tight against the sides that he might have given himself splinters.

The leather of the lash trapped sawdust in the coating of blood and bits of flesh as it moved over the ring floor.

Maya panted as though she'd run a half-marathon. Sweat had bloomed on her shirt. Her hair had frizzed, although she'd pulled it tightly back from the dampness on her forehead and scalp. Her cheeks had flushed, but her lips were still too close to the color of her skin—not colorless but muted.

She approached him, passing the handle from one hand to the other, her mouth parted, the dark light in her gaze like staring into the glow of a crocodile's eyes in the marshes at night—an oddly specific comparison that struck him with perfect clarity.

Some people found reptiles cold, but just because they needed external heat didn't mean that they were heartless. Crocodiles were survivors, their species varying little from millions of years ago, and they could grow and live indefinitely as long as they didn't get sick and their environment provided them the food sources required. Only the lack of enough food to sustain growth stopped crocodiles from growing out of control.

Here in the Arcanium ring, Bell gave Maya infinite sustenance for as long as she could consume it. He allowed the healing to speed up a little — to give her another canvas, now that she had destroyed this one. To give her options.

She used the end of handle where the braiding attached to lift his chin and guide him upright. She flitted her consideration from the smooth skin where his nipples had been down to his cock, which was slightly erect, but not due to the kind of arousal that had warmed him before.

A naked human had a tendency to diminish, even seem comical. A naked demon rarely did. But through the Ringmaster's eyes — not hers, because he still respected her autonomy in what she was doing tonight — Bell appeared more human than usual after a hundred lashes. He had diminished.

In his pain, in his weakness, in his detachment, all the world narrowed to the light in the ring, as though nothing else existed and there was only this dungeon.

And it *was* a dungeon, this place she had made for him.

Without his psychic connection, he couldn't read her. She was as inscrutable to him as stone, the pass of emotions in her eyes and over her face unreadable, enigmatic — not in a fortune teller way but in the way most people felt about the Ringmaster.

Which, right now, she was. She was the master of the ring, with the owner of Arcanium under her whip and the Ringmaster himself at her beck and call. Bell wondered whether the Ringmaster realized that he'd handed over his own leash to her without protest and that she could use that power against him another, more unfortunate day. At least she didn't know his name to chain him completely. No one knew his name, and Bell hadn't needed it to snap the chains around him. Brute power did just as well in a pinch.

Where was Bell's power now, and that of the terrifying Ringmaster? In the blood-specked hands of a little girl with frizzy hair, stained clothes and dark circles under her eyes.

"I'm. Exhausted. I knew it was going to be hard, but no one could have told me just how exhausting this is. I won't be raising my arm for a week. Aren't you going to ask me to stop?"

Bell leaned forward on his hands so that his back didn't have to hold him up as much. "You can stop at any time."

"I'm definitely done with the whip for now." She held it out from her, regarding the blood and dust with distaste. "I'm not sure how to present this to you again," she said to the Ringmaster.

The Ringmaster stood from the partition and took the handle. Usually, he wouldn't bother cleaning anything until it was time to put them away, but he shook the lash, sending several waves through its length, until the blood and sawdust disappeared, leaving the leather beautifully black and glossy once again. Maya had said she was done 'for now'. She might want another go at it, and if that was the case, the Ringmaster would present her with a whip ready for its closeup.

Hands empty, Maya touched Bell's face, inspecting him with a guise of indifference, but he could read enough to know that indifference was the last thing she felt when she looked at him. The face he knew she saw had surely lost some of its own color, like hers, under the cold sweat, and the amber of his hazel eyes had probably faded, like resin stone instead of a lantern, because he'd tamped his magic down to be the victim she needed him to be. The whites of his eyes would be red, but although he was capable of producing tears, tears were not generally how jinn or demons expressed sorrow or pain.

"How long will it take you to heal?" she asked.

"At the present pace, ten minutes."

Maya glanced over at the Ringmaster. "Do you have a rack somewhere? Something to spread his wrists and ankles like quartering rather than just pulling him in two directions, please."

The Ringmaster nodded, transporting Bell from the bloodstained bench to a smooth, well-oiled, polished frame. He shackled Bell's wrists and ankles to chains attached to a roller at both ends of the frame. Bell had been flipped onto his back, which was still raw and exposed. He hissed, every shift from the pain offering no relief, but he didn't speed up the already-increased healing. He would heal soon enough, and lying on his own nerves had been Maya's design.

Maya ran her fingertips along the grain of the wooden frame. "This, I remember." She found the handle that turned the roll. The ratchet clicked, and his arms and legs stretched taut—not enough to strain his joints or muscles but to keep him from shifting. Then she adjusted the frame to tilt Bell up about forty-five degrees.

She took a drink from her water before offering it to Bell. He lowered his head, although the strain against his shoulders, which pulled the wounds on his back wider, made that position excruciating.

Maya allowed him to gulp down three deep swallows before withdrawing the straw. He could go all night without water, but it soothed his dry, hot mouth, and he didn't have to work so hard at replenishing his blood with water absorbing into his system.

Maya set the cup back down. "I need something sharp," she said to the Ringmaster. "Your entire collection, whatever you have—knives, scalpels, boxcutters, spurs, broken glass, the works."

"I thought you'd never ask."

Next to the rack, the spotlight gleamed over a large table of every sharp implement that the Ringmaster could think of, including a sparkling pair of knitting needles to honor Kitty and a full set of thick-gauge sewing needles that Maya would also recognize. In addition to knives, swords and scalpels, he'd also thrown in the iron nails and fish hooks that Misha had once used in his act as well as meat hooks, a tongue tearer, an Iron Spider, a paper spike, several railroad spikes and an assortment of hammers, if any were necessary. He didn't limit the options to manual. He'd included a fully loaded nail gun and a staple gun as well.

Maya raised her eyebrows at the possibilities but bypassed the guns. She lingered at the sewing needles for a moment then grabbed a scalpel instead.

"Most of your favorites were booked for years before Locke even stole Arcanium," she said as she inspected the blade's shine, "but twice a month, he had open auctions, which guaranteed he'd get four or five times what he'd sold the pre-bookings for. Do you know what almost all of them did to me?"

Bell could have answered yes, but she wasn't really asking.

"Even though there weren't a lot of ways for gossip to reach beyond the borders of Arcanium — because who the hell were we going to tell? — everyone knew who your favorites were, who you'd claimed as your own more than the others. You staked your claim in some indeterminate way so that any demon who entered Arcanium would know that they were extra-protected to make up for the extra attention. As a way to show us that we weren't yours anymore, they would…*carve* their names into us."

Maya pressed the ready edge of the scalpel to his ribs, where the close bone would enhance the pain and give her something to push against as she cut her name into his skin. He didn't scream, but every breath, every hiss, brought him closer to her. She didn't start small, and she didn't bother making sure she didn't cut something she shouldn't. She sliced until some of the lines scored bone.

"One man carved his name onto me over and over again for half the night, from my forehead to my ankles, before he convinced me in another way to whom I really belonged. Do you know what it's like to have something carved into your lips, Bell? What about your tongue? I had a ring attached to my tongue for one session, connected to the headboard while the demon fucked me with both his dicks." Maya brought the bloody scalpel to his lips. "*Slave.* That's what I was, and that's what you are tonight. You belong to me. Everything you have, everything you are, is mine."

From his lips, she dipped back down to his chest, where she tested what designs she was capable of creating with a sharp enough edge—spirals, paisley, flowers, crosshatch. She had to keep wiping the blade on her shirt, like an artist dipping her brush in water.

"Very good." Maya set the scalpel back on the table, gravitating back toward the needles. "You remember these, I'll bet. No one else used needles against me quite like you. There was an art to what they did, of course—like acupuncture but the other way around. What you did to me was visually stunning, stimulating and didn't hurt like what they did. What you did was surface. They sent the needles deep. Before tonight, I didn't know how they managed to find every single pressure point and a few I'd never even thought of."

"I think I'd quite like to see what you make of me."

Maya hesitated before gathering the needles into her palm and bringing them to the rack. His cock was still slightly erect, not even half. The acid-sting of the cuts had done nothing to lessen or increase it. He reacted to systemic stimulation, regardless of what that stimulation was. When he was truly aroused, she wouldn't question whether it was happening.

"This isn't working, is it?" She prodded at one of the crosshatch marks on his abdomen—a particularly effective method, because it had required her to slice over an existing cut that had already started the nerves singing.

"I have bled for you. I have screamed for you." He couldn't touch her, couldn't smooth the dark cloud of her hair, smudge away the blood spatter from her cheeks. "I cannot cry—at least not the way you do—and I cannot stop my healing if you're to take the full measure of your revenge. What more do you wish of me?"

Maya leaned in, almost close enough to kiss. The way she glanced at his bloody lip, he wondered if she would, and he parted his lips in reactive anticipation, his emotions raw, and with them, his desires, despite the inevitable denial of the night. The pain she'd dealt had sewed her like scar tissue to him, violent but inexorable connection — craving underneath the rawness.

"I don't know how to make you despair," she whispered. Her lips brushing his captured some of his blood like the lipstick she'd always worn on circus days. It was her color.

"I am capable of feeling multiple things at once. What makes you think I don't despair?"

"Because you know this will end, and it was your choice. Your choice to accept it, your choice to continue accepting it. I never had that choice." She caught his lower lip between her teeth and sucked it with an exaggerated passion.

The flesh was already so sensitive, bee-stung under her tongue, although it hadn't swelled much. All the cuts she'd made over him flushed at the edges, inflammation framing the thin lines of blood that followed the contours of his body down to the rack.

In her false tenderness, Maya smeared a few of the clean blood lines with her palm, wrist and elbows. If she hadn't looked like a serial killer after she'd finished whipping him, she certainly did as she pulled back from her bloody kiss. Or perhaps a moonlighting surgeon with a penchant for suturing, although she wasn't holding a curved surgical needle — just a plain, shiny sewing needle with an eye at the top.

"I guess I have to keep trying." She plunged the needle into his navel.

The rack held him down…but only barely.

When she was done with sharp, he had seven needles in his navel—torture's answer to how many angels could dance on the head of a pin—two in the crook of each elbow, two through each wrist, and two rows up his neck from his collarbone. She'd found a place between his fingers in the main part of his hand that made him throb like advanced rheumatoid arthritis.

She'd used one of the silver knitting needles to pierce between two ribs and puncture a lung. When she'd removed the needle, the lung had collapsed. He'd struggled fruitlessly against the shackles until his magic could patch the puncture and reinflate the lung.

Then she'd dotted needles in the middle of the cuts she'd made, places already lit with little fires.

After she'd used all the needles, she stepped back, taking in the crimson and silver brushstrokes in the work of art she'd created.

"What time is it?" she asked the Ringmaster, as emotionless as the demon himself.

"A quarter past midnight."

"I'm sure Kitty's wondering where you are. I have some things I'd like to do, and I don't think I can do them with an audience."

A demon on her shoulder would only remind her of the angel she was supposed to have. The hellborn made her think too much of heaven.

"But I am the only audience who can appreciate what you do." Of the two of them, the Ringmaster exhibited the most emotion—disappointment. It would have been amusing had a swarm of hornets not been living in Bell's flesh.

"Another time, perhaps."

The Ringmaster straddled the partition between the ring and the entrance. "Shall I leave you anything before I go? Thumbscrews? A pear of anguish, perhaps?"

"A pair of pliers and the whip, please. The rest should do in a pinch."

They were an eerie match, the Ringmaster and Maya. They appeared cut from the same cloth, so cavalier and polite, although the Ringmaster was normally polite with no one—other than his usual exception—and Maya wouldn't actually be cavalier about torture.

She'd erected a series of plexiglass walls between herself and her feelings. It was no wonder the torture didn't satisfy.

The Ringmaster made the collection of pliers—from large, blunt instruments to smaller ones meant for more delicate work—available among his array of sharp things. But the whip he handed to Maya personally.

"A brimstone heart swells with pride to see such things. I would very much like to see it again."

Maya accepted the circle of leather tucked in her arm. "You never know."

The Ringmaster didn't necessarily appear to surprise her, other than that he lowered down to her at all, but a wall cloud cycling down to the ground would alarm anyone. When Maya visibly tensed, the Ringmaster seemed to allow her time to withdraw. She didn't.

He licked Bell's blood on her lips then delved into her mouth to give her a taste as well, steadying her chin with a finger, the only other point of contact.

"You have no idea how much I would like to see more one day," he murmured against her lips. "Perhaps I shall let Katharine know, hmmm?"

Maya didn't say anything else, and the Ringmaster needed no acknowledgment. He left with an even stride, as though he hadn't been sitting on an uncomfortable wooden partition for four hours, watching a jinni tortured to what would have been his death at least twice, were he a weaker man.

"I told you, Maya, that you can do anything to me," Bell said quietly. "No matter what you do, I will not judge you for it."

"Maybe I'd rather not be celebrated for it."

"If you're ashamed, love, why are you doing it?"

"Because it has to be done." Maya picked up the nail gun. "I'm trying. I'm trying to make you understand what this was like. But I don't think it's getting through. You're giving honest reactions. I know you too well to believe you're faking. You don't fake reactions. You hide them, sometimes, like everyone, but you don't fake what you're feeling."

She brought the nail gun to the center of his chest, right in the middle of his sternum.

A nail punched through the bone as though it were balsa wood. Bell jolted from the lightning bolt of pain and the glancing damage to his heart. His shout grated through his throat like the prongs of a rake.

"Like that. That was real. But the problem…" She aimed the nail gun dead center on his forehead. "The recovery's too fast."

She squeezed the trigger again, and this time she kept it squeezed, sending nails one after another deep into his skull.

* * * *

When he woke from the black, the nails had been pushed out of his head and chest to roll down the frame to the ring floor. They'd been joined by the needles as well.

Maya had dragged the bench over to the rack. She cradled the garish orange nail gun in her lap like a cat and held her head in her hand, her eyes closed.

The metallic click from the shift of his limbs in the shackles alerted her that he was awake, but she didn't open her eyes. She'd seen him recover from a crushed skull and disembowelment. It took more than most mortal means to kill him, and it would require a near-complete obliteration of his magic to manage it. While he'd been unconscious, he hadn't been able to hold back his magic anymore. He woke up almost pristine but for the stains of blood left behind, with only ghosts of the burning and stinging of his wounds.

"I can slow the healing down, but if I were to strip it away entirely, you'd kill me. I don't think that's what you want." Bell tilted his head, trying to see her face behind the hair from her ponytail hiding her. "But I might be wrong."

"It's not your physical recovery that bothers me. It's not getting through because you're not begging. You keep reassuring me that I can do anything, like a Master telling his new sub it's okay to cry. This isn't *doing* anything to you. It's not enough of a mindfuck."

"Only because you're afraid to take me there."

Maya looked up. Tears streaked her cheeks, and her eyes were red. She'd waited until he was unconscious to cry.

"It's clear to me why you told the Ringmaster to leave," he said. "If it was for my untimely demise by nail gun, I'm sorry to disappoint you. But I don't believe you tried to permanently kill me. You're just building up the strength to do it, because it doesn't come naturally to you."

"You think I should do it. You're actually telling me to do it." Maya pushed herself off the bench, leaving the nail gun on the plank. "That's the whole goddamn problem!"

"Do you think I've always been this powerful? Do you think the reason I've given you this place and time to do whatever you want to me is because it doesn't affect me, has never affected me? This was never about me, but this is far from the first torture session I've endured. And I can endure another one. *You* endured it. It may not feel like you did, but you're still here, love. There's only so much you can do to deny that."

"I died hundreds of times from what they did to me. If we'd been anywhere but Arcanium and under the influence of anything other than demons, we all would have died within the first week, within the first few *days*. The first night, he *crucified* me, Bell."

"I know what he turned Arcanium into, just as you know why I couldn't give you what you begged for last night, even if you didn't remember why then." Bell shifted on the rack, but really, there wasn't much he could do with his body, taut as it was. All he had was the mildness in his voice, the memories they'd shared that she now had in abundance. "What I make of Arcanium and what he made of it are fundamentally opposed, but they were different sides of the same coin, which was why it was such an insult on every level."

"Yes, we can't have a demon insulting you by turning Arcanium into a proper demon brothel. Better to be an occasional human brothel. Less rude."

"I'm not talking about epithets. Words have weight, of course, but when I say insult, I mean he subverted and perverted everything that made Arcanium unique and wonderful. He made it a place where his guests rather than his cast had all the power, where desires were twisted into torture. They may have seemed the same from the outside, but can you look me in the eyes, Maya, and say that what I did to you was the same thing? You have the pliers here, my dear. There's no need to fling a lie in the hope that it'll stab as deeply as a knife."

"No. What you did to me wasn't torture. I know that, even if I didn't then. What the Ringmaster did was, but ten to twenty lashes weren't anything in comparison, and I went to him for my own reasons."

Maya trailed her fingers over the beautiful line of almost sensuous knives — some utilitarian and unadorned and others curvaceous, with handles made of expensive material, steel etched with elaborate designs. "For a long time, I thought the reason I was in Locke's Arcanium was for the same reason you took care of me and the reason I went to the Ringmaster. He was so fond of using religious imagery with me *because* I thought I deserved it, punished forever for thinking that there was anything I could do to return to a state of grace I had no intention of staying in."

She picked up a dagger, slender, elegant, less gleaming than the others because the steel was dark instead of silver.

"That's not how absolution works, and I knew it. So did he. He spent most of his time with Neve and the

Spider, of course. He devoted so much to them, as you once devoted so much to me. But sometimes he took time out of his busy schedule skull-fucking Neve to take me to one of the guest rooms."

Maya brought the tip of the knife to her wrist, where scars from after leaving Arcanium and before joining Illumina already marked her. "That's a mortal sin, too. I had to bring this one up to the priest Fairuza knew, which was the most fun ever, along with every other mortal sin I had to confess. He told me that anything that happened during Locke's Arcanium required nothing. He gave me penance for what happened before and for what happened after. I did everything he told me to do, three times over. It wasn't enough. I'm not forgiven, and I never will be. Locke wasn't wrong about that."

Bell kept silent, even as she breached the flesh next to the scar and drew it up her arm. She didn't appear disturbed when blood failed to flow from her as readily as it did from him. She stared at the cuts, open, red but not bleeding, parallel to the ones she'd made months before.

"People think repentance means asking for forgiveness or saying you're sorry. But to repent literally means to turn back your way of thinking, to change course. To repent from your sins means promising to God, the way you wish to jinn, that you'll never do it again. Maybe you will, but you don't repent if you intend to run right back to the sin you asked absolution for. And if you don't repent, absolution is meaningless." The cuts closed, sealed over as though they had never been there, without even an echo of the scars. "Kind of like trying to cut yourself in Arcanium when you know the jinni's magic is just going to close it again. Meaningless."

"Maya..."

She held up the dagger in lieu of a finger to stop him from talking. "I left everything behind. I repented when I asked Fairuza to take my memories. I thought that would excise the worst of my worst. But I repented again, didn't I? I sought it out, knowing instinctively that what I uncovered would be worse than the most terrible thing I was capable of imagining. I sought it out anyway, because something was wrong with me when I didn't have the worst of myself. I missed it without even knowing what it was."

She plunged the dagger into his abdomen, just under the temple of his ribs, catching his diaphragm so that every gasp and cry shredded deeper. Still holding the dagger, just short of cutting her palm, she brought herself close to him, more intimate at that moment holding the blade inside him than when she'd kissed him.

"You want me to do to you what Locke did to me?" Maya drank in the sight of him, from his healed face down to the new blood welling from the wound like a fresh spring.

"Yes," he hissed, his teeth bared and eyes narrowed against the pain. "It's what you need to do."

Maya jerked the knife out and brought it to Bell's throat. Even if she slit it, that wouldn't kill him, although slicing an artery would eliminate his blood faster than he could replenish it, weakening him. In the meantime, his abdominal wound gushed, nothing left plugging the hole she'd made. For the sake of keeping his consciousness this time, he quickened the healing process. His whole body was bloodstained now, but that didn't appear to repel her. She'd been bloodstained enough herself during the course of Locke's reign.

"Did you know that when a criminal threatens with a knife instead of a gun, people are more compliant? A bullet is separated from you at the barrel. A knife is more personal, more primal, no matter the technology that goes into making it. We think a knife to the throat will cause a more painful death than a gun to the head. Maybe when Locke eventually opened us up to humans as well as demons, he would have made more trigger-happy weapons available, but nothing could make us go compliant like a knife. When Locke took me aside, everything he used on me was sharp."

In his true form, Locke had been taller than Bell in his, with longer limbs and flesh deep red and veiny beneath nearly transparent skin. His teeth and claws had rivaled Ciarán's, prehistoric in scale. He wouldn't have needed instruments of torture when his body had been weapon enough, the tips of his claws scalpels, teeth his daggers. What he'd done with them when he and Maya had been alone had been much like what he'd done to Neve and Lizzie, because agreeing to be his slaves had provided them a certain amount of protection, even from him. But Maya had denied him.

Maya withdrew the knife from Bell's throat. Although the damage wouldn't have been permanent, Bell let out the breath he'd been holding. She set the knife aside and picked up the whip. Then she shifted the frame to lie horizontal once more.

"Of course, there are things that he did that I'm simply unable to do. We'll get to that in a minute. First…" She turned the handle on the rack.

The ratchet clicked a few grooves. His already taut muscles stretched in every direction. Bones strained in their joints and muscle fibers protested the tension, a few in his arms and legs tearing.

Then she turned the handle again.

Four nearly simultaneous pops marked the moment his legs and arms jerked out of their sockets. Bell shouted then bellowed again as she climbed onto the table between his legs, jostling the already indescribable pain that couldn't be healed because the rack held him apart. If she released him from the shackles, he would be able to make all the repairs, but until then, he could only endure — and he *could* endure, because he *was* enduring, as she had endured the same fate a dozen times with her mortal body.

Maya lowered the bulbous end of the whip handle to Bell's lips. "You have one chance. Use your saliva, use magic, it doesn't matter, but this is your opportunity to make sure this is ready enough. I would have stuck it into your stab wound, but you healed that too quickly."

"I can open it again," Bell tried to say, but she pushed the leather into his mouth.

The knotted strips were tough, with little give against his teeth, and it was almost the same size and thickness as his own cockhead, a comparison that hit him suddenly and hard, in spite of the bolts of pain with every slight movement. She'd rendered him a being of sensation — already his natural state, but pain inhibited reason, enhanced his sense of his solely physical self. His cock, which had deflated while he'd been unconscious, didn't just awaken but came alive.

There was a reason the Ringmaster had been so proud. Bell was in so much pain that he wanted to shatter iron, splinter wood and crush Maya beneath him until she realized how small she was in comparison. She'd brought him so low that only the hair's breadth of will left within convinced him to remain enslaved — for her.

Bell coated the end of the handle with his saliva as best as he could with a dry mouth. When she pulled it out, he also coated it with a thick layer of magical lubrication, the kind he would apply to his cock before doing what she planned to do with that whip. It hadn't been the Ringmaster's intention in giving it to her for the night, but this also wouldn't be the first time that the whip had been used in such a manner — on a much more receptive partner and with a much more loving spirit.

"Does this excite you?" She knocked his thighs with her knees to give herself more space to work with and make him scream again. "How the fuck can this excite you? How can you be broken beyond your ability to repair and still your cock is growing because you know what's coming? I'm not going to be gentle. I'm not going to care. I'm not doing this for you. Whether you go slug-dick or come your brains out is irrelevant to me. I didn't have a choice. You do. But the fact that you're still *choosing* not to have a choice is even more pathetic."

Her affect and voice remained flat, but her wrist threatened to go slack when she brought the knot behind his scrotum. Her belly quivered as she struggled to convince herself to breathe.

"Do it," he whispered. "I'm asking you to."

"You're a damned fool, Bell. We both are."

She didn't prepare him, and unlike Bell, she had no magic to make room. She grabbed him by the balls and shoved the end of the handle into Bell's ass.

Once inside, in spite of the way it seemed to *rip* through and he *pushed* back as tightly as he could, she pushed right back, working the handle inside him like a cock, forcing it almost halfway up with each thrust inside. She grunted from the effort, but her eyes hooded as she stared down at him, meeting his gaze, although she had to see that his cock grew, and grew, and grew, in spite of the excruciation from each jostle of disjointed bones and torn, strained, useless muscles.

She filled him without mercy or consideration, thrusts designed to punch inside him like a spike-knuckled fist. Pain took him from every direction. There was nowhere to strain away to or escape. He hadn't felt anything like this in four hundred years, not even in his battle against Locke and everything the demon could think of to destroy him.

She'd propped herself over him, but the faster she forced the whip handle in, the more she lost the strength in the rest of her. She lowered and lowered until her forehead almost rested on his, in spite of his deafening screams. Her tears struck his face. The more tears, like warm rain, the harder she fucked him.

Even in the midst of the all-encompassing pain that wracked him from every side and the taste of her tears hydrating the blood on his lips, salt on his tongue, his erection drew up heavy and tight against his abdomen. The head bumped just above his navel whenever she shoved the handle in as far as she could.

It wasn't like when a demon took someone, the way they displaced anything in their way and entered a place no longer physical. Maya was eminently physical, and the whip handle was just a blunt instrument. She could only go so far without stabbing through his intestines. For him as opposed to her, this was far more real. It shamed him to be taken so crudely, in such a feral, grounded, human way, as she had been shamed in a demon's bed.

Maya's forehead pressed to his now, and she fell against his dislocated body — new strain, new avenues of pain — but she didn't stop fucking him. She moved her hips with the rhythm, the lash tangled around her leg, until it really was like *she* was fucking him, with none of the pleasure it could have given her if she'd felt what his pain could do for her, as it was doing to him. There was no way she couldn't feel how large he'd swelled, how insistently his pleasure made itself known, like black clouds streaking a red sky.

"God, you're disgusting. Are you making yourself do this? Are you hard because you think that's what I want from you, that it's secretly what I need?" Maya shook her head and tried to turn away from him, even though there was nowhere to go. Her hair smothered him, but it smelled so thickly of her and her shampoo that it wasn't an unpleasant way to lose his oxygen.

He managed to form words in the midst of his screams. "No. This is just me."

In the miasma of pain, pleasure became more and more substantial, coalescing low in his abdomen and gathering in his cock. It really was going to happen. He was going to come his brains out while she tortured him, and that wasn't something he'd planned to happen at all.

He'd always called Maya a true masochist. He hadn't known he was one himself. In a distant recess of his mind where he could form thoughts unrelated to what Maya was doing to him, he filed that away to peruse later. After a demon lover, after the Crusades and the Inquisition, after Locke, it had taken a human girl with guilt issues to show him he could love pain just as much as pleasure, that he could revel in all extremes to which a body could reach.

As she fucked him with the bulbous end of the handle, she was rubbing herself against the leather-wrapped wood, moaning through her tears in time with his screams. When the urge quickened in her, so did she in him. Bell made no effort to hold himself back, because the pain and the healing distracted him and he was too curious about what would happen in its own time.

She came first, with less to hinder the build of arousal. Disgust, guilt, shame, humiliation... None of those had ever stopped her from reaching her climax, only bolstered her desire in ways that he hadn't shaped but had used when she'd just been discovering what she was capable of.

Maya turned her head back toward him, her mouth against the corded tension in his neck, and sent her cries vibrating through him as she bucked harder to the dysrhythmic clenching of her orgasm. She stopped for a moment after it ended then resumed fucking him, faster, angrier, heavy over his broken body. He wrenched toward his own orgasm like a car without a driver, lifting his hips involuntarily now to feel her against his cock.

Even if he couldn't be inside her, he remembered. With her fucking him and with the memory of her surrounding him, he finally came, his cock heavy, full and oversensitive, the pressure in his balls and deep in his abdomen like fists.

And it seemed to go on forever, pleasure lighting up within him with the pain, sheet lightning in the storm that had been and was still raging. The harder he came, the more he wrenched his limbs and the more pain drove his pleasure—until pain and pleasure were the same and he couldn't tell which one wracked his body anymore, why he was screaming.

He could come for a long time, replenishing himself through each pulse, but it eventually had to end. Blood, sweat, tears, semen... They were filthy from the side effects of love and torture.

Bell snapped open the shackles. With a growling shout, he forced his limbs back into their joints then sewed up the fiber damage to his muscles, reviving his strength. The whip was still in his ass, but Maya had gone completely still now, and it wasn't the biggest thing he'd ever taken. After repairing himself, it didn't bother him that it was there, and with the full measure of his magic available, he could more than bear anything else if she decided to take the handle again.

But she didn't, nor did she order him back into the shackles, although he would have done it, stretched his muscles to the breaking point and dislocated his arms and legs all over again. She also didn't wrench away from his nakedness and the cum he'd marked on her, more symbolic than all the blood she'd shed. When he lowered his arms to cradle her gently through the continuing tears in a room that had otherwise gone silent, Maya instead let go of the whip handle and tucked her hands under his shoulders, burying her face in his neck.

"Even with his cock inside me and my bones torn out of joint, muscles stretched into uselessness, he made me come. But he didn't make me, did he? He didn't make me any more than you do, or the Ringmaster. You found it, but it was always there. He took it and showed me exactly what I am. I deserved what happened to me. He put me in hell, and I came for him every time. And not just for him. I didn't even need Sasha and Mikhail, did I? They forced us to watch, sometimes, if we were bought with others. I know it was only me. That's where I was supposed to be. I went to his hell to show me what's coming."

Bell knotted a fist in her hair and pulled her back. "No. I can't tell you whether this was part of a grander plan, but you were there because I failed in my promise to keep you safe. You weren't there because you belonged there, any more than Joanne did, or Seth, or Valorie, or Neve. You weren't the only one to come in a position you wouldn't have imagined you would."

"I know they did sometimes, if the demons wanted it of them, if half the fun was making them horny before hurting them or if the demons' own desires weren't tied to pain. But coming while tied to the rack, bleeding from my mouth and down my thighs from bite marks and claw marks? Did any of them come in the midst of the worst that a demon could devise, things meant only for the most excruciating pain?"

Bell slid his other hand into her hair, holding her up and tugging at the roots to soothe her as much as to make sure she looked him in the eyes. "You and I, *azizam*, are unique. You always have been, before anyone would have known what to do with you. But the way your body reacts to pain doesn't make it wrong, and having a body at all doesn't make you impure. You came when he tortured you. That's *why* he tortured you like that. There is no morality in pain, Maya. It's the very definition of extenuating, and it *was* hell, my dear, the world he brought you into. You were there because of chance, fortune and a cunning demon taking advantage of my weakness—nothing more.

That's not where you belong, under him, in that kind of pain, whether you came for him or not."

"How can you know that?" She shoved at his chest, but he didn't budge, and he didn't let her go. "How can you know that, when I'm no longer under your protection and the knife blade works next time, I'm not sinking straight under some other Ringmaster for the rest of eternity?"

"Because you've suffered and been punished and punished yourself far more than you could ever deserve. And because I would never send you there in the first place. Am I more merciful than the Creator you follow? I only ever punished you because you derived pleasure from it, in spite of yourself. I gave you what you needed, everything you ever desired. I would spare you everything if I had that choice. Am I more merciful, Maya, than your God? You are not meant for hell. You're meant for Arcanium."

Bell pushed the whip out now and discarded it to the side before raising himself up on the rack frame and gathering her into his lap, still holding her by the hair. The mess didn't bother him, and she barely noticed.

"Arcanium *is* hell," she said. "I've seen the hell that you and the Ringmaster made, before and now. The Voodoo Torso is still in the haunted funhouse. The Man-Doll. I can tell who's still in hell by the look in their eyes. It's the same look we saw in each other, through distance and glass, in Locke's Arcanium, the same hell we tried not to see when you kept so many prisoners."

"A dungeon is supposed to be hell on earth. I changed it to suit my needs, which was never permanent torture. Locke's Arcanium expiated any debt they had with me and more, which was why I released all except those I promised Elizabeth I'd keep.

Otherwise, I required service and, yes, repentance. Misha paid his debt and repented, yet he was tortured by Locke just the same. Arcanium isn't hell, Maya. It's the purgatory that you first believed it was. You were part of that purgatory only when you were first whipped, because you transgressed. That was it. Every other punishment, you asked for because you sensed impurity and corruption in yourself that was never there. I became your demon because that was what you required of me, just as I became your victim."

"You weren't my victim. You escaped the shackles. Nothing's broken anymore. It's not the same. It wasn't the same." She grabbed his wrists to pull him away, but he still didn't let her go. "It's...not...enough."

"This wasn't about punishing me. This was about punishing yourself. Again. It's not dolls and drawings, love, but this was your psychodrama. You haven't been able to talk about this with anyone, even Fairuza, even yourself, because shame has always been rooted in every part of you like a parasite."

He shifted his hold on her hair to massage her scalp. The rack tilted to the side as Bell brought them down onto the cushion that appeared in the middle of the ring. Not a bed, because she would resist a bed—more like a giant pillow atop an equally giant ottoman, something soft on which to land, with blankets that he gathered around her, eliminating the filth from both of them at once.

"So you think I'm fixed now? Everything's going to be fine because I said something out loud? It hasn't changed anything. Everything's still rotten inside me, and you are still fucking incapable of understanding what it was like—"

"I apologize in advance." He pressed his forehead against hers again, creating the contact that made it so much easier to connect to her mind in turn, although it was such a familiar place that it wouldn't have taken much more effort. It was good, having her this close again—chest to chest, skin to skin, even with her still clothed—without her wrenching away from him.

With his forehead to hers, he sent her what it had been like when he'd wrested Arcanium back. The demons and monsters who had populated the stadium had been contained and silenced, leaving only the tortured cast of Arcanium in the empty parking lot he'd created over the razed building. He'd been able to ignore his people in the white noise of evil around him to focus on Locke and on Neve, because the demon's power had been linked to her. When the white noise had disappeared into crystal prisons, he hadn't been able to ignore them anymore.

In that moment, their pain had been his, and all he'd been able do with his phenomenal power was try to make their bodies hurt less. He'd witnessed them in every bit of their agony—hooks, infected amputations, lash marks, blood and bars and holes where there shouldn't have been. And that had just been the damage he could see at that present moment, which would have been enough without the screaming, wailing, crying and dead silence that had stretched through the months of Locke's Arcanium and which had invaded him without filter as though it were his own. All the sharp things had stabbed into in his skull, pierced him inside and out as though he'd swallowed then injected ground glass—from everyone, from those he loved most down to the meanest prisoner. Regret had cut jagged on his tongue and in his throat.

Maya had accused him of not being able to understand human pain because he wasn't human, but that couldn't be further from the truth. He'd just endured too much of it.

Maya tightened her grip on the cage of his ribs until her nails dug into his skin and drew blood, but that was nothing in comparison to the pain he sent her, the pain he shared. Not just her whole experience, day by day, in Locke's Arcanium, but everyone else's all at once *and* day by day *and* at that moment, layer upon layer of individual hells. Her mouth dropped open as she struggled to breathe, her eyes open but unseeing from the depth of what he had felt and continued to feel.

He carried her through the tumult, gave her a soft, warm place to land when it receded. She cried again, this time in wails and screams of her own. Her mortal brain couldn't hold that many feelings at once like his, but it could remember with a mortal's naturally fading memory what it had been like. And now that she wasn't crying for herself, she could express without feeling dead, without feeling like a mockery of suffering.

"It's not that I don't understand what you went through, that I'm incapable of feeling or comprehending human pain because I'm not human," he whispered, his breath hot so close to her. "I was there with you, through everything—not as it happened but after I found you again. I didn't continue Arcanium because I care so little but because I care so much. I've lived through so much suffering over all my thousands of years on this earth. I've learned not just to endure but to persist, and I wasn't going to let Locke destroy something that I loved any more than he already had."

He wiped her tears, cleaned the blood and the mess again, because even though crying always felt like it would never stop, it always did. "There might be a time when Arcanium shuts its doors, but not when there are people who still need it. I don't create these relationships to trap people here. Relationships make it easier to burn through the purgatory, sometimes of their own making. And sometimes of mine. I don't deny that. But my dear, beautiful woman, it's not forever. And even those who develop attachments leave. Fairuza left. Valorie would have left within a few years on her own. I would have let you go when you asked for freedom. I did let you go when you walked away. I'm not a monster, Maya, and I'm not a demon just because you think I enjoy myself too much. All I ever tried to teach you was that you don't have to beg forgiveness from the saints just to live. After living through hell, how can you still believe that you deserved it, that pleasure condemned you to the pain that you experienced? Is Kitty a saint, that she was spared in the hands of another demon? Her desires run almost as deep and dark as your own. What of the others of mine? Did they deserve their fate?"

"You and I will just have to agree to disagree on theology," Maya said thickly. "We always have."

"No. You disagreed and sought to be punished at every turn because you couldn't stop yourself from wanting what you wanted. Then you kept going in spite of the punishments giving you the same pleasure you sought to punish yourself for. We can disagree on who created the world and why, but I won't feed your desire for atonement anymore." He kissed her forehead where he had sent the memories through her, apology and devotion at the same time. "If you want pain,

Maya, I will give you pain. If you want to cause pain, I will give you something to torment. Those are your desires, and I can feed them forever, my love. But if you want to be punished for those desires, I will no longer indulge you."

"Then what fucking good are you to me?" Maya struggled from his arms and onto the overly soft pillow, rolling until she found the edge of the cushion and fell to the sawdust on her hands and feet. She stood and immediately strode for the big top entrance, leaving the torture implements behind for the Ringmaster to retrieve later.

Bell appeared behind her. When she turned, he drew her against him by the wrist. Although he was also still naked, she didn't stiffen.

"You came to me when you couldn't remember Arcanium — mine or Locke's. When you were in Illumina, with no memory of a demonic circus and what it had made you question, you invited yourself into Fairuza's bed. And it made you happy, happier than when you first came to me in the company of your dearly disjointed ex. Because Illumina harbors a few, you knew that real demons existed, yet though you continued to go to Mass and confession, you still found room to take pleasure from life. Guilt hadn't taken such a strangling grip upon you. It's why you came to me in the Funhouse."

"You refused me," Maya said quietly.

"Not because I didn't want you. I want you more than the sun, moon and stars, my love. But even if you don't return to me, *golam*, I want you here in Arcanium now, because it's safer than it ever was and because you crave what it provides. It's no coincidence that you went to Fairuza when you thought you couldn't come back to me. You crave something you can't get out there, something you only had while part of a demonic circus."

"If I'm craving something from a demonic circus, then I've no business staying. You'll have to find someone else to coax into your web, dissolve into something you can consume until there's nothing left."

Bell slapped her cheek, more sound than substance, but it shocked Maya into staggering back. "I told you to bite your tongue, Maya. I won't have you cheapen yourself or what we had. *Wishes* are what I feed upon. People are not my prey, and you should know better than anyone that you were not destroyed by what I did. Fairuza didn't bring Illumina to Arcanium because she thought her people needed a little predation in their life."

"No, you just think I do," Maya retorted, stepping toward him again.

"I think you have unique tastes, and there are very few places in the world where you can indulge in them without danger."

Maya laughed without humor, throwing up her hands. "You don't get it. You just don't get it."

"You thought that about pain, too. You've thought that about a lot of things. I understand more than you think. I was there when belief started. I've seen how theologies were shaped. I myself was the subject of worship for quite a long time when human beings looked for the divine in magic. Would you like to see the beginning? Would you like to see them worship? I watched them bow to the volcano to beg it not to destroy them, pray to the winds and rivers to keep their houses upright, to the earth to give them good crops. You think I don't understand your theology, but the truth is that I dismiss it. Is the reason you've never asked the Ringmaster whether hell is what you've believed because you secretly fear how wrong you've been?"

Maya stilled.

"You had absolution from your priest, but even when you weren't planning on committing the same mortal sins, it wasn't enough. This isn't about belief. This isn't about God and whether He is merciful to those who stumble into hells on earth, run by demons or man. This is about you being afraid — afraid of what you desire. It was why you chose men who undermined you before you came to Arcanium. It was why the only way you could tolerate my love was if it was also punishment. And it's why you've never escaped Locke's Arcanium, even though Locke is a shriveled miniature of what he was. He's *nothing*. He's nothing, and you are infuriating and strong and extraordinary and the only one pulling you deeper into his hell is *you*. Not God. Not me. *You*."

Maya raised a hand, calling a thick hunting knife to her palm.

Bell spread his arms, giving her an adequate target. "I'll do it again for you, Maya. I'll be your victim and slave for weeks. It doesn't matter what you want to do to me, what you want me to do to you. The only thing I'll *not* do is punish, not the way you want to be punished. Not anymore."

She advanced on him. In the shadow, she could have been the demon again, dark-eyed and bright-toothed. "You'd let me do it all over again. You'd let me play demon. You'd let me *be* demon. Or you'd be demon to me."

"Whatever makes you happy, love."

"You always called this a demonic circus." She lowered the knife but continued toward him. "It was never a jinn circus."

"I don't have to explain demons to Americans like I do jinn. Easier to use the word people associated with horror."

Maya brought the curved knife point up to his cheek, the serrated edge inches from his mouth. "You said you'd be demon for me. How can you be demon if it's not inside you?"

"How can *you*?"

She raised an eyebrow for a split second then jerked him down by the back of the neck, shifting the knife, but not fast enough to keep from nicking him. It was the very definition of a surface wound, and after the hell she'd put him through, he barely noticed it.

Especially when she let her arm fall altogether and kissed him. It wasn't gentle or slow or soft. She kissed him hard, giving herself neither time nor room to talk herself out of it. The events of the night and the memories of her own hell were still very much present, shuddering through her into him. But so was the fact that she'd dreamed of him, and not always in nightmares, although every dream about Arcanium had been a nightmare when she hadn't wanted to remember.

Kissing her now wasn't like kissing her during the Funhouse, although that had been achingly lovely, so close to what he'd lost. This Maya—harder, sharper, darker, colder and hotter at the same time, crueler and guiltier because of it—was still very much his Maya, because when she kissed him, it was with the flavor of every single day and night that they'd spent together. She knew who he was, everything he'd done and everything she'd done, and it was so much sweeter that he could kiss her like this when she knew what she was doing.

He wrenched the knife from her hand, the cut she'd made nothing but a smear on his cheek now. Maya gasped into his mouth, but she tightened her hold to keep him close, parting her lips more to take him deeper.

He brought the knife to her shoulder. She cried out, reactive fear adding an edge to her moan as he pulled away from her mouth and followed the messy cut he made across her shoulder, slicing and ripping the exposed bra strap over the wide neckline of the shirt. The wound was only a little deeper than the one she'd given his cheek. He had no intent to torture her as he licked back across the line, gathering her blood, before closing slightly sharpened teeth into the base of her neck. She moaned again, this time without a trace of fear.

He sucked on her skin, on her blood, then let it gather to drag up her neck to her lips. "Maybe a little bit of demon," he murmured, before dipping down to give her a taste.

They stumbled back toward the light of the ring. He stopped them when he reached the wooden partition, but only to lift her up so that she could wrap her legs around his waist. Then he rocked over the partition – a delicate procedure while nude, but something he'd done before – and they landed back in the sawdust.

Still holding her up, Bell stared into those dark eyes that hadn't lightened, although the red in the whites had faded some. Color had returned to her cheeks, to her lips, and not only from the smears of blood. When he looked into her, he didn't just see desire or a need to kill what hurt inside with a different road to endorphins than the knives she'd used. She was lucid, present and prepared to regret, but she expected the torture to hit her harder.

Bell brought the blade to her lips. She licked the blood at the tip, careful not to press too hard. That was permission enough for him.

He tossed the knife back to the table.

Maya depended on the strength of her legs and his hold on her as she pulled her T-shirt over her head. The fabric was stained again from her blood, but it hadn't been something she'd needed to preserve. She removed her ruined bra with the same disregard.

She brought herself back against him with some trepidation, the kind of fear that came from respecting his power, which he had over her whether he wielded it or not.

It had always been his task to remind her that, although he had power over her, she had nothing to fear from him, no matter how dark the hole into which he drew her, at her own request.

Bell stroked her hair from her face as she tucked herself close to him again, her arms around his neck.

"I'm here. You have me. Everything you wanted." Her disgust hadn't quite left, but it hadn't led to aversion, and she didn't jerk away from his fingers as he continued to stroke her hair.

"You are here. But I don't have you, and this is not everything I wanted. You are not owned. Whatever I do to brand you is impermanent, not a mark of property." He lowered her onto the cushion, urging her to release her legs from around his waist. "You were free as soon as you wished it. If you're here now, it is your choice, *golam*, not mine. Let neither of us be confused who has the power here."

"You."

"I've yielded my power to you for quite some time, Maya."

"If you have power to yield, that doesn't mean it goes away." She pushed herself up, bracing herself with her hands behind her, her legs hanging over the side of the cushion.

"I've always chosen my limitations. Just because I can revoke them doesn't mean that I'm not limited." Bell climbed onto the cushion to sit beside her. She pushed down her leggings and underwear, leaving herself as naked as he was. He took the last of her clothes and tossed them onto the floor with the rest. "While you were wearing your clothes, I couldn't touch your skin directly. Oh, I could have torn them away, slipped my hands underneath. But the clothing you wear is still a limitation you choose. Just because you can take them off doesn't make the limitation irrelevant while you are clothed."

"You know, that made a surprising amount of sense." She crawled backward toward the center of the massive cushion, beckoning him with the parting of her legs.

Like the slave he had made of himself tonight, he obeyed, stalking after her as though he wanted to consume her. And he did want to consume her, though not to nothing, like she'd believed. He wanted her to keep every ounce of substance that he now followed.

She took his hand when she could reach it to guide him next to her rather than above. She crossed her arms over herself but shifted closer. He aligned himself with her as well as he could, relishing her proximity more now than the sex she'd been willing to give him during the Funhouse. It was all he could do not to take her in his arms again, embrace her as though he would never release her from warmth and safety and the love that she'd never known what to do with. He would never forget the sight of her walking away from him — not from Arcanium, not really. She'd been walking away from *him*, and she hadn't looked back.

Tentatively, she uncrossed her arms, tracing the cut he'd made, unsettling the dark red to reawaken the wound. "I don't know what I am anymore."

"You don't have to know what you are. What you were five years ago is not what you will be five years from now, and if you fear what happens after you die, you needn't fear it yet, because here you will not die. There will be time to figure out what you are and what you want to be. If you want biblical references, I can —"

"No, I know what they would be." The slightest humor curved her lips, even if it was more self-deprecating than anything else. "Hebrews in the wilderness, prodigal son squandering money, Jonah with…everything. I get the picture. But things happen, Bell. You can't promise that again."

"Yet I have. Locke broke my last promise, but so many more of them are kept, locked and hidden."

"What I did to you…"

"I asked you to do to me."

"You agreed to do it. That's not the same thing. You didn't want it for yourself. If you hadn't been doing it for me, you wouldn't have done it at all. You wouldn't have chosen to be stabbed and broken and…" She couldn't say it. It was trapped in her throat, so poisonous that she nearly choked. "And I did that. I got off on it. Even when I was hating myself and nearly throwing up, I got off on it anyway. How could I... When I know what it was like for me, how could I do that to you and still come to it, as strong as I came to receiving it? What the fuck is wrong with me?"

Bell closed his hand around her throat, but he didn't squeeze, just drew her in to kiss her, startle her into less-complicated arousal—although not as uncomplicated as it could have been. When he wrapped his leg around hers to draw her closer still, she moaned, stroking down his back to his ass, to the strong thigh that held her.

"That's a question that Neve asks herself every day," he murmured, peppering her chin and jaw with more kisses. "But she knows the answer to that question is me, so she can dismiss it. Lizzie doesn't have it so easy, and neither do you. But I'm going to spend all the time that I have with both of you, love, to convince you that there's nothing wrong with you at all."

"I guess at least part of the question should be what's wrong with *you*. After what I just did..."

"Unlike you, I don't question what gets me off. I confess, that way will never be my favorite." Bell licked a line up her throat back to her mouth, where he delved in slowly, gently, before guiding her to her back so that he could raise himself over her. "It was a singular experience that even I didn't know I was capable of. And for that, you have my boundless gratitude. But don't believe that just because you *can* come to something you don't like, even actively hate, that it's the only thing you can love. We had such times together, Maya, some with pain and some with pleasure. Thrilling in one didn't mean you couldn't thrill in the other. Our bodies will feel how they feel, but we can still choose what we do. What Locke did to you, what you did to me, what we shared in that moment that you hated and loved at the same time... None of that has to mean anything now. You are strong. You are here. You are alive. And you are never boring, my dear."

"I don't understand you at all. I don't understand how you could have been on this earth as long as you have and ended up like you are. And I don't know why your impulse after tonight is still to seduce me." But she stroked over his chest, finding the nipples that had grown back, touching the places on his ribs where she had carved her name, where she had stabbed him, shot him.

"I'm seducing you? You kissed me first."

She pulled him down by the nipples, her intent pleasure rather than pain. He laughed as she kissed him again, this time taking control of his mouth instead of letting him take hers. There was far greater joy in yielding to her in this than the rack, and when he made his pleasure known, she took his cock in hand instead of shying away from it.

Bell knotted his fist in her hair to pull her head back. He lavished attention from the stinging base of her neck up to the lobe of her ear and the sensitive place just beneath it. He teased her with teeth, although he didn't bite her again. One mark would be enough tonight, after all the other marks on him that hadn't so much as scarred. He didn't fool himself that they were gone, though, that the circumstances that had created the events of that night had healed. Those wounds were still raw and angry, but he gave them what soothing balm he could as he stroked her in turn, trying not to confuse her pleasure any more tonight.

She tensed when he entered her with his fingers, two at once. She'd had sex with more than just Fairuza since she'd left Arcanium, but that had been when she'd had no memory of Locke and every other demon inside her. Bell used his magic to ease his way so that there could be no discomfort, even in her tension.

"Why do I still want this?" It was almost a moan, but plaintive, and she shook her head as she gasped and arched up into the beckoning of his fingers against the spot he could always find. It wasn't even a point of pride, just a point of fact, knowing where on a woman or man gave them the greatest pleasure. "Why do I still want you? I hated you. I'd go to sleep hating myself but hating you more. I blamed you for everything. You *were* to blame for everything. How can I let you...? How can I want you to...?"

He didn't let up on the thrusts and curl of his fingers inside her, though, because she gave no indication in word, deed or thought that she wanted him to stop — quite the contrary. "I told you, love. I stopped analyzing why I want what I want and love what I love a long time ago. You would have a lot more peace if you did the same."

Bell quickened his pace in her cunt, but he kissed her slowly, an aching counterpoint to make her chase him to match the pace.

"I don't want to think anymore," she said between kissing him, each break in her sentences lasting forever and no time at all. "I don't want to care. I don't want to hate myself. I don't want to hate you. I don't want to feel anything. Please. Take it away, just for a little while."

"I'll do my best."

Her cunt clutched at his fingers as she came, but he already knew that wouldn't be enough. He brought her through and over the orgasm then slowly withdrew, allowing her to adjust rather than leaving her empty.

As much as her memories abhorred contact, she still needed it, needed to feel safe even if she wasn't entirely certain that she was. As ever when they were alone, everything within him oriented almost solely toward giving her what she wanted and what she needed — what she needed more than she wanted, but if he could give her both, he would and did. Her wellbeing interested him so much more than his own needs, although he served them by serving hers.

"Don't be alarmed. I'm removing my limitations." He normally wouldn't warn her. She'd interacted with his true form far more often than most of his companions — with the exception of the demon, Elspeth, because he'd interacted with her true form more often as well — but Locke's Arcanium had given her too many memories of other large bodies over her, within her, although most demons chose their human faces for torture.

Maya nodded, sinking into the cushion, and he raised himself back up. Cleansing magic fluttered around them as he released the human body that contained him and shifted into that of the jinni. He shadowed the sun of the spotlight, shook his head as his hair lengthened and darkened, adjusted his position above her as his arms and legs grew and thickened — as *all* of him grew and thickened. In his true form, he was an ash-blue giant larger than Ciarán in every way, almost cartoonish to a human who had never encountered gods.

Except when someone touched him, they touched something more real than they, dense and hot, the fire and water from which he was made emanating like a furnace—but not hellfire. He was sunlight and a bonfire in the autumn, the blessing of a fever finally breaking, hot springs in the wilderness.

He had revealed himself to his whole circus when he'd fought Locke, but not all of them had noticed, so he could keep some of his secrets a little longer. It wasn't something that shamed him, but it was something that not all human minds could comprehend, and in the midst of humanity, he felt little need to appear extraordinary. Sleight of hand required his audience to believe in him, trust him and underestimate him so that he could show them wondrous things. If he was a god in their eyes, there could be no wonder greater than him.

But Maya knew this form intimately, had been taken by it in every way, possessed as a god could possess a woman. He had used his true form on her when she'd needed to be overwhelmed, when she'd needed permission to let go of all the fears that plagued her when she was near him. She'd since gained new fears, new troubled thoughts, but she was still a woman, a small, lush jewel in a jinni's bed, and as he lowered himself over her, using the pillow to keep from crushing her, he still overwhelmed her.

He gathered her like flowers against him and worshipped her as he had once been worshipped, leaving no part of her untasted. Under other circumstances, he would bring her off with his tongue on her clit and his massive fingers stretching her cunt much more than they had before, but she needed her mind taken. For that, he had to take all of her. He distracted her mouth with his then guided her kisses down to his chest so that he could bring his cock to her entrance. He split her in a way that would literally tear her apart if he weren't jinn, if he didn't open her like jasmine to the moon and take her beyond her physical body.

He bent down to kiss her again, moving his body in impossible ways over her, inside her, to give her everything he had. Every time she tried to get purchase, every time a thought tried to take root, he unbalanced her, shifted inside her body, reaching every sensitive nerve that lit her in flame with his own.

The big top tent no longer resounded with screams or sobs within the vast emptiness but her moans, his too deep to be anything but vibration beneath them, rattling the bleachers, shuddering the earth.

How many times they came was immaterial. There was no time in the arms of jinn when they took their pleasure. He could always make them clean, make them new, and a body never tired under his touch. Maya was exhausted, but this was better than sleep. Her thoughts were no longer her own, as though she were unconscious. She was in his hands, and he would not let her have bad dreams.

Chapter Thirteen

They did sleep, though. Bell gave Maya space in the aftermath, once he was sure that neither his touch nor its absence would distress her. He clasped her hand and nothing else before closing his eyes and shrinking back down to his human form. She fell asleep hard, sinking to deep sleep like a stone, and he allowed her to drag him under so that he could keep her dreams empty.

Maya woke him, tugging on his hand and squeezing it to coax him. Though there was no urgency, Bell opened his eyes quickly, unsettled for a reason that had nothing to do with what was inside the big top tent.

His mind was too quiet, even when he reached out on every spell thread to confirm everyone's presence. They were all there, but something blocked his mental connection to them, and fate itself blocked him from seeing forward or backward to know why the connection had been snuffed. But even the web of spells didn't seem right, the way an empty room echoed when furniture had been removed.

Maya had already dressed, her expression solemn. Guarded. Sad. "Something's happening."

Bell didn't invade her mind. Just seeing her like that aroused his suspicion. He abruptly released her hand then climbed from the cushion and gathered his clothes around him. Shuffling footsteps suggested that Maya followed him more slowly.

When he struck open the tent flap of the big top entrance, the bright midday sun strove to blind him, but his eyes adjusted far more quickly than those of a human.

The commotion—a low hum in a distance, punctuated by the occasional, abrasive shout—came from one of the few places in Arcanium that could be seen from the big top entrance.

The inhabitants of the Illumina tent city overlapped with the Arcanium cast, evident in the color of their clothes. Arcanium had unconsciously adopted a more monochromatic, dark palette, even for their casualwear, while Illumina preferred lighter and brighter colors. There were exceptions on both sides, of course, but it was clear that the conflict was between some members of Illumina and some of Arcanium, while the others mingled and tried to calm the turmoil in the center. No one had come to blows, or else Bell would have awoken on his own and the crack of the Ringmaster's whip would have broken the buzz of the argument.

Bell ran across the heat-brittle grass. He tried not to seem urgent but struggled against the impulse to run faster, to clench his teeth and his fists. He couldn't even put a finger on why, which was as much a reason for the feeling as knowing why might have been. That he couldn't tell who was at the center of the conflict disoriented him. It reminded him of when Locke had stolen Arcanium, leaving him too weak to hear the thoughts of cockroaches, much less the humans in his care, and severing him from every last thread of Arcanium. This wasn't as abrupt and complete, but Bell couldn't help but think that a few lines had been cut — only a few, but a few that he couldn't find, and that was bad enough, because he thought he'd made Arcanium impregnable.

Except Arcanium was still his. And it wasn't quite impregnable, was it?

Not when I let people in.

His disquiet deepened.

At the center of the conflict, Kitty stood on one side, with the Ringmaster silent and furious behind her. Fairuza, dignified and unfazed in a sleeveless white dress, stood on the other, and not only Illumina cast had joined her. More concerning to Bell was the number of Arcanium cast that hadn't chosen Kitty's side. Illumina had no hesitation. Not a single one of them had stepped across the line for Arcanium.

At Bell's arrival, the people milling uncertainly in the center jumped back, unable to look him in the eye.

Fairuza was expecting him. Only when near enough to feel her, because she'd always kept her power and her thoughts close and private, could Bell determine what had changed about his spells. They'd been mirrored, and all the duplicated threads flowed through Fairuza. The duplication was imperfect, because so much of the magic in Arcanium was bound to wishes that had no connection to her. But they were close enough to be almost as effective at manipulating Arcanium. Almost.

The entire crowd, both casts, went completely silent, until Vivian said, "How the fuck could you not know?" Because of course Vivian would be the one to say it out loud.

"Don't blame him for that," Fairuza said. "He's always had blind spots and always will. All the more reason why this should happen."

Bell didn't bother asking questions. As soon as he'd sensed the duplication of his spells and Maya's approaching ambivalence, he'd understood. "I've been looking for a demon to rip Arcanium away from me or an army to set fire to canvas and velvet. But it's not a thief in the night or an arsonist army, is it? This comes from within."

Maya passed him from behind, her head down, although her steps were steady.

"You. You did this?" Betrayal caught in Kitty's throat.

Fairuza placed a hand on Maya's shoulder as Maya crossed her path, guiding Maya behind her in case Kitty or one of the others decided to retaliate. No one had yet another reason this had flown under his radar. But although Maya stayed behind Fairuza, she raised her head and stepped to the side. Not quite *behind* Fairuza, which gave Fairuza pause.

"She didn't do anything but provide the distraction," Bell said quietly. "She was always a good lovely assistant, wasn't she, Fairuza? The perfect illusion to lure attention away from the real trick."

"It helps when she isn't an illusion at all," Fairuza replied. "But you always knew when to use an illusion and when the real thing was more spectacular. I deliberately didn't give her all the information, no matter how much of a blind spot she is to you as well."

Just another facet of how to manipulate him, one that Locke had used, a loophole that he had failed to completely close. With Maya out of the picture, there had been no point in closing it, but he should have known better once she'd returned. "No, but you gave her enough to know you had intentions for Arcanium. That was the plan all along. Not to join in alliance with Arcanium or become part of it but to take Arcanium for yourself."

"Yes." If anyone in Arcanium or Illumina had missed what was going on, Fairuza left no room for ambiguity. "But if this is a coup, it was always meant to be a peaceful one."

"I opened Arcanium to you. I sensed no ill intentions, or else I would never have opened it. I still sense no ill intentions."

"Because there are none." Fairuza raised her chin to point at the circus proper. "You have a good circus, Bell. I wouldn't change that. The problem is you."

"Because you managed to sneak in here? I'd say like a snake in the grass, except I'm much fonder of Sasha's serpents than you at the moment."

"That's part of it, yes. I expose that you have holes in your security, that there are still ways to take Arcanium by force—through those you love, because you can't see their futures as clearly, because anything to do with Arcanium's future related to them is obscured, because you don't peer into them as deeply as those you care less for. And I've proven that if you have no ill intentions for Arcanium, you have the capacity to take it. Again, my darlings, don't judge him too harshly. If someone has no ill intentions, then most wouldn't be interested in taking Arcanium at all."

"You haven't taken it yet," Bell said. "Just because you've mimicked the magic doesn't mean you can interfere with what I have in place."

"I can."

Bell pointed at her, fighting the impulse again to make a fist. Magic shuddered in the iron core at the base of his spine, threatening something darker than he was used to considering with someone whom he had loved. "I granted you your power. I can take it away. You are not infallible."

"Neither are you, and you can't take it away anymore—at least not as easily as you could have twenty-five years ago. And in the time it would take to divest me of that power, I could do damage that neither you nor I would want to do to Arcanium. Arcanium hasn't rejected me, Bell. I tripped none of your alarms or suspicions, and neither did Maya. Do you know why?"

"More loopholes that I need to close."

"Arcanium isn't protecting itself from me because I'm not the one it needs to protect itself from. I'm not the danger here. You are."

Bell lowered his arm. He didn't blink at all. "You're less than a century old, and human for most of it. What makes you think you can protect Arcanium better than me?"

"I can protect it in all the same ways. I think you already know that. The problem here isn't what's coming at Arcanium from the outside. The infrastructure for that is all in place. The problem is you. And the reason Maya agreed to help me distract you was because she trusts me, not you. Very few of them do, Bell. When you make Arcanium their purgatory before their time, when you imprison and torture in the name of *helping* them, how can you possibly expect your own people to trust you, to love you, without fear?"

Bell turned toward Maya. "Do you not trust me?"

She didn't say anything. She didn't have to. He could see with perfect clarity that Maya trusted him, or else she wouldn't have done anything to him the night before or let him do anything to her when she'd finished.

The worst in his circus trusted him, because he didn't lie. They didn't always like him, but they knew what to expect. Did she mean trust him not to hurt them when they put themselves in the position for pain? Because they certainly trusted him to mete out punishment. When he called for it, they were never surprised.

"They trust you to protect them, although that's on shakier ground these days, isn't it? No, I'm not talking about that kind of trust. I'm talking about the kind of trust that has them withholding wishes, biting their tongue when some random fool lets loose a slip of the tongue. It's one thing for the people who come in here willingly to love you." Fairuza nodded to Kitty to acknowledge how she'd entered Arcanium of her own free will.

Then she turned to the Skeletons, to Skinless, Rebekah, George, the Wicked Nurse, the Sphynx and the Man-Doll, the Spider and Neve. "But he stole you from your lives, ground you beneath his heel and said it was for your own good. I won't deny that you're stronger for the trials and tribulations. I came out of mine stronger, too, but it took me fifteen years to fully extract myself from Bell Madoc, to understand how poisonous his love could be. I won't pretend he wants to harm you, otherwise he would be held to account by his own laws. He has his own twisted sense of honor, but it's still just that—twisted.

"As I said, I will change very little about how Arcanium functions. The demons are welcome to stay—the same rules apply. The Ringmaster will deal punishments when someone in Arcanium puts another in danger. But I can only grant one wish, and I do not grant them as he does. I will not use the wishes tied into Arcanium to continue doing anything to you at my capricious whim beyond the initial granting of the wish. And with the aid of Illumina, I will make the circus itself better."

She turned back to Bell, who had gone completely still—stiller than a statue, which was, at a fundamental level, crumbling. "Arcanium is a beautiful machine, Bell, but I've felt for a while that you are no longer fit to lead. When members of Arcanium came to Illumina, it gave me further cause for concern—not because of what Locke did to them but what precipitated the capture. You've made adjustments since then, which shows that you realize some of your errors. I might have contented myself with an alliance and mere oversight, but after what you did to Maya…"

"How dare you." He stayed quiet, almost inaudible.

"Not last night. I wouldn't deny either of you that. But you dismantled the walls around her memories, Bell. That was when the canary dropped dead in this mine."

"You want me to walk out and just leave you behind with *everything*—everything that *I* built. Because of what I did to her. But when she came to *you* and asked to have her memories removed, you didn't do what I did with all the others and wall off the memories only of Locke's Arcanium so that she would have a better sense of what she'd left and what she'd lost." He shook his head, movement returning to his limbs with angry jerks. "No, you took them all and left her with too great a gap for her unfractured mind to stand. Then you brought her back to Arcanium, *knowing* what it would do to her, knowing that she would eventually have to get her memories back, because you didn't want to let go of what *I* found. You deliberately overstepped because you wanted the mistake to be mine, because you wanted *all* of it at no expense to their love for you."

"If you want to start placing blame on who is responsible for Maya," Fairuza said, chill returning, "we could keep going back to what led to Locke taking Arcanium, because you just had to dangle live bait in front of a hellborn demon, and you had to compromise your relationship with Maya to do it. Or shall we go all the way back to the beginning? Back to when you saw a woman you wanted, used another person's wish to bring her in then broke her like you break everything you love—so that you can fill in the cracks with gold and call it better."

"Bringing her into Arcanium was inevitable. You understand this better than anyone. You have hindsight and foresight. Maya was bound to Arcanium."

"Because you always had to have her! Because you made it so!" This time she raised her voice not to be heard across the crowd but out of fury. "Just like you had to have me. Just like you had to have Valorie. It was only etched into fate because you would always have made it so. Don't pretend you have nothing to do with the past or the future, Bell. Your actions are your own, whether prophesied or not."

She took a breath then approached him with deliberate determination. Oh yes, he could take her power if he chose, but she was right. Without his influence, she had removed many of her ties to him, created fail-safes and knots of magic that would impede him and give her the time to challenge him in other ways. He also couldn't take her power without seeming petty, like he needed to keep others weak for him to lead. No one else could rise up in her stead, because none of them had the power, but it would undermine the trust he'd built, striking someone down when they weren't a legitimate threat to Arcanium — simply to him.

"She isn't your only mistake, but she might be the only one you can see," she said more gently. "Look at her. You are responsible for what she has become. Not Locke. Not her poor choice in boyfriends. Not me. *You*. She had a chance to be free, but you stripped that from her as well, knowing that once you brought back her memories, you wouldn't be able to free her again. You may believe I manipulated you into an inevitable end, but you had a chance to deny her. Instead, you handed her the key to lock herself back in. If you'd had an ounce of honor, you would have walked away then. You would have realized the error you'd made with her, with everyone here, and dissolved Arcanium. You would have dissolved Arcanium the second you got it back."

"I love Arcanium." Bell wouldn't let the fact that she was inches away intimidate him into moving.

"And you always damage what you love the most. I don't know whether it's your nature, Bell, or just you."

"I love Arcanium," he repeated. "You want this to be a peaceful coup. You want me to hand it over, contrite, leave with my head hanging low to contemplate my life choices in some remote desert. You want to bring a more compassionate jinni to the helm of Arcanium, in concert with Illumina's fare. But you don't have the resources, and if you'll forgive the sexist phrase, you don't have the balls. You couldn't even handle a circus of humans. You won't know how to contain a circus of demons. You'll relieve suffering when it needs to persist. You'll break my promises. And you don't have the experience to combat those who come to Arcanium to take it with more insidious force. You'll wear Arcanium like an expensive necklace, Maya like a bracelet, then you'll be simply shocked when someone rips them away. You'll run it into the ground, Fairuza, just like you did Illumina."

Fairuza recoiled — almost imperceptible to the human eye but not to his. "It's past time for a regime change. I think you know that. That's why you submitted to her. That's why you gave her your pain. That's why you seek the absolution she taught you to seek. Because you know you fucked up, but you don't know what to do about it. I know what Arcanium needs to be, better than anyone. I don't have to be soft to be compassionate. You can entrust her to me. If you love Arcanium, Bell — if you love Maya, Elizabeth, Neve, Kitty — you'll let it go."

"You seriously didn't see this coming?" Kitty said, echoing Vivian as she gestured to Fairuza. "You didn't have to see the future to tell she was plotting against you."

Bell didn't take his gaze off Fairuza and, by extension, Maya. "I don't make a point of digging that deeply into the people I know. It's a courtesy that has backfired before, just not so spectacularly."

What disturbed him more than anything was that no one was interjecting on his behalf. He sensed uncertainty that he needed to leave but no certainty that Bell was the jinni to lead Arcanium — this beautiful thing he had created, this masterpiece, this reimagining of something destructive into a forge's fire, something that had produced stronger and better people upon release. That the process was slow was to be expected, even for those born into a world that expected much faster results, yet was what he did not enough to justify it in their eyes?

Their opinions of him had never concerned Bell, but with Fairuza presenting a viable alternative, even Kitty considered all the things she didn't like about how he brought new cast in, the trials, exchanges and negotiations, the control he wrested.

"You didn't detect my intentions on the surface of my thoughts because my concerns are nothing more or less than your own," Fairuza said. "I worry for Arcanium, for those of mine who have entered it, for those of yours who came to me before returning. I will take care of Arcanium. I will grace it with the spirit you intended, even if your execution is flawed. I might be several decades removed from my humanity, but I have the benefit of having been both human and jinn. I've picked what I think is best from both. You never had that luxury. There will always be something inhumane in the things you've done. You've embraced being an agent of chaos. I didn't have to. Please." She cupped his cheek, tracing the bone with her thumb. "Make this easier on everyone, on yourself. Don't make this a battle that will damage you to win. Do what's best for Arcanium, not yourself. I know it's hard to distinguish the two, but they are not one and the same."

She lowered her voice so only he would hear. "Look back at your mistakes. Elizabeth. Maya. Neve. Valorie. Vivian. Shane. You know I'm right. You *know* it, or you would have shot me out of Arcanium the second you realized what I was doing. You've feared that you are inadequate. You have a good heart, Bell, in spite of the cruelty you commit and inspire. If I believed that we could coexist peaceably, I would allow you to remain, but we both know you don't work like that. A collector without the collection in his possession would lead to blows between us eventually."

Bell stepped back — not in retreat but to widen his gaze from her to the people he'd tended and cared for like a night-blooming garden. Demon, human and monster looked back at him, waited with undefined tension between the two potential ends. Doubt simmered among some of his cast that Fairuza would keep Arcanium as Bell had created it, but there was also doubt with him in the center of the web. The memories fueling their trepidation surfaced in disjointed images.

Sasha, Maya and Kitty walking away from him backstage after he'd brought Neve into the circus.

Mikhail being whipped for stalking Joanne and Jane then for doing the same to Seth.

Valorie holding a knife, chasing Maya across the tightrope.

The group of boys pretending to be men splitting the circus' attention to attack Kitty, and the Ringmaster's interrupted attempt to drag Arcanium into his hell in retribution for the actions of the men and Bell's inability to stop them all.

Neve in tears, with silver piercings digging into her flesh.

Elizabeth becoming the Spider for everyone to see, terrified of herself, ashamed by her nudity because Dez had put her through the same shame.

Vivian undergoing the worst lashing he'd ever permitted the Ringmaster to give a human and the whispers that followed as people learned why.

Shane screaming bloody murder because her mouths were so hungry.

Fae surrounding Arcanium's borders, a bloody Horned God standing in front of Carlo and Sera because Bell hadn't taken point.

And it went without saying that visions of Locke's Arcanium filled the circus — his ultimate mistake, one he could never rectify, no matter how many passes the Ringmaster made over his back, not even with Maya taking the whip and other assorted implements. Nothing he did could fix what had happened, change that his Arcanium had been nearly destroyed there on the empty lot where Locke's stadium had been, because Arcanium wasn't the circus. It was his people – broken, suspicious, adaptive, adventurous, fierce, infuriating, beautiful.

Fairuza wanted to take his people. And every last one, at least part of them, wanted her to.

The Creature adjusted his gargoyle wings, calling attention to the Spider, who had perfected her own art of stillness. The extra limbs gave her a steadier foundation, but it also came from the subtler qualities of a spider that he'd given Elizabeth when he'd transformed her from a modest, head-covered nanny into the sexy femme fatale she'd hidden underneath the garb of her religion. She'd been discovering herself ever since. Bell taking her abuser into Arcanium as the limbless, sightless, earless, mouthless Voodoo Torso had helped greatly with her trust in him and her willingness to explore in safety and strength what Dez had once exploited. She'd entered Arcanium a phobic, fragile, struggling saint. In the hands of the fear-consuming Creature and the patient but questionable probing of Bell, she'd become a goddess, despite a lack of natural immortality or magic. Kitty was the heart of Arcanium. Lizzie was its elegant, black-diamond claw. Her transformation was one that Bell was most proud of.

But Elizabeth wasn't only accompanied by the Creature. On her other side, she'd tucked her two left arms around the elbow of Thomas Petros.

A self-styled charismatic cult leader who called himself a prophet was usually a confidence man of the first order — seeking attention, acclaim, the favors of beautiful women in the guise of innocence, the modest earnings of his congregation in his coffers and, above all, control. From Lizzie's recollections of her biological father, Bell hadn't noticed any glaring red flags in the Petrosian church beyond the usual isolationist and sometimes fundamentalist views of the church itself. Bell had assumed that Lizzie had been left alone by her father because her status as the bastard child of a saint had been described in great detail in many sermon illustrations, which did nothing for Elizabeth's reputation as a child but had also shielded her, perhaps, from the potentially predatory acts of leaders such as he.

However, when Petros had entered Arcanium at Lizzie's earnest behest, Bell had been startled and thoroughly enchanted to learn that Thomas Petros was a true prophet—an imperfect holy man profoundly aware of his own imperfections and refreshingly nonjudgmental, the intrinsic judgments within Petrosian theology notwithstanding.

Since then, Petros had developed something of a long-distance relationship with Elizabeth, akin to that which they'd had when she was a child and mostly had to watch her father from afar, while her familial dad ignored her and her mother found her inadequate as both a daughter and saint. Like Maya, Elizabeth was too much of a creature of flesh and blood to achieve the perfection they'd been expected to maintain.

Bell didn't pry into the Spider's mind and life much anymore, now that he didn't have to worry about her, even with her propensity toward drowning her sorrows. He'd assumed that she was the reason why her father had kept his distance, in spite of Petros' threat to come after him if Bell ever hurt his daughter— and he had, in his failure to protect her. But Elizabeth had chosen to remain in Arcanium when her father had first rushed to her rescue, and she'd chosen to stay in Arcanium when Bell had offered his cast the choice to leave. The absence of an army of angry saints at his gate had suggested that her father had respected that decision.

Bell didn't normally allow family into Arcanium at all hours, but he was more permissive of family than strangers, and as long as Petros had entered Arcanium at Elizabeth's invitation and with no intent to steal Elizabeth or attack Bell with the aforementioned army, he would have been able to enter without tripping any wires. Bell had been too distracted by Maya and Fairuza to notice a genuine prophet in Arcanium, but now the hot, righteous anger that Fairuza had stoked inside of him dimmed — ashes on the flames.

Fairuza had been there for the original thought, remembered it with him as he met the dark eyes of the prophet.

On the day Thomas Petros finally comes for me, perhaps then it's time for Arcanium to end.

Bell's prophetic gift was quite different from that of Petros. He'd never before delivered a prophecy to himself that he only understood in hindsight.

It wouldn't be Arcanium ending. Just *his* Arcanium.

Bell briefly ignored Fairuza as he approached Petros.

In spite of his status as a prophet and cult leader, Petros was still just a man, but unlike most men, he was completely aware of what approached him. He shifted his arm to around Elizabeth's shoulders, although he couldn't do anything to protect Elizabeth that she couldn't do better.

Bell bowed to Petros, out of respect for the man's unique gift if not his standing in his congregation. Petros bowed back, although reluctant to lower his eyes. Still, it was smarter to be polite with jinn.

"What brings a Petrosian saint to purgatory, Father?" Bell asked. "Have you come to collect what I owe?"

"God told me to call my daughter. She invited me." Thomas Petros' voice was richly resonant — like the Ringmaster's but with far more warmth — made to fill a church without the use of a microphone. "I know what I promised. But I made a promise to her first, and she told me to spare you. God had no say one way or the other on the matter, so I deferred to Lizzie. No matter how they speak of apostates, they could stand to learn mercy from her. I don't know what you did to deserve that mercy. I don't want to know. I didn't want to know what happened to her, either, but after she was taken, God gave me that vision. If I'd had the power, I would have damned you then for making me that helpless, to know what had happened and that there was nothing I could do to help her."

"We shared that helplessness, Father. I can't apologize to you, any more than I could apologize to her. There isn't enough forgiveness in the world to balance out the error that led to her pain." Bell was all too aware of his audience, attuned as he was to attention, but he'd shown contrition before.

"Don't pretend to know what it was like, jinni. Don't pretend you know what it's like to lose your child to that…twice."

Bell didn't respond. Prophets were allowed to be wrong, and he wasn't interested in repeating the argument he'd given Maya.

"It's just a coincidence that he's here, Bell." Elizabeth shrugged off the arm from around her shoulders. She had many and mixed feelings about her biological father, which included love, but accepting closer affection had not been part of their relationship. She didn't accept much contact from anyone other than the Creature and Neve these days, the latter more platonic than the former. "He's not here to oust you. That would be the jinni you made who's standing right over there."

"But it isn't coincidence, is it, Petros?" Bell tilted his head, searching for Petros' answer in his stony silence. Prophets were always harder to read, which seemed a special kind of irony. On an ordinary day, he would enjoy the challenge, even enjoy the failure. But the silence from him deafened Bell as he strained to hear. "It's time, isn't it?"

Petros looked away from Bell to Fairuza. His troubled expression—enhanced by strong, black, bushy eyebrows and an equally defined jawline—remained. "Do you know what you've done?"

The man had learned from hours of Petrosian confession—more therapeutic than compulsory as a sacrament—to withhold judgment in his tone. That he extended the same courtesy to Bell touched him. "Yes."

Petros returned his attention to Bell. "No, you don't. But you will. Spiders always make their webs."

"Not all spiders make... Never mind." Elizabeth held up all four hands to beg forgiveness for the interruption. "That's irrelevant to the metaphor. Although the metaphor itself is kind of insulting."

"I'm sorry, sweetheart."

Bell got the message, whether it came from the Creator or the Father. Far be it from a prescient jinni to ignore signs.

Elizabeth narrowed her eyes then blinked, dismay multiplied by her extra limbs. "You can't possibly be thinking about leaving Arcanium."

"You *can't* leave Arcanium," Kitty interjected, stepping into his peripheral vision, although he didn't need to see her to feel her close.

"The spirit of the circus will remain the same, Kitty," Fairuza said gently, although she stayed back to give Bell and his people their space.

Kitty glared over her shoulder at Fairuza.

"She's given her word," Bell said. "You know how binding a jinni's word is. It's not Arcanium she wants to get rid of, Katharine. Just me."

Kitty grasped his shoulder before he could step away. "Yes, I know how binding a jinni's word is. I also know a thing or two about how you get around it."

"That's exactly what I'm hoping to avoid," Fairuza said. "I've been where all of you are. I was involuntary when I was brought into Arcanium. I'm not going to force anyone to stay, but please, I do ask you to give me a chance. Give yourselves a chance to see what Arcanium could become."

Bell cradled Kitty's face in both hands and kissed her lips gently. "I love you, pretty thing. I don't want to go. You know I've tried to find my footing again, and Arcanium itself is something I've never been surer of. But my place in it, how I have erred and would err again... Perhaps it's time for fresh eyes. She has power, she matched my spells, she can only grant one wish and she's inclined to grant it well."

Kitty gripped his wrists. Although her strength alone wasn't enough to hold him, the tears threatening to spill over onto her cheeks nearly did. "Do you know how long I searched for Arcanium?"

"Arcanium's not leaving." He couldn't cry like she could, but an obstruction formed in his throat nevertheless, rendering his reply a whisper. "I am."

Bell stepped out of her hold and turned, fixing his sights on the opening Arcanium gates so he wouldn't have to see anyone watching him leave, and he shut his mind so he wouldn't hear their sorrow...or their glee.

He gathered his few belongings — not his RV, which was just a place to sleep, but his fortune teller tent with its trappings and the chest of crystals, because they were his prisoners and not Arcanium's. Then, as he crossed over the threshold, he dissolved the strong, silken strands of his Arcanium behind him.

The same or similar spells sewed into place behind him — just as strong, just as impregnable by antagonistic forces, but more lenient on those within Arcanium who wanted to leave. Already, he tasted the differences like powder on his tongue, and he swallowed against the bitterness.

Bell refused to look back. He just...disappeared.

Chapter Fourteen

Bell hadn't suffered dreamless nights since Arcanium had been taken from him the first time. In spite of the terrible content of Arcanium's dreams since Locke, dreamless sleep unsettled him far more. He slept even less than usual these days.

At first, he'd found Renaissance faires where he could pitch his tent. Arcanium had a reputation among the various faires around the country, even the ones they'd never attached themselves to. They'd always welcomed him in. He just had to avoid the ones that Arcanium joined in the summer so that they would never cross paths.

Faire season generally extended all summer, which in the South and Southwest lasted much longer. Once haunted houses had started sprouting up with more frequency, Bell had abandoned his nomadic existence and lived isolated until everything had transitioned to Christmas lights that illuminated reindeer instead of monsters.

Winter found him in a rented shopfront, taken over from the previous psychic who had married and moved to a coastal town with her husband. She'd passed on a good number of clients to him with enthusiastic recommendations to them, although Unfettered Fortunes didn't quite cater to long-term clientele the way that Madame Nero had.

More people left the shop with troubled expressions these days, the ringing of the brass bells over the door heralding increasing unease. People were rarely ready for real psychics or the readings that they gave.

It helped that Bell had no use for any money he received. He didn't even know why he continued as a fortune teller, other than it was what he knew best. During the Thanksgiving and Christmas festivals, he'd gone out among the modest parade crowds and done close-up magic, both illusion and real. That satisfied him a little more, because magic of that kind inspired wonder—a better feeling for him to feed upon.

Really, all he'd done was return to earlier form. He'd been a one-man traveling show for several centuries, taking lovers where he desired.

In spite of dozens of potential affairs—of both the married and single variety—Bell kept his solitude and disregarded the rumors about him because of it—more rumors than if he *had* taken lovers, because people wanted to be more discreet under those circumstances. Some called him a white whale in their quirky, touristy small town. Others just called him strange and probably gay, which amused him, because women weren't the only lovers he denied.

He'd return to his old ways eventually. Grief had settled over him like fog between mountains, and grief always needed time.

His apartment above the shop was blissfully quiet, with only his own magic for company. He reveled in the lack of incubus and succubus magic working its chaotic will on him night and day. As much as he'd enjoyed it when he'd had someone to share it with, the novelty wore off when he didn't. Without it, he became much more in tune with his own desires, stripped of any enhancements, and those desires remained largely dormant. If they didn't arise on their own, he knew better than to force them. He was no one to grace a man or woman's bed lightly.

December brought snowfall, which slowed his already peaceful days.

Bell invited the stray cat, which he usually fed in the alley behind the shop, into the building, where he kept his fire burning and didn't mind when the cat brought in dead birds. Cats and gods got along splendidly, because a cat worshipped neither gods nor kings and demanded alms instead. When people did it, it was a sign of disrespect. When cats did, it was a matter of fact. As Bell lay on the sofa in front of his fire, the cat jumped up to join him and curled against his chest.

However, the jingle of bells, too dark in tone for holiday sleigh bells, called him down from his apartment to the shop.

The cat arose with him, ran down the stairs in a winding, unsuccessful attempt to trip Bell on the way. With a cat's tail regularly flicking under his soles, Bell had learned care where he stepped.

Despite the weather, he'd changed little about his attire from when he'd been an outdoor fortune teller. He still went barefoot and wore the cotton pants — rarely leather these days. Instead of going shirtless, though, he wore the Henley during store hours, and

301

instead of donning another gold arm bracelet, he'd pierced a small gold hoop into one ear — a nod to what he'd been long before he'd taken a human guise.

No one sat in the waiting room, called cozy by the generous. It wouldn't have been the first time that someone had entered Unfettered Fortunes only to back out less than a minute later, either from the scent of incense or from the creepy-crawling feeling inspired by the many skulls set in curio cabinets and on the walls that some religious residents deemed satanic. Or from a general fear of the fortune teller. Even for those who didn't really believe in psychics and patronized them for entertainment alone, a nagging doubt sometimes dissuaded them. He had that effect on people. They couldn't see his magic, couldn't feel it like touch, the way he felt magic in others. They could, however, sense it if it was especially absent in their lives elsewhere. When faced with the possibility of altering their entire view of the world, not a few chose to flee. Not everyone was ready.

Bell started back up the stairs but hesitated when Del Toro — what he'd been calling the stray — scurried into the reading room with the eagerness he usually reserved for mealtimes and the shaking of a catnip container.

The shop had no security other than the bells and Bell himself. He didn't need a security system. He didn't even need a spell web, which had been to preserve his cast's safety rather than his own. He could sleep in the most criminal-infested park and not fear harm, because he was more dangerous than most of the things that might wake him.

He rarely looked forward or reached out during business hours to see who was coming. He had no reason to be suspicious, not even with demon prison crystals lining his reading room like trophies to ward off other demons who thought he was more vulnerable without Arcanium's spells protecting him.

Bell followed the cat into the reading room. "Can I help y—"

"I see you still like to be surprised."

Unlike him, she was dressed for the weather in a sweater, scarf and coat. Del Toro rubbed his cheeks on her boots.

As Bell slowly stepped around the parlor table to sit across from her, she shrugged off the coat and unwound the scarf. A fresh twenty-dollar bill had been put in the previously empty jar he kept next to his favorite crystal ball and modified Magic 8-Ball.

Maya picked up his enchanted version of the tarot and did a standard shuffle before setting it in front of him. "Would it surprise you to learn that Elizabeth was the first to leave? Turns out that when the chains were loosened on the people who hurt her, she didn't feel so safe anymore. Compassion has its place, but it also has consequences. When she left, the Creature had to leave with her. He can drink fear all day from the haunted funhouse, but after imprinting, he needs her."

Bell took the top card and flipped it over in front of him. The Spider. He turned over a second card. The Cat and the Cauldron.

"Kitty was next, and with her, the Ringmaster followed. The loss of Kitty's confidence would have been bad enough, but losing the big stick of Arcanium himself lowered the morale of the original Arcanium cast all the more. You were always right about Kitty, though. Without its heart, Arcanium died. Kitty's exit led quickly to Delilah and Dom bowing out, because without Kitty tethering the freak show, the oddities ended up the odd men out, so to speak, in a circus suddenly crawling with skilled acts. The clowns left when their source of food dried up by Fairuza's decree. Lennon left, which started the Skeletons dropping like flies, plus Melanie. Jonas left, which convinced Vivian out as a solo act. Caroline, Riley and Colm took longer, but they left around the same time as Neve, and when Neve left, so did Sasha and Mikhail. Fairuza couldn't stop the bleeding."

Bell turned over the last card. The Bell. He never drew that card as often as he did with Maya.

"Kitty saw it coming the whole time. With Arcanium run by Illumina, the focus shifted. It was beautiful for a while. No one denied that. But more and more guests and patrons came for the new performances, for the Illumina cast of pretty people, and Arcanium's oddities seemed all-the-more out of place, freakish, unrelatable, mockable. When the oddities were the center, you forced the guests to adjust to a different normal. You made *them* beautiful."

Maya turned over a card of her own on top of the deck. The Queen of Skulls.

"Some of them are still there, but their heart isn't in it anymore. Fairuza did what she promised. She keeps the oddities safe from the worst that outsiders bring in. But without demons and monsters, a demonic circus just isn't what it used to be. Without Kitty, the Spider, the snake charmer, the strongman, the Tall Man and Short Man, the possessed contortionist, what the hell kind of freak show can Fai offer? She brought in a new oddity cast after a call. Give her time and she might be able to create a facsimile of what Arcanium was. But it's not the same without you, without what you made."

"You mean what I made of people's wishes, often against their will and to their great distress," Bell finally said. "That's why I left. That's why no one stopped me."

"Since when has anyone stopped you, Bell? They didn't say anything because they never thought in a million years you'd actually leave."

"I was only ever a fortune teller. Arcanium was always its cast. If they had stayed, Arcanium would have survived. But leaving was the right Fairuza gave to them. It should have come as no surprise that they did."

"Arcanium wasn't us." Maya leaned down to scratch Del Toro's cheeks and head. "We were cogs. You were the machine, Bell. *You* were Arcanium. It had all the same moving parts, but it stopped being Arcanium when you left. That's why it fell apart. Fairuza is capable, and you're right—if we'd given her more time, she could have made something of those moving parts. But it wouldn't have been Arcanium. It *wasn't* Arcanium."

"I was under the impression no one wanted my Arcanium anymore." Bell gathered the tarot cards and put them back in their place.

"Bell, look outside."

Maya gathered Del Toro in her arms at his insistence, standing with Bell as he labored around the narrow space between the walls and the table to the bay window seat that comprised his shopfront—decorated with the carved idols, crystals and candles that had once adorned his tent.

Across the snowy street stood the most unusual crowd that the downtown square had ever seen, which was no small feat, since the Pride Parade went down Main Street every year.

Del Toro demanded to be let down, his love tanks full. Maya lowered him to the floor. "It took me a while to find them all again. Being psychic helps."

Fairuza had broadened Maya's abilities to fill in the fortune teller role, because Fairuza had needed to focus on running an abruptly higher-maintenance circus. Maya's magic had none of the depth of that of immortals, but its richness overlapped with his own when she touched his hand, first with only her fingertips, trailing the length of bone and vein, then covering him with her warmth.

Bell still couldn't find words. His thoughts swelled with emotion after emotion too strong to define, but contact allowed Maya to share them. She bit her lip, swayed down to the shallow cushion of the window seat.

Elizabeth had lost her extra limbs, but the Creature made up for her more normal appearance with his complete inability to feign normal. He had to conceal himself from the view of anyone passing by, although they still did a double take for the ones who didn't hide, like Ciarán, with Moss sitting on his usual perch on Ciarán's shoulder.

Separate from the rest for their protection, Mikhail and Sasha stood on either side of Neve, who was as scarred as when he'd left her. Colm and Riley flanked Caroline. The stitches were gone, but she still didn't open her mouth. Victor, Troy, Delilah, Dom, Vivian, Jonas, Lennon, Alicia, Lily, Nasreen and Shane clustered together on the sidewalk. Vivian, Alicia, Lily and Shane had lost their skeletal definition, and given that hair had grown in over the complete lack of a monster mouth on the side of her head, Shane appeared to have shed the Tooth Fairy.

The Mountain loomed over Mayumi and Selena, and the Gentleman loomed over him. The Horned God hid himself from unready eyes, but he stood with Sera, who led Salem by a leash. Salem carried Carlo on his back, because even with gloves, the snow was too cold for Carlo to walk his normal way.

The clowns prowled the shop roofs above, too odd to walk among humans without face paint and too tempted by the children taking the sidewalks with their parents to visit the shops.

And in the center of it all, the Ringmaster smoldered in his unbridled, fire-and-brimstone glory, possessively embracing the bearded woman in front of him.

Many of these people had been involuntary, torn apart and sewn together again. They'd resisted him at every turn, would have been first in line in justifying their escape from Arcanium when they finally had the chance and never stepping within a hundred miles of Bell, if they'd known where he was.

They had no reason to be here today, except that they didn't want to be in Fairuza's Arcanium.

But they still wanted to be a part of *something*, something that only Bell could create—the haunted haven, the purgatory they would have given their right arms to have never entered in the first place. A place for demons and humans to live in something approaching harmony, dissonant though it might seem to some.

"Interesting place you've set up shop." Maya interlocked her fingers with his. "Do you think it could use a haunted funhouse?"

Bell tore his gaze from the people—*his* people—across the street. He should have been the first to know when something was real rather than illusion, but even though she held his hand, he almost couldn't trust his senses, the physical and the psychic.

"Why are you here? Why would you leave what Fairuza built?"

It had been tailormade for someone like Maya, with her acrobatics, fortune telling and illusionist skills, not to mention how much more beautiful she had become. If she'd been desirable before, she was nearly irresistible to him now. Even those who didn't know what she'd endured would crave the taste of tragedy on her skin like salt.

"Before my memories were restored, I wouldn't have. Fairuza's Arcanium would have had everything I needed, as Illumina did. But after returning my memories, after what you let me do, she offered nothing to...to fill... I tried to repeat what I'd been in Illumina. I tried to be..."

"Good," Bell finished for her.

Maya slid her other hand up the side of his neck and brought his mouth to hers, moaning as though he were the first meal she'd tasted in months of foraging in the desert. She released his other hand to slip hers under his shirt, skin to skin, no obstacles to her contact other than the layers of clothes between them as she climbed over him on the window seat. She straddled his hips with insistence he hadn't expected, and that aroused him as much as the sensation of her tongue caressing his. Catching his lower lip then his tongue with her teeth, she kissed him as though she wanted to swallow him whole, sent him sinking back on the window seat until she lay on top of him, canting her hips shamelessly against his.

She raised herself up to yank off her sweater. With fire under her skin, the heated room was stifling, and Bell shared her impulse. She helped him pull his shirt over his head. Together they reached down to push down Maya's jeans so that she could kick them off, to push down the waistband of Bell's so that Maya could position him and sink herself down on his still-growing cock. No foreplay. No hesitation. She'd had all the time in the world to think, to second-guess herself.

Bell had pulled her into Arcanium against her will. Locke had done the same. Fairuza had kept her under false pretenses, however well-meaning.

But Maya had come to him now on her own.

Although it was bright outside and the windows were tinted, anyone at all could see in. Bell concealed them from view — not out of modesty or the concern of narrow-minded citizens but because this was something he didn't want to share. Not now. Not when Maya was riding him hard enough to hurt herself, moaning as she leaned down to muffle herself in his kiss.

He cupped her breasts, still in her bra, then smoothed his palms down to her ass, where he gripped bruises into her flesh as he fucked her just as hard as she fucked him, using him, compelling him to use her. It was fast, messy, awkward on the window seat and unenhanced by sex magic, unlike any of the sex they'd ever had before. The incubus and succubus' magic was more or less contained within themselves across the street, perhaps catching on the breeze now and then, but it had been free for months instead of kept within the bell jar of Arcanium and didn't need to reach as far as the shop.

This was just them, more real than real, only confirming how real it had always been.

Bell pushed them upright again then stood, nearly tripping over their clothes as he brought them to the parlor table. She wrapped her legs around him, crossing her ankles above his ass, still kissing him furiously, her nails carving bloodless lines down his back. He lowered her to the velvet tablecloth, covered her then gripped the other side of the table, his arms, back and thighs flexing as he pulled himself into her, the slap of his hips striking her thighs loud in the small room.

He wasn't gentle, his magic barely making room for him inside her, but he still found what he needed, as he always did. She broke away from the kiss to cry out as his cock stretched her and hit the spot again and again and again.

Bell only needed one hand to grip the edge of the parlor table, which barely held them but which he reinforced to ensure that it would. With the other, he stroked around her clit, tormenting the place just above and near the bone in the way that made her writhe. He kissed her again, this time claiming her, each groan vibrating through her lips almost like *mine*.

"Bell, I'm..."

Maya screamed without regard for who was on the other side of his wall. She tore her nails through the skin of his back. This time, she drew blood in a delicious fire that joined with the fever low in his abdomen, tight in his scrotum, hottest where she squeezed around him, slickening his way. With no magical aid, nothing but his body inside and around her, he called her orgasm up and up, as far as it could go. Then he plunged his raw magic deep inside of her, binding them together, to bring her higher, to bring him with her.

No one could see inside the bay window, but let them talk about what they heard through the walls — her feral cries, her name on his lips before he kissed her again, releasing the edge of the table to sink his fingers into her hair and just taste her, remind himself through the sheer carnal aftermath that she was here. She was here because she wanted to be here. *Wished* to be here.

"Maya..." He breathed her in, the scent of her hair, her skin. "I gave up Arcanium for you. My beautiful, dangerous flower. My Maya."

She brought her bloody fingers to her mouth over his shoulder and sucked her fingertips. He chased her tongue, mixing his flavor with hers.

When the last of her climax, if not her arousal, had faded, he yanked her up, him standing, her sitting on the parlor table, both of them entwined together in a hot tangle of limbs. He didn't want to let her go, and she didn't seem to either, biting his neck hard enough to leave marks as she rocked against his cock, still thick and deep in her cunt.

"I don't know what I am anymore," she murmured into his skin. "I don't know whether I'm lapsed, chaotic or evil. I don't know what I believe or what I'm going to become if I let go. But I know that I've never been more at home or more myself, whatever that is, than when I'm with you. I thought that if you weren't there, those things would go away because you made me that way...but they didn't." She bit the cord of his neck hard, sucked at the light sweat of his flesh. "Neither Illumina nor Fairuza's Arcanium satisfies. Out there, they all understand. That's why they're here. That's why *we're* here."

She pulled back from his neck, guiding Bell's face to hers as she moved to kiss him again. But she licked her reddened lips, swollen from the roughness of his mouth on hers, and looked up at him. "The prophet was right. Spiders always make their webs. And you were right, too. It *is* time, Bell. Time to make another one."

Not Arcanium. Arcanium was taken, at least in name, and it would limp along for a while in an attempt to recreate the spirit that he'd built with the cast that had abandoned it.

Arcanium was gone.

But he could build something new. Something better.

Untempered, unrestricted. Beautiful and strange.

Dark. Like her. Like them together.

"The things I'll make of you, Maya," he whispered into her. "The things I'll do for you. The web we'll weave."

It had already started. Their magic bound, twisted, spread like smoke, darkening the room that had been bright with sun and snow only moments before.

"You'll see."

Want to see more from this author?
Here's a taster for you to enjoy!

Intervention
Aurelia T. Evans

Excerpt

"Land, what time is it?"

"It's seven."

"What do you mean it's seven? Why didn't my alarm go off?"

"You needed the sleep, Em," Land replied.

"So you decided to go off on your own at night just so I could get a little shut-eye? Land, we've watched enough horror movies to know that splitting up is *not* a good idea."

"I know. But we've also watched enough reality TV to know that not getting enough sleep also isn't a good idea."

"Touché. Did we get a call?"

"No, Em. I found him."

Emily sat straight up in bed. "You found Matt?"

"The lures worked. He's in the trap."

Emily rocked out of bed and yanked on a pair of leggings. Then she did some fancy moves to get a sports bra on without taking off her long tank sleep shirt. "That's great. That's really great. Is he okay?"

"More or less," Land replied.

Emily stopped rushing through their dark bedroom. "Is something wrong? You sound weird."

"The important thing is that we found him. You should come down. We need to do the intervention together. He won't listen to me. He'll listen to you."

"Um, okay. I'll get my coffee and drive right over."

"Love you, Em."

"I love you, too, Land. Are you sure —"

The call abruptly ended.

Land had never hung up on her like this, not unless they were in a knock-down, drag-out kind of fight, and they'd only had that twice in their relationship. And both times, Emily had known they were in one.

Her stomach tightened, but she forced herself not to overanalyze.

That didn't mean she couldn't hurry. By the time she made it to the warehouse, it would be full-on dark.

She grabbed a large bottle of iced coffee from the second shelf of the fridge. Then she hopped into her subcompact. Land had the company car, but hers had an extermination kit or two for emergencies, so she wasn't going out to the warehouse district half-cocked.

As she drove away from the glittery, bustling part of the city, the blue velvet of the sky went black.

"Ladies and gentlemen, lock your doors," she whispered.

* * * *

Three years ago, if someone had told Emily that she was going to be in pest control, she would have laughed in that person's face while spraying a line of Raid around her apartment.

These days, she could pick up a cockroach without flinching. They were nothing in comparison to the kinds of infestations she, Land and Matt had to deal with in addition to the usual suspects. It just so happened that the usual suspects tended to hang around the unusual ones so often that they'd get paid on the books for the usual, then off the books — cash, goods or services — for the unusual. Because how were they supposed to put 'rat-sized cockroach demon spawn' on the invoice without raising some red flags during an audit?

Their unconventional night job had started as an accident, evolved into a hobby then turned into a full-on occupation.

The accident had happened during a bit of urban exploring that had followed Land's side job at the time as an exterminator's apprentice. When rats started having red eyes and a person didn't have holy water on hand, they'd better hope they had a cross necklace or a rosary. Emily had. Land hadn't.

Back then, it had been a good thing the vampire family hadn't really been interested in bothering or being bothered, otherwise Land might have died then and there.

After that encounter, though, they'd felt like they had a responsibility. 'Once seen, never unseen' and all that. Balancing the work with school had meant creative hours, cat naps, copious amounts of caffeine and a few prayers, but it was totally worth it.

They hadn't even thought about making a profit out of the hobby until after Land had gone solo with extermination.

Around that time, they'd stumbled upon Matt at one of those bars that discreetly catered to hunters — demon hunters, vampire hunters, regular hunters looking to score on exotic creatures…the scene took all sorts. Emily and Land had largely been viewed by that community as newlywed newbies, cannon fodder that wouldn't last a year. They hadn't taken it personally.

Matt had been new himself, drawn to the supernatural underbelly of the city by the promise of an unconventional thrill. He'd been the first one intrigued by the idea of not hunting the big game. And he'd been just charming and enthusiastic enough about the idea that Land had eventually welcomed him to the extermination team.

Para-exterminators, Matt called them, for when a job came along that was too small or too damn infested. After all, what did the other demon hunters know about corpse beetles, ectoplasm residue and specter slugs, except that they seriously stained leather boots?

Emily's parents were still trying to figure out why she hadn't gone running the second Land had become a full-fledged exterminator instead of something more ambitious and less icky, and why she'd actually gone and married the bastard. Or why she and Land had opened up their house to another man. Emily knew the whispers, the bets on who was going to cheat first.

But it made financial sense for Matt to contribute to the mortgage and for them to work out of their house instead of renting an office somewhere. Let the hens and roosters cluck in their narrow little barnyards. The three of them were fiscally sound, would be out of debt in less than five years if business kept up, and they didn't drive each other crazy.

If Matt had a crush on Emily and Emily admired Matt too, what did that matter as long as they kept their hands to themselves and out of each other's bedrooms?

That's how it had been, anyway.

It wasn't like Matt to just run off. He was a thrill-seeker, yes, but if he'd decided to go to Louisiana for an alligator-wrestling lesson or to Florida to swim with bull sharks, he would have left them a note. The only clue they'd had was a bunch of bloody footprints at a warehouse where a hunter had said he'd seen Matt. Some of the footprints had been human, some of them not. No bodies to be found.

Emily and Land specialized in the small, but that didn't mean they were clueless to the larger problems. A creature that size wasn't a Texas chupacabra or a werecat. Those paw prints could be nothing other than a werewolf.

Their local urban sprawl didn't have much in the way of werewolves. The small forest area that ran through the center of the city with the river could only ever hold the territory of a single small pack. There were a few in-city packs as well, but they weren't like vampires or other demons. They didn't thrive in a concrete jungle, and those that did take up residence there were usually pretty passive and self-policing, for their own protection.

However, that only meant that werewolf attacks were *less* common. Not that they didn't happen.

In general, most hunters left the city werewolves alone, as long as they didn't start killing things they weren't supposed to. New wolves, however, weren't always good at toeing that line.

And that was the best-case scenario for Matt—that he'd been turned. So they'd set the traps outside the forest, hoping to lead him in with game and blood to one of the many abandoned buildings in the warehouse district, hoping against hope that he was still alive and that he was the one they'd catch.

Well, Matt *was* still alive, and he *was* the one they'd caught, thank God.

Now that Matt had been captured, what she and Land needed to do next was convince Matt that he was still a part of their family, fur and all. That they'd help take care of him.

No matter what.

TOTALLY BOUND

Home of Erotic Romance

Sign up for our newsletter and find out about all our romance book releases, eBook sales and promotions, sneak peeks and FREE romance books!

About the Author

Aurelia T. Evans is an up-and-coming erotica author with a penchant for horror and the supernatural.

She's the twisted mind behind the werewolf/shifter Sanctuary trilogy, demonic circus series Arcanium, and vampire serial Bloodbound. She's also had short stories featured in various erotic anthologies.

Aurelia presently lives in Dallas, Texas (although she doesn't ride horses or wear hats). She loves cats and enjoys baking as much as she dislikes cooking. She's a walker, not a runner, and she writes outside as often as possible.

Aurelia loves to hear from readers. You can find her contact information, website details and author profile page at https://www.totallybound.com